# HOUSE OF THE FLYING SNAKES: OPERATION ALGORITHM

# HOUSE OF THE FLYING SNAKES: OPERATION ALGORITHM

**Written By P. W. Hand**

**Wilhelm Libertaire series**
Volume Two

**Foreword and Haiku Poems**
**Written by Claire L. Hand**

**Cover Illustrations**
**By Claire L. Hand**

**Edited by Claire L. Hand**

**Second Edition**

House of the Flying Snakes: Operation Algorithm

Wilhelm Libertaire series

Volume Two

Second Edition

Library of Congress Control Number: 2021904507

ISBN-13: 978-0-9960673-5-5 (pbk)

ISBN-13: 979-8-9864162-1-2 (HB)

ISBN-13: 978-0-9960673-6-2 (eBook)

Illustrator, Haiku Poet, and Editor: Claire L. Hand

Printed in the United States of America.

Second Edition, 2021
Second Edition First Printing, 2021

Second eBook Edition, 2021

First Edition, 2019
First eBook Edition, 2019

Imprint: P. W. Hand

pwhandbooks@gmail.com

# Foreword
## By Claire L. Hand

P. W. Hand continues his modern spy tale in a captivating style that we have come to expect from him. He uniquely intertwines world facts, action, martial arts, family, and high-style with the intelligence world. He dramatically reveals answers to many questions plaguing the hero Wilhelm Libertaire, his colleagues, and his antagonists. Even more, he fully develops his characters as realistic and integral members of their communities i.e. Libertaire staff, CIA, mercenaries, martial and secret societies, and world nemeses.

P. W. Hand's espionage fantasy carries the reader away through intrigue and passion and is astonishingly believable. Our favorite players have grown into their roles by surviving past missions, learning the spy game, developing innovative techniques, and taking on new assignments. Additionally, new players are introduced and are highlighted as they interact with the core players. Undoubtedly, with each victory gained, many losses are endured. Ultimately, in this spy game, with every question answered, more questions emerge and at times the hero's information is vulnerable.

*Wilhelm Libertaire*
*Eliminating his foes*
*Master of the game*

# Acknowledgements

To my wife Claire who is my muse, my staunchest supporter, and the best editor who a writer could ask for. Without her, there wouldn't be a Libertaire series. She is my most honest critic even if I don't like what she says. She keeps me honest and helps me write the best that I can. Thanks Dear. You're the best!

# Table of Contents

# Table of Contents

# Preface

Master spy Wilhelm Libertaire is back and is as exciting and intriguing as ever. In volume two of the Libertaire series, Wilhelm faces two challenges that will test his skills to the fullest. The highly secretive criminal organization, the Council of Five, has made great gains with their plans and has become increasingly bold. Meanwhile, Wilhelm's next mission is taking place in the land of the flying snakes now known as Angola. There, he will confront three worthy adversaries the Chinese, a double agent who has crossed both the Russians and the United States, and the Council's hit team.

As Wilhelm runs two important, unrelated, and complicated missions with two different teams, he has to stay alive to complete them. With the Councils special hit team on the hunt, his mission just got a lot more difficult. So he enlists the aid of a democratic underground organization to help him. He finds them more than up to the task at hand. He even discovers a sexy, smart, young Angolan woman who proves to be quite adept to the spy game and to potentially become his protégé.

Volume two has more twists and turns than the first volume and has even more action and intrigue. The story reveals more about Wilhelm Libertaire than before. In it, he proves to the CIA once and for all his purpose for training his special security force the way he did and his need for them to continue to pull off the impossible, time and time again. This volume will set the stage for the final showdown with the Council of Five who has broken a cardinal rule within the intelligence community.

# Drinks & Information
## *Chapter One*

### *Belgium*

"Oh, that's it, baby. Fuck me harder," the pretty blond said into the ear of Ralph Crinkle, a 55 year old diamond director.

"Is that how you like it?" He gasped as he tried his best to satisfy her and pumped harder into her.

"Oh yes! That's what your baby likes. Fuck me, baby. Fuck me like your life depends on it," she said. An hour later, Linda woke up. Before getting out of bed, she checked on Ralph. "Good, sleeping like a baby," she said as she patted his ass. He stirred, mumbled something, and turned over. She walked into the living room and took out a small camera and cassette-sized black case. She paddled barefooted and bare-assed into his office and swung open the picture of horses on the wall which revealed the wall safe. Then she opened the black case, attached the wire and suction cup, and turned it on. After waiting for 30 seconds which it took for the machine to give her the combination, she opened the safe. Linda looked for and found the paperwork that she wanted. She took the folder out and placed it on the desk. Then she took photos of the platinum shipments that Ralph's company was making. She also recorded the routes, times, and dates. After collecting the information, she put the papers back, closed the safe, and went back to bed where she found Ralph still sound asleep.

### *Armenia*

Shadow Two looked at the ten-foot wall in front of her as she knelt down in the dark woods forty meters away. She was dressed in her

1

work clothes, all black yet stylish and functional. Once over the wall, she only had six guards and the target to kill. Why Armenian arms dealers like to live in big houses in the middle of nowhere was beyond her. This asshole had to go and change the deal that he had with the C.I.A. Didn't he know he was replaceable? Her job tonight was to remind him of that. Too bad, he had to die to learn that lesson. She walked to the wall, put her back to it, and started counting paces. When she hit her mark, she stopped. Next, she took out a collapsible trampoline and set it up. Then, she put on her light weight backpack and paced off the distance again. When she was ready, she pulled her mask down, took a deep breath, let it out, and started her run. She had to be precise. The trampoline had just enough room for both of her feet but only if they were perfectly aligned and together. Never mind it was pitch black and the trampoline was black as well. She began her run and then jumped when she hit her mark.

The silent springs stretched and propelled her up and over the wall. Her single summersault helped straighten her body out for the landing. She made no noise when she landed. While looking around and getting her bearings, she saw the house lights and headed for them. When she was close, she was greeted by a fifty-meter open area of grass that was well-lit. Staying in the shadows, she circled the house until she found the two outside guards. They were standing near the side entrance smoking cigarettes and holding their AK47s casually in their hands. She took off her pack, took out a carbine rifle, and put it together. Next, she screwed on the silencer, inserted a five-round 9 mm magazine, and took aim.

She shot the first man in the face right in the nose causing him to be thrown backwards. Before the second guard could sound the alarm, she shot him in the head. She moved across the grass at a run and stopped at the side door. She tried it and it opened. Going inside, she found herself near the servants area where she heard them talking in a room to her left. She crept up to the room, peered in, and saw two maids folding clothes and gossiping. According to her diagram, she had to go twenty-five meters to get to the living room. If he wasn't there, then she had to go upstairs. Not to mention, she might run into the six house guards. So she started down the hall towards the living room. Before she reached the open area just before the living room there was a small alcove. She carefully approached it with her pistol at the ready and quickly looked in. She found one of the guards getting his dick sucked by one of the maids. She shot him. Then she looked at the maid who was on her knees dressed in her uniform, and she shot her. She continued towards the living room. When she got there, she found two more guards playing X-box. So she killed them. "Fuck," she thought. Now she had to go upstairs. As she headed for the stairs, another guard appeared. She double tapped him in the head and kept going.

In a flash, she changed magazines and was up the stairs at the arms dealer's bedroom door. Putting her ear to the door, she listened and heard a woman's voice then a man's. She tried the handle; the door was unlocked. So she took a deep breath, turned the handle, and walked in. There, she found her target standing in the middle of the room. He was talking to a woman who was lying on the bed in her underwear. The two stopped and looked at her.

"Who are you?" he said in a thick Armenian accent. Shadow Two didn't answer. She just shot him then the woman and left. Since she didn't run into the last two guards on her way out, she took one of the sports cars in the garage and made good her escape.

### Libertaire Manor

While enjoying the cool breeze on this July morning, Wilhelm sat under a large shade tree and watched his horse graze. He was wondering if Rodney would talk about what was going on in Europe in today's meeting. There was no way he could keep ignoring the events over the last few months. Someone was doing a number on the agency and no one was talking about it especially Rodney. He stood up brushed the grass from his jeans and mounted his horse. He swung by the east fields before heading home to check on the crops that his chief agriculturist was growing with his new farming method. His new organic formula would hopefully double the yield of this year's crop. The whole time he was listening to his agriculturist, his mind was on the upcoming meeting. So he did a lot of head nodding and saying, "Whatever you think is best." Afterwards, he climbed aboard his black Andalusian stallion and rode away at a cantor.

Wilhelm cleaned up, dressed in a blue summer wool pinstripe suit and went to the library. Anthony appeared at the door and informed him that they were ready and the driver was standing by. Wilhelm listened as he checked his Walther PPK/CCP then dismissed him and began to place some files into his briefcase. He did one last check and headed out to the awaiting car.

As he approached, he saw who was assigned as his driver. He knew this man; he knew his capabilities. He was a good choice, he thought. Then Wilhelm turned his attention to the car. Anthony had chosen the Audie S6 with the custom Phantom Black Pearl paint job— another good choice. This car was equipped with bulletproof glass that could withstand several direct hits from a 338 caliber round. The body had been sprayed with Kevlar fibers to reinforce the Kevlar plates and was equipped with run flat tires. Its armaments included two M4s in 7.62 x 39 caliber and a Sig Sauer in 45 caliber. Anthony had made a good selection from all of the cars at his disposal. Wilhelm could see George's influence on him. So far, he made all of the right decisions.

He got into the car. The driver closed the door behind him, got in the car, and sat there looking at him in the rearview mirror.

"CIA headquarters," he said. The driver started the car and headed down the driveway. As he rode up Route 64, he thought about the meeting and wondered what devilment George was up to on his vacation.

"CIA headquarters, sir," the driver said over his shoulder pulling him out of his thoughts. Wilhelm pulled out his I.D. and pass from his briefcase and showed it to the guard at the gate.

"Good afternoon, sir," the guard said as he took the I.D. and pass to look over. "You are cleared to proceed, sir." Then the guard handed back his papers.

"You can drop me off in front." The driver pulled up, got out, and opened the door for him, all the time never saying a word.

Wilhelm walked up to the turn stile, swiped his card, entered the inner sanctum, and headed to Rodney's office. He walked in, said good morning to the AA, sat down on the couch, and listened as she informed her boss that he was there. A few minutes later Rodney opened his office door and beckoned him to come in. Wilhelm walked in closing the door behind him; he placed his briefcase alongside the wingback chair and then sat down crossing his legs and waited.

"The final report on Frank is in," Rodney said as he looked through the files on his desk. "But that's not what I wanted to discuss with you. What is foremost on my mind is who has the secrets that once belonged to the Stanleys. We came up with nothing to connect Frank to it but he did say he had seen that type of torture before. So I want you to put some people on it. If the person or persons who have this information break the code, they could cause a lot of problems for a lot of people and not just in this agency."

"Are we still keeping tabs on Linda?" Wilhelm asked.

"Yes, we are; she's in Austria sunning and generally enjoying herself. She's had no contact with anyone in the intelligence community thus far and seems to be enjoying her early retirement," Rodney replied. The conversation then turned to the ongoing operation that Wilhelm was running. So he opened his briefcase and pulled out the information. The meeting lasted an hour then Wilhelm was back in the car headed for the office.

As he rode along, he wondered why Rodney hadn't mentioned the killing of the eight agents in Europe. The CIA had lost three agents;

the Germans lost two, and MI6 had three killed as well. This wasn't business as usual yet Rodney was treating it as such. His driver pulled up in front of his new office which was renamed to coincide with the export office in Turkey. The driver got out and scanned the area before opening the door for him. Wilhelm got out and looked around. It was late morning close to 11:00 a.m., and the early lunch takers were all over the place. But he failed to spot the three sets of eyes that were watching his every move.

Wilhelm walked in, said good morning to Gladys, and headed straight into his office seemingly ignoring the young lady sitting opposite Gladys' desk.

"Gladys! Who is our visitor?" Wilhelm barked into the phone's intercom.

"The young lady I told you about, the one applying for the assistant position, sir."

"Could you come in here, please?" Gladys got up and signaled to the young woman to sit still as she headed to his office. Wilhelm waited until she was standing in front of him before he began. "Since when do we need and assistant and why am I just hearing about it?"

"I put that information on your desk a week ago and I informed you of my need for help around the office," Gladys said as she pointed to the file. "You also told me that the person I selected was fine with you as long as you give final approval, sir."

"Alright Gladys, give me ten minutes then send her in."

Gladys left the office without saying anything else, and Wilhelm opened the file and began reading. The young lady had scored high on her tests and passed all of the security checks thus far. He would run his own check, of course. But he didn't see any reason not to hire her, not to mention Gladys' reaction if he didn't. After all, Gladys was the only person taking care of the nine people that worked in this three-story building. He heard a soft knock and the door opened up.

"Ms. Bradley told me to come in," a soft voice said as she came into view. With an expressionless face, Wilhelm looked at the young woman. She was five-foot-five in her flats. She wore a long skirt and loose-fitting blouse in earth tones that complemented her skin tone. Her hair was braided. She stood quietly in front of his desk and looked him in the eye. Wilhelm looked at her for a minute then spoke.

"Gladys wants you so I'll give you a chance. You will take your orders and project assignment from her. Any questions?"

"No, sir," she responded in that same soft voice. He dismissed her. Then she turned and left the office. He listened to Gladys and the young lady celebrate as he sat back and smiled.

The rest of Wilhelm's day passed uneventfully. Since his promotion, he found himself doing a lot more paperwork and holding meetings than planning missions. Most days, he couldn't wait to get out of the office. But this time, it was different; he was extra anxious; he was having dinner with an old friend at Cee's. He left the office and headed straight to Cee's. He arrived with time to spare so he had a few shots of scotch with Cee and caught up with him. Scott arrived on time precisely at six-thirty. Wilhelm rose from the booth and greeted him.

"Scott, it's nice to see you."

"You could image my surprise when you called. How did you know I was at the embassy?" Scott said as he shook his hand and smiled.

They waited until the waiter finished setting up. He poured them a glass of house Sangria and left the pitcher. During that time, Wilhelm ran Scott's record through his mind.

Born Scott Boulstridge, recruited by MI6 after finishing graduate school at Oxford. Expertise: counter-intelligent. Currently, he was posted in Germany a week ago. He was called here for some meetings.

Wilhelm wanted to know what those meeting were about, and if these talks had anything to do with the problem in Europe.

"When you called and suggested dinner at this spot, how could I refuse? I've tried to get reservations here every time I'm in town with no luck. So talk slowly and let me at least enjoy the food and ambiance before I say no to whatever it is that you want," Scott said before taking a sip of his drink.

"It's nothing like that, Scott. I just wanted to thank you for your help in Cyprus."

"I don't believe you; you still haven't told me how you knew I was at the embassy."

"Let's enjoy a meal together. I ordered Cee's surf and turf: rib-eye rare, of course, with the area's best seafood along with his special sauce."

"I'll drink to that," Scott said raising his glass. This time, he took a longer sip of his drink. Wilhelm did likewise. The two drank and ate. It truly was a magnificent meal. As they ate, they talked about nothing important.

Over the years, their paths had crossed several times in the field. And each man had at least on one occasion upset the plans of the other. Wilhelm has known Scott for fifteen years. He was very good at what he did for MI6. Somehow, Wilhelm had to get him to talk. After dinner, he invited Scott back to the townhouse for some fifty-year-old scotch. If Scott had any weaknesses, it was very good, very old scotch. Wilhelm waited until their third shot before asking Scott what was going on in the European Union. Scott looked Wilhelm in the eyes and said very seriously,

"Somebody is killing my agents."

"Only MI6?"

"No, some of your agents as well and your boss seems to be ignoring it. I mean Rodney is an alright guy and all but he seems to be ignoring the picture that is being painted. Some of these agents have been in deep cover for five years and now they're dead."

Wilhelm listened to the information that Scott told him; he didn't ask too many questions; he just let him talk. He knew Scott wouldn't tell him any sensitive information no matter how drunk he got. As he listened, he started to put together a picture of his own. With what he already knew coupled with this new information, he started to understand. A few hours later, he walked Scott to his car and driver and watched until they were out of sight. Wilhelm headed straight to his office where he pulled out a few files and added the new information.

# Treachery Times Two

## *Chapter Two*

"MARs!" Wilhelm yelled through the open door of his office—he called her that because of her initials. Her name is Monica Angela Robertson; it was clear her mother hadn't put a lot of thought into it at the time. Although she claims nobody in her family calls her MARs, he naturally started doing it. She walked into his office.

"Yes, sir."

"Where's Gladys?"

"She's running those blueprints you wanted, sir."

"Then I need you to go up to Joe's office and get the report on Angola and make sure it has the latest intelligence reports in it." Then stop by the print room and bring me the blueprints Gladys is running and tell her to print out a chart of the coast." MARs nodded then left the room; Wilhelm listened to her hurried footsteps as she went up the stairs.

He spent the rest of the day going over the updated information and putting the beginnings of the operation together. He liked Joe's plan. But he needed a diversion so the assault team could accomplish their mission. At the moment, nothing was coming to mind. He glanced at the clock; it was getting late. Only he, security, Joe, and one of his assistants were in the building; the others had gone home hours ago. He notified his driver, locked his safe, closed his briefcase, put on his fedora, and went to meet. His driver was waiting for him at the side entrance. During the ride home, he had an uneasy feeling—nothing he could put his finger on but it caused him to look over his should out the back window. Neither he nor his driver spotted the car that was following them. The driver was careful not to get too close when Wilhelm's driver turned onto the private lane. The man following him went an extra mile before he pulled over and called in his report. Then he dismantled his cellphone and threw it out the window as he drove away.

## Sol del Oriente en Peru

Number 1 sat in his bungalow at the hotel Sol del Oriente looking out at the pool watching his companion floating and sunning herself. He liked this hotel, and the weather in central Peru was perfect this time of year. As he drank his bourbon ice tea, he thought of his upcoming meeting when he would introduce the newest member to the Council. He knew they would have their reservations. But after they hear what is brought to the table, they would accept his decision.

Just then, he heard a knock at the door. His bodyguard rose, took out his pistol, and went to the door. He looked back at his boss who nodded; then he opened the door.

"Mr. Royce," his bodyguard announced. The guard stepped aside and let him in, all the while keeping his gun on him. Number 1 turned around to face him but he didn't speak until his bodyguard finished frisking him. Then he got up and extended his hand as he greeted him.

"Mr. Royce, it's so nice to see you. Thank you for coming; we have much to talk about." He showed him to the sitting area just off the pool area. "Can I get you a drink?"

"Yes, vodka ice tea," he replied.

"I am pleased with the work you and your people have done in Europe but I am concerned about the silence I am hearing," Number 1 said.

"I don't understand it myself. My people in Europe assure me that the U.S. has tightened its security and changed habits. So I know they are feeling the pressure. Besides, MI6 sent their German station chief Scott Boulstridge to Washington for a meeting."

"Then we'll just have to wait and see what develops. In the meantime, I want your program of eliminations to widen its scope. I want you to send people to Luanda and Juba, and this is what I want you to do." Number 1 spent the next two hours telling Royce what he wanted him to do. Then he paid him and sent him on his mission.

*The New Number 2*

Number 1 sat at the head of the conference table and looked at the other members. For the first time, they didn't wear their disguises. This was his new order. He knew this would bind them together permanently. He wore a poker face as his eyes peered through each one of them. He knew that each and every one of them would slit his throat and Number 5 would probably shoot him a couple times for good measure if they thought for one moment he was weak. But the removal of Number 2 had dispelled all thoughts of a takeover. He was sure his pick for the new Number 2 would be accepted and he would gain a new ally in the process.

"I called this meeting to inform you that today you will meet the new Number 2," he began. He paused a moment while looking at their faces. "This person brings access to a very unique organization one

13

that will fill a need that our organization can utilize. We will have an intelligence network par excellence and one that is already in place. So gentlemen, I give you Number 2."

Number 1 stood up and faced the large double doors at the other end of the room while the others looked on puzzled. They looked at each other not saying a word but their looks said it all. The doors opened and in walked a woman. She is five feet, ten inches tall, 165 lbs. and has an athletic build with shoulder-length brown hair framing her face. She had an easy, graceful walk but purposeful, and the soft pink spaghetti-strap silk chiffon dress showcased her body in all the right places. As she approached, the remaining members stood up. Next, they noticed her diamond pendant earrings, bracelet, and rings on each of her fingers. But what really caught their attention was the sound of the bell that rang softly every time her camel-colored three-inch gold heel on her right shoe touched the floor.

"Gentlemen, please be seated," she said as Number 1 helped her with her chair. She looked up the table at the other three Council members and smiled. Then she addressed them. "Gentlemen, I know this may come as a shock to some of you. I'm sure you never thought a woman would be selected for this position. Let me start by saying that I have admired your work from afar for many years now. When Number 1 asked me if I would be interested in joining your group, I jumped at it. What I'm bringing to the table is an intelligence network that has been in place for fifteen years. All of its operatives are female, and I have eyes and ears all over the world. I can and will provide up-to-date and real-time Intel on any continent twenty-four hours, seven days a week. I will live up to my part of the bargain, and I have no doubt that this Council will live up to theirs."

"Does anyone have any questions for Number 2?" Number 1 asked. When no one spoke, he continued. "Then I will show our newest member to her quarters. We will meet again in two hours; I have some news I wish to share." Number 1 and Number 2 got up from the table and left the room. "Right now, they are going crazy. But they won't say anything to each other until after I inform them of my plan," he told her as he walked her to her suite.

"What are your plans?" she asked.

"Oh, you are going to fit in just fine around here," he said with a laugh. "You have to wait like the rest of them. And Number 2, memorize the rule book. Those guys won't cut you any slack." Then he handed her a card with the door code and kept walking down the hallway.

# Sanaa's Interview

## Chapter Three

### The Farm

Wilhelm and his oldest son were fencing in the open area of the exercise room when George appeared in the doorway with bag in hand. He waited quietly and watched as his boss instructed Junior in the finer points of how to use the epee.

"How long are you going to stand there?" Wilhelm said as he turned around and removed his head gear.

"I did not want to interrupt just in case Junior got the best of you," George replied with a great big smile.

"You're back early. What? Trouble? Or should I say who are you dodging?" At that moment, Junior walked by George.

"I think he missed you. Welcome home."

"Meet me in the library in an hour and welcome back," Wilhelm said has he left the room. George smiled, shook his head, and headed to his room. Anthony joined him and filled him in as they walked.

Once in his room, Anthony looked around slowly taking in as much as he could. He couldn't believe he was there. No one he knew that worked there had ever been invited except the boss, of course. He saw pictures of George as a young lieutenant in the Green Berets and as a captain in the French Foreign Legion. Knives and military swords lined the wall. A silver forty-five in a case lay on the shelf along with two unit flags neatly folded in the military manner. His room was large; everything was in proper order and immaculately clean. George put his bag on the bed, walked over to the bar, and poured two bourbons. He handed Anthony one and said,

"Tell me what's been happening around here while I've been gone."

*Peru*

"I called this meeting to bring you up to speed on phase two of the resources control plan," Number 1 said.

He pressed a button on the control panel in front of him, and a seventy-inch liquid TV screen came down. He pressed a few keys, and the image of South Sudan appeared. He continued manipulating the controls. Next, a camp was shown from the top view.

"This is the beginning of the research facility that will house the test facilities concerning the recent scientific information we acquired. We now have the protection of the Sudanese government in exchange for their access to this technology. I don't have to tell you what this means for us. This facility will be completed and online in two months."

Number 1 slid his fingers across the control panel tapping lightly. As he did so, he placed images and text on the screen. Next, he hit one final button and a hologram of a man at a building complex in 3D imaging appeared on the large conference table.

Number 2 placed her hands in her lap and looked at the table; she could hardly believe her eyes. She had some idea of the reach and resources the Council had but she couldn't have fathomed the depth and implications of their plan. This meeting was revealing an unbelievable plan. If the Council could somehow control the natural resources in Africa, they would be more powerful than any first world nation.

"Let's start with the gentleman, shall we? This is Mr. Royce; he is carrying out an operation on behalf of the Council in Europe. His mission is twofold: First, he is to keep certain intelligence agents busy. Second, he is to draw out Libertaire. Now you are viewing what the finished facility will look like. Please feel free to look it over."

The members got up and walked around the table talking to each other and pointing out things of interest. Number 1 sat and watched. He waited patiently for them to finish their inspection. When they had retaken their seats, he began again. "As you can see, this will be a vast complex; it will be constructed from modular components saving us time and money. The foundation has been set, and the equipment is sitting in a warehouse in-country waiting to be delivered.

"And we have our own private army, of course, to keep the local warlords in line. Fellow members, this will be a crowning jewel in our achievements, and it is only the beginning. When we start to offer the surrounding countries this technology and they see what it can do for them, they will give us whatever we ask for. Just think about it, the wealth of a continent at our finger tips."

The others were looking at him. Now they could see the gleam in his eyes as he talked along with his sinister grin which said it all. But he was right. They would be very rich and powerful and protected by multiple governments. He may be a little mad but there was no doubt about his genius.

"Number 3," he began again, "I want you to start talking to certain countries' leaders and certain people; I will give the list later. Number

4, I want you in Africa immediately; you will be in charge of the facility. Number 5, I want you to find and hire the *Three Craftsman of Death;* I will give you their info after the meeting. Number 2, I need you to track Libertaire; he doesn't know about you or your organization yet. Put only your best people on this. And Number 2, take extra precautions. Libertaire is a totally different animal than you're used to dealing with."

℗

Wilhelm stood a few yards away from the platform that was erected between the two-story security personnel living quarters. It is 5:47 a.m. on this Thursday morning. The July air was cool and perfumed with scents from the nearby meadow. Men and women began to gather; they each had a medium-sized duffel bag and a rifle case. They were dressed in black cargo pants bloused around their boots in Marine Corps fashion, black t-shirts with the Libertaire crest over the left breast, and utility belts. Today was their annual competition when they would shoot and fight against one another. Men and women going against each other head to head on the pistol, shotgun, and long-range precision shooting courses. The hand-to-hand portion was the only competition that would be gender specific.

Anthony stood on the platform and began to talk.

"My fellow employees, today is the day that I kick all of your asses. And if you don't agree with that statement, meet me at the starting line of the pistol course where I will begin your education."

The staff burst into laughter. Everyone knew that Anthony came in seventh last year. Wilhelm attended every year. When he couldn't be there, he reviewed the tapes. He looked at this competition as an opportunity to gauge the effectiveness of his security forces. He needed to see what to improve and which staff to replace. He knew George and Anthony would be doing the same.

At 10:00 a.m., Wilhelm heard the sound of a helicopter headed for the helipad and looked up. Then he saw George jump into a jeep and speed off in that direction. Wilhelm went back to watching the match. It was getting hot now and the humidity was rising. The last four shooters drenched in sweat drank water as they waited for the word to begin. They were competing for the championship which would be judged by their time and number of hits on target. This pistol course would take three minutes to run and required sixty rounds to cover all the targets. They would be allowed only sixty rounds—four magazines of fifteen rounds each.

Wilhelm waited for the third contestant to begin her run. The previous two had put up good times but missed a few targets. He was watching as George approached. George walked up and informed him that Rodney and a woman named Sanaa were at the house waiting for him. Wilhelm told him to call the house and have Colleen keep an eye on them until he arrived. George made the call and informed his boss that she was already babysitting the two in the living room. Wilhelm waited until the last contender had finished the course before he left. He didn't want to know who won because he had to shoot against him or her as was tradition.

He and George walked back to the house. Wilhelm briefly wondered what brought his boss out here.

"Good morning, Rodney," he said has he walked into the living room. "And who do we have here?"

"This is Sanaa, someone I want you to meet." Wilhelm knew what that meant—Rodney wanted him to put her to work. "As much as I would like to sit here and enjoy all of this ambiance and talk with Colleen, this is a business call."

"Shall we continue to the library," Wilhelm said then turned and left the room. George waited and walked with the two of them. When they arrived, they found Wilhelm patting and talking to a rather large dog. "Come in! He won't bite you; he's just a pup."

"Pup my ass! Look at the size of that dog!" Rodney said as he walked by him and the dog stopping at the bar.

"That's the real reason you wanted to talk in here—to drink my booze," Wilhelm said as he walked towards his desk.

"Not actually, I have a bit of news and a mission for you. I know what you are going to say. You just finished a job and are planning your next one. And a job well done. But now, I need you to take on this job, and *this* young lady will be working with you on it."

Rodney paused and took a sip of his gin and tonic and looked at him then at her. Sanaa was patting and playing with the dog not paying attention to what the two men were talking about. When she looked up, she saw them looking at her. So she stood up, straightened and smoothed out her lined knit dress, and adjusted her jacket. Wilhelm looked at her. The short afro, coral-colored dress that stopped a few inches above her knees, and matching jacket with post earrings went well with her dark complexion. In turn, Sanaa was taking a good look at him. She looked at the brown-skinned man dressed in loose-fitting linen pants and tunic in light brown and wearing braided leather summer sandals. So far, what she had heard about how he lived was

22

true. But, was he really as smart and ruthless as they say? Wilhelm walked around his desk and sat down.

"Alright, let's hear it. What is so important about this mission?" Rodney sat down in one of the chairs in front of his desk and motioned to Sanaa to sit in the other. Rodney told Sanaa to give Wilhelm the file. She opened the briefcase that she had beside her and took out the file. She closed the briefcase, got up, and handed him the file across his desk. As she did so, she wondered why he was behind his desk instead of sitting out here with them. There was plenty of seating in the library, and Rodney was his boss after all.

Wilhelm opened the file and was greeted with an 8x10 glossy photo of Sanaa. He turned the page and began to read.

Name: Sanaa Amina...born August 17, 1987

Place of Birth: Rhode Island, USA

Education: Master's in Electrical Engineering,

Dartmouth University

Service: Five years field experience

Last Posting: Namibia

Expertise: Cyber Intelligence, CQC (close

quarter combat), Pistol, Knives, Poisons, Plum

Flower Fist Kung Fu

Languages: Bantu, Portuguese

Wilhelm stopped reading and looked at the young woman sitting in front of him and looked down at her shoes. She looked down at them also then looked back at him a little puzzled. Wilhelm wasn't looking at her legs; he was looking at her heels. They were two-inch pumps well suited for her work, yet stylish.

"She seems qualified—not green not overly exposed—from her file. I take it you want me to go to Africa."

"Yes," was all that Rodney said. Then he rose and refilled his drink. "I want you to go to Angola, in fact, and retrieve certain information then blow up the equipment. For the first part, you will need Ms. Amina. You pick the rest of your team to carry out the second part of the mission. After all, you're already working on a project concerning Angola. Just interject yourself into this mission. The information you already have will serve you well."

"What is the mission or is that a surprise," Wilhelm said as he looked at Sanaa.

"You are to take a team and blow up a three-story building belonging to the Chinese. We have Intel that this location is of great importance to them because it is a central location for their hacking activities in Southern Africa."

"And Ms. Amina's role in this mission is what?"

"She will be photographing certain equipment and retrieving data and if possible bring back an encryption machine. I believe there is a picture in the file somewhere." Rodney waited as Wilhelm looked at the picture of a small silver device three inches tall, nine inches long, and five inches wide.

"What does this do exactly?"

"I will explain that later. So now that you have this information, what do you think?"

24

"I think I have no choice in the matter. But it was nice of you to ask. Second, I'd like to test her out ... not that I think Ms. Amina isn't up to the task at hand. As you know, today is keep or lose your job day. We like to call it, 'Libertaire's Game Day.' I'd like to run Ms. Amina through the courses, if she doesn't mind. Then we can have a late lunch or dinner whatever the time dictates."

"I'm sure she wouldn't mind a workout before we eat. Do you, Ms. Amina?" Rodney said as he looked in her direction.

"No, sir. But I didn't bring any workout clothing."

"Nonsense! I'm sure Wilhelm can come up with something for you to wear," he said with a devilish smile. Rodney loved doing this to Wilhelm and it showed. He knew this was his competition day. Springing this on him on this day would allow him to see what new tricks he had come up with for training his private army.

Wilhelm pressed the intercom button and asked George to come in. "Will you show Ms. Amina where she can change? She will be trying out the courses."

"The fighting portion, as well?" George asked.

"Yes."

As Sanaa got up and headed for the door, Wilhelm asked, "Ms. Amina, before you go can you show me what sidearm you are carrying?" She said nothing as she turned around and walked back to his desk. She reached into her purse, produced a Kahr P380 Black Rose edition, and handed it to him. Wilhelm looked at it closely. He removed the magazine and then the bullets, seven in all counting the one in the chamber. He reloaded the pistol and handed it back to her.

"Nice weapon, and the black rose is a nice touch," he said in a flat voice.

"Thank you," she replied and placed the pistol back in her purse and then left with George.

Wilhelm and Rodney talked about the mission while waiting for her to return. There was a knock at the library door; then it opened. In walked Sanaa; she was dressed in the same uniform as his security personnel.

"Well, look at you," Rodney said as he looked her over. "Are we ready? Then let's get this started. I for one can't wait to see what Wilhelm has in store for you."

"George, would you escort our guests over to the competition field? I will join you there in a moment," Wilhelm said as they all left the library. Then he closed the doors behind them.

Sanaa was quiet as they walked to the competition area. She was in deep thought. She couldn't tell if he disliked her or liked her. One thing she was sure of was he didn't like surprises like the one Rodney just pulled. She was also concerned about what she was walking into. His security force was known to be brutal and unforgiving.

"Would you like to warm up?" George asked her.

"What, I'm sorry; I didn't hear you," Sanaa said as she snapped out of her thoughts and realized they had arrived.

"Would you like to warm up?"

"Yes, I would. Where can I do that?"

"Anthony will show you. Just follow him."

"Will she be fighting?" Anthony asked.

"Yes, and Anthony, walk her through the courses."

26

"Okay."

Anthony looked her up and down, shook his head in disbelief, and told her to follow him.

As George was showing Rodney around, Wilhelm was telling Colleen that they will be having company for dinner. Then he changed into the uniform of the contestants: black t-shirt with crest, black boots, and black cargo pants bloused low at the ankles. He headed downstairs. As he was exiting the eastside door, he saw his young mastiff chewing on a large bone.

"Put that bone down, pup, and come with me. I have to watch a young lady get schooled, and it isn't going to be a pretty sight." The dog got up and walked alongside him. When Wilhelm began to jog, the dog kept the same position. Wilhelm looked at him with admiration; he was training up just fine.

When Wilhelm arrived, Sanaa had warmed up and was out walking the pistol course with Anthony.

"Where are we on the stages and what is the ranking so far?" he asked George. George handed him the clipboard with the results. As he read, he was glad to see that the winners had changed from last year, and the scores were close. It looked like he would keep everybody if these scores stayed in the same range. Just then, Anthony walked up and told him they were ready to start anytime he was ready. Wilhelm walked up onto the platform and stood there. His security people stopped what they were doing and gathered around. He waited until they all gathered before addressing them.

"I just looked at the scores, and I must say I am impressed. All of you have improved and meet the bar set for this competition. Today, we have a special guest with us. Her name is Sanaa, and she will be running the course against one of you lucky people. I expect you to be just as tough and fair as you are with each other. Also she'll participate in the hand-to-hand portion, and I expect the person whoever it is that has the honor of fighting Sanaa not to hold back. That being said, the winner of the knife and pistol courses step up; I believe we have a date."

A man and woman stepped forward. The crowd roared and Wilhelm roared along with them. Rodney watched and took mental notes: Wilhelm's people are loyal. They like their boss maybe even love him. One thing was sure; he had a highly trained unit, and there was no doubt they would follow and defend their boss. He of all people understood why Wilhelm had such a force but it didn't make him feel any better about it. As the crowd headed for the pistol course, they passed the kitchen staff who was setting up and could smell the barbecue beef, mutton, and goat which had everyone licking their lips.

Wilhelm ran the pistol course first, then his opponent. They were shooting Sig Sauer pistols in 40 caliber. Afterwards he watched Sanaa run the course. She was quick and agile and her magazine change was smooth. When he compared the hits on target, Sanaa lost by five targets missed. But her time was faster. During knife throwing, she tied with fifteen bullseyes at all three ranges. They took a short break so Sanaa could prepare for the last stage of the course—the fighting portion. Anthony walked her over to the platform where the matches took place. The platform is round, approximately ten-yard in diameter, and four feet in height. It has no ropes or barriers to protect the person from falling off.

28

"We fight with a mouth piece. No eye gouging or breaking of limbs is allowed. Everything else is fair game. There is a three-fall rule. And of course, if you are knocked off the platform, you lose. There is one ten-minute round. If it goes the distance, then the boss and George make the decision," Anthony said.

"Do many matches go the distance?" Sanaa asked.

"Sometimes, you never can tell until it's over. I'll get you a fresh mouth piece. You better warm up and stretch; we'll start soon." Then he left. Sanaa started to stretch. As she did so, she watched the others warm up. Some were hitting a heavy bag; others were shadow boxing; all looked formidable. Wilhelm walked up the stairs to the platform and announced the order of the matches and who would be fighting whom. She was in the fourth match with a woman named Dee. She searched the crowd hoping to spot her with no luck.

Sanaa stood and watched the matches. When sitting, she couldn't see anything so she had to stand. The first match had to be decided by the judges; but it was bloody. While she continued to watch, she observed techniques and fighting styles that she didn't know anything about, let alone had seen before. Then her name was called. As she headed for the stairs, she glanced at Wilhelm talking to a woman. He stepped away, and the woman ascended the stairs. Sanaa walked up and faced her; both were barefoot. She looked down at the canvas and noticed the blood stains. She listened to Anthony remind them of the rules, and then he yelled, "Fight!" Dee came straight at her with hands in a boxer's style. When she was in range, she fired off a fast combination. Sanaa slipped the jab and blocked the right cross. But the front kick to her stomach got through.

"Ugh," she murmured then danced to her right.

Dee followed Sanaa throwing a straight right hand and followed up with a roundhouse kick to her ribs; both strikes connected. Sanaa winched but pressed forward showering Dee with body blows. Sanaa did her best but Dee countered with a left hook and a knee—and she went down. She expected Dee to pounce on her. Instead, she backed off and allowed Sanna to get to her feet. She shook off the pain as much as she could and headed for her opponent. This time she was more precise and patient. Her plum fist techniques worked flawlessly—this time Dee went down. She returned the courtesy by backing away and allowing Dee to get up. Dee immediately attacked by kicking and punching her body and punishing her legs with her low kicks. She was careful not to hit her in the face; her boss wouldn't like that. She kept up her attack even when Sanaa landed solid punches to her face and body. Then she heard Anthony yell, "Time!" Dee broke contact. Sanaa looked down from the platform and saw Wilhelm looking at her. Rodney was waiting for her at the bottom of the stairs.

"You did pretty good. For minute there, I thought you were done. But, you came back in good fashion. I must say, I even think Wilhelm was impressed."

"Sir, I hurt all over. Can I skip dinner?"

"No, you can't. Besides, he has a fantastic spa complete with sauna and hot tube. You'll be fine by dinner," he said as they walked towards the house. Wilhelm watched as Rodney and Sanaa approached the house. He took out his cellphone and called Colleen.

"They are on their way back. Have Afra take Sanaa to the spa and stay with her. I want you to keep Rodney busy. As soon as I finish up here, I'll be there." He hung up. Colleen put her cellphone in her dress pocket and went to find Afra.

Wilhelm handed out cash prizes and trophies to the first, second, and third place winners of each event. He made a short speech and announced that the wine, beer, and whiskey bar was now open and that the barbecue had begun. He stayed long enough for a few toasts with his team. Afterwards, he and George got in the jeep and headed to the house with the dog riding in the back. Rodney and Sanaa were greeted by Colleen and Afra when they arrived at the east entrance. Moments earlier, Colleen had given Afra her instructions; all was ready for their guests.

"Hello, Colleen! Afra, how is that beautiful little girl of yours?" Rodney said with a warm smile; he was being sincere and she knew it.

"She's growing like a weed and is such a happy child. Thank you for asking," she replied.

"This is Ms. Sanaa Amina. Colleen has already met her."

"Pleased to meet you," Sanaa said.

"Afra will show you to the spa. I hear you played with my husband's security personnel. I hope you fared well."

"She didn't do too badly, I have to say. I'm proud of the performance she put on," Rodney interjected before she could answer.

"Good! Then she can follow Afra, and *you* shall retire to the salon for drinks before dinner. Ms. Amina can join us later," she said. Then she hooked her arm with Rodney's, and they walked off.

"If you would follow me, Ms. Amina, I will show you to the spa."

"Please, call me Sanaa."

"Okay," Afra said sweetly as she took her to the spa.

31

On the way, they passed the music/dance room and the gym before going into the spa. Sanaa walked in and looked around. The space had blue Indian marble tiles with white swirls covering the floor and walls. On the ceiling, a hand painted tile mural depicted an island scene with people playing and lounging on the beach and surfing. Two individual hot tubs were positioned in the center of the room. Wet and dry steam rooms were located along the back wall. A masseuse table was situated next to the towel rack on the opposite wall near the shower.

"You can undress over there," Afra said as she pointed to the bench next to the towel rack. "Do you prefer a wet or dry sauna?"

"What do you recommend?"

"I suggest you sit in the tub with cool water for half an hour then a warm shower.

"Then it's a plan," she said and started to disrobe. When she was naked and about to get in the tub, she looked in the mirror and saw the bruises on her body.

"Shit! She really did a job on me," she said half out loud.

"Yes, she did. Who did you fight?"

"A beast named Dee."

"Oh, I understand. I know she is tough but a nice person. You'll do better next time."

"I hope I never have to fight her again. If I do, I'm bringing a gun," she said as she slid into the cool swirling water. "Your boss is nice but he's kind of serious. And those *courses* he ran me through were a killer on the body, and it didn't neglect the mind either. The twists and turns, the targets jumping out at you from all angles—I don't think they missed an angle. I have never run a course like that nor have

32

I ever heard of one. Who in-the-hell designed it?" Sanaa was talking with her eyes closed so she missed the big smile on Afra's face.

Afra picked up the white wall phone and told a house attendant to bring Sanaa's clothes to the spa. When she hung up, she continued the conversation.

"So you think my husband is a nice guy who is a little too serious." Sanaa's eyes widened; her mouth fell open; she couldn't make a sound no matter how hard she tried.

"I didn't mean anything about that. You are his wife? I thought the other woman was his wife?" Afra smiled then laughed.

"I'm sorry, but if you could see your face you would be laughing also. Yes, Colleen is also his wife. Didn't Rodney tell you?"

"No, he forgot that bit of information."

"Will you be working with my husband?"

"Yes, I will be, and I guess tonight was a test of my abilities. Can I ask you something?"

"Yes, of course."

"Is your husband this hard on everybody who works for him?"

"Yes, I'm afraid he is. Are you ready to come out of that tub?" Sanaa climbed out and headed for the shower. When she stepped out the shower, she found her clothes hanging near the mirror and a tray filled with scented lotions and perfumes, combs and brushes, and an afro pick. "I hope you find something to your liking. When you are ready, just open the door. I will be outside." Then Afra left the spa closing the door behind her. Sanaa stood there for a moment then the scent of the lotions caught her attention. Twenty minutes later, Sanaa emerged. She found Afra talking to Afef. Afra turned and addressed her.

"You look good and I love the color and cut of that dress. Shall we join the others?" Afra didn't bother to introduce Afef because she had left as soon as Sanaa appeared.

The four of them had dinner. Afra and Afef did not attend. The conversation was light; then they left. On the ride back, Sanaa thought about her day. If this was an indicator of what it was going to be like to work with Libertaire, she better bone up on everything. Wilhelm and his young male mastiff walked down the hall towards his private room.

"I'm going to have to give you a name. I can't keep calling you pup but for now it will do," he said to the dog as he leaned over and patted his head. He entered the music room and headed for the left corner. There, he pressed a panel, and a door opened up. He walked in with the dog ahead of him and closed the door. "Welcome to my sanctuary, pup! Pull up a rug and take the load off." Then he sat down on his lounge chair, took a small wooden box off the little table, opened it, and looked at the five compartments. Each contained a different strain of bud. "Ahhh, that's the one—White Widow," he said out loud. He took the joint, closed the box, and picked up a gold lighter. He turned on some jazz, lit the joint, laid back putting his feet up, and forgot the world.

# Shadow on the Mountain

## *Chapter Four*

### *South Africa*

Royce sat on the stone veranda in an overstuffed wicker chair drinking vodka lemonade and watching a young brunette swinging gently from the living room ceiling. She was tied in intricate knots and rope designs, and she seemed happy and horny.

"I didn't know you were into bondage although I'm not surprised. I thought you were more the normal pervert," Royce said to Talaus.

"Fuck you, don't forget I'm not that fond of you. What brings your sleazy ass to my doorstep?" Talaus replied.

"Now no need to get touchy. I have some information I think you'll want to hear. Of course, I can thank you for your hospitality and be on my way and let your B&D ass along with your murdering whores find out for yourselves what the Council is up to."

"Alright, Royce, don't go off the deep end; I'm all ears." But before you begin, I need a refill." He told Taylor to get him another drink and to give Stacy a spin.

"Where-the-fuck did you learn to tie people up like that?" Royce asked.

"I picked it up in Japan. With the kind of work I do, it seemed like a natural progression. Now tell me what our friends are up to."

Royce began to outline the Council's plans in Africa and how they were scheming to double-cross him with Libertaire. Undoubtedly, the later part was a lie but he had his reasons for telling that lie. If he could get Talaus to throw in with him then he would have the muscle he needed for the next stage of his *own* plan.

"How long has she been up there?" Talaus looked at his Rolex.

"Two hours," he replied.

"How long are you going to let her hang there?"

"Three hours…anything less, she gets bitchy. Don't worry, Royce, she's enjoying herself."

"So as I understand it, the Council is setting up some type of research base that will allow them to control certain resources. And they know or are hoping that Libertaire won't be able to resist snooping around. Then they can kill him."

"Are those guys stupid or something? I have good reason to want to kill him but I can wait. I've replaced Theresa with a very capable killer. She's the gifted sex partner you see before you. Their plan didn't work last time; I doubt it will this time around either. That fucking Wilhelm! There is no other cocksucker on the planet I would love to kill very slowly, very painfully. But he is a charmed motherfucker; he has escaped many attempts on his life as well as his bodyguard George. Let me tell you something about that motherfucker; he will kill you faster than Libertaire. That is one guy you don't want on your ass. Libertaire is the one that got Frank Depore. Did you know that?"

"No, I didn't. I heard it was a special job ordered by the Council to clean up," Royce said looking somewhat perplexed.

"Bullshit! It was Libertaire and one of his secret killers."

"What secret killers are you talking about…some secret CIA assassin team?"

"No! Man, you're not listening. For years, there's been a rumor that Libertaire has a secret assassin...not even the CIA knows the identity."

"I never believed those stories. Granted, the highest honor we can give to someone in our business is stories like that one."

"Libertaire also took out Bryda and her organization. Did you know that?"

"No, but this ultra-secret assassin shit is taking it a bit far. Don't you think?"

"Whether he does or doesn't, I have my hands full. I have more contracts than I can keep up with. So thanks for the information; I do appreciate it. If I can return the favor, I will."

"If any info comes to mind that you think I'd be interested in, you know where to reach me," Royce said as he stood up.

"Taylor, show our guest out."

Talaus walked with them to the living room but stopped by Stacy. He began spanking her progressively harder until he heard her moans through the ball gage she had in her mouth. Taylor returned and stood in front of her and watched in silence. Talaus looked at her as he continued spanking Stacy. He knew she was getting wet and horny as he watched her pupils dilate and her breathing quicken.

Talaus stopped spanking Stacy and rubbed his hand over her now reddened ass. Then he turned her around to face him.

"Would you like to watch me and Taylor fuck, baby?" he said to her as he stroked her face and hair. She responded by nodding her head and smiling around the gag. He walked to the wall and loosened the rope then gently lowered her to the cold stone floor. He left her tied up but removed the ball gag. "Stripe for us," he said. Taylor began to grind slowly moving her hips; then she eased into a sensual dance. As she moved to the music that no one else could hear, Talaus and Stacy looked on getting turned on. As Taylor removed her clothes, Talaus got harder and harder until he couldn't take it anymore, and he began removing his clothes.

He lay down on the floor in front of Stacy and motioned for Taylor to sit on his face. Taylor positioned herself over his face then lowered. "Mmmm," she moaned. Then she leaned over and took his cock in her mouth. Stacy lay there watching. They were close enough to her that she could smell the sex which made her orgasm.

P

As Royce rode away, he thought of the meeting and started to replay it word for word. By the time he reached the airport, he had figured out where he had gone wrong with Talaus. He boarded his private plane and told the pilot to head for Spain.

*Austrian Alps*

Linda walked down the street of the little village where she had chosen to lie low after she left the CIA. She knew the agency would keep an eye on her. So this little village allowed her to keep track of the few strangers that came through. Today was a perfect sunny day in the Austrian mountains. A slow steady breeze brought the scents of fresh baked bread, beer, food, and flowers. She was shopping for dinner because she was expecting special company tonight. She dressed in a yellow sundress, a wide brimmed straw hat, and sandals. She carried a large straw bag instead of a pocketbook which she wore across her body left to right. With her lightly tan body and her easy demeanor, one would think she was a resident of this mountain village.

But Linda didn't notice Shadow Two sitting in the open air café drinking a beer with a young man. She had been watching Linda for two weeks now, and Linda was a *boring* girl. In all that time, she didn't have any outside visitors; only the locals stopped by.

On the other hand, Shadow Two was having a good time on this assignment. It was a cake walk. The tall gorgeous man-friend whom she selected for cover purposes was *perfect*.

She watched Linda walk from shop to shop filling the basket that she carried in her left hand with bread, three bottles of wine, cheese, vegetables, and meat—lamb in particular. Then she thought, "This is Tuesday, so she is either shopping for a couple of days or expecting company." To be on the safe side, she would watch her closely tonight. Then she looked at Paul. "I think I'll fuck him extra hard tonight. That should knock him out, and I can work late," she thought.

Shadow Two looked back at Paul and watched his slow steady breathing. He hadn't awakened while she showered, and she was sure he would sleep through the night. She dressed in a black catsuit, black skullcap, and black, non-slip, treadless, rubber footwear. She pulled out a black pouch with draw strings and checked the contents. Satisfied that she had all she needed, she slipped out the front door into the darkness. She made a complete circle around Linda's house then sat up where she could observe it in safety; it was 8:30 p.m. At 10:30 p.m., she watched three figures walk down the road towards Linda's place. At first, she thought they were locals come calling. Then she put on her night goggles and took another look. "Oh, what have we here," she whispered to herself. She saw three men—medium build, fit, and professional. Two of them were flanking the third man in the middle. Their heads swiveled slowly surveying the area as they walked, and they walked with a purpose. She picked up her camera and waited. When they hit the light of the porch, she began to snap pictures. The tall older looking European man was greeted by Linda with kisses and hugs; she ignored his two companions. After the man entered the house, his bodyguards left.

Shadow Two wondered why they left him unguarded. She sat, waited, and watched. At 2:45 a.m., the guards returned and escorted the mysterious man back into the darkness from whence he appeared. She made a sweep of the grounds. Next, she looked in a bedroom window. There, she discovered Linda in bed so she decided to do the same. She slipped back into her room and found Paul still sleeping. She undressed, put her equipment away, and slid under the covers. As she lay in the darkness, she thought about the strange male visitor. Maybe he was a wealthy man on a booty call. She would send her report in the morning, and maybe the question will be answered.

Shadow Two was eating breakfast and joking with Paul when she noticed the mysterious man from the night before. He was eating by himself and his bodyguards were eating nearby. Now she finally had a good look at him. Just her luck, Paul's camera was aimed in the right direction. She casually started playing with it. As she talked, she turned it on and looked at the back view finder. "Great!" she thought. "These pics are going to be good." Now her boss can't possibly ask for better. Then she began clicking away. She caught him in every angle that he presented. Even when he stood to leave, she didn't leave out the bodyguards; one of them was a real hunk.

As they were leaving, one of his guards called his name, Mr. Cinq. She wondered who would be named the Number 5 in French. She would add that bit of information to this evening's report. Then she went back to her breakfast and toying with Paul. "She could use a morning romp," she thought as she smiled sexily at him.

P

Wilhelm sat in front of the computer screen in his secret communications room under the library and looked at the picture of Mr. Cinq. He wondered, why now would Linda decide to start seeing someone and how did they meet. She and older men wasn't anything new; in fact, it was her preference. So who was Mr. Cinq? He had an uneasy feeling when he looked at the picture like the feeling he got when a spy was around. He told the computer the message that he wanted sent and set the protocol to use. Then he went back to the picture and had the computer run a face recognition and comparison test.P

Linda looked at the balance in her Swiss account and smiled; the ten million dollars was a good start. With the second installment coming, she could disappear for a while—drop of the radar so to speak. Now if Number 5 is consistent and he usually is, tonight she would give him the second part of the list. Thereafter, he will transfer the rest of the money. "A good meal, a good fuck, and our business would be concluded ... not a bad way to end a business deal," she thought as she stared at the number.

P

Shadow Two sat in the bathroom reading the message from Wilhelm.

*"Audio needed on any conversations target has with subject."*

"How in the hell am I going to get a bug in there? She rarely leaves the place. And when she does, it's not for long," she contemplated. She burned the message and flushed the ashes. She walked into the bedroom and lay on the bed staring at the ceiling. She had to find out who this person was; he had piqued her curiosity. "And how in the hell did Linda meet this guy," she wondered.

Shadow Two set up where she had a good view of the front door and the road leading to it. She hoped the stranger would repeat his approach. She looked at her watch which read 9:20 p.m. So she opened up a power bar and began to eat. At 11:17 p.m., she noticed the men coming down the lane. She knew it was them by their walk. She set up the camera and took pictures. Now if those two goons would leave as they did before, maybe she could get some audio. Linda greeted him at the door with a lot less enthusiasm this time, and his bodyguards left like before. Shadow Two waited until the lights dimmed. Then she made her move while staying in the shadows and taking the long way around to Linda's bedroom window. When she got into positon she paused and listened to the darkness and the faint sounds coming from within. Reaching into her bag, she took out a long black rubber-coated cord with a male plug at each end. She attached a small suction cup that was the size of a dime to one end and an earpiece to the other. Next, she quietly attached the suction cup to the window and placed the earpiece in her ear; she heard instant sound. After disconnecting the earpiece, she connected the cord to the recorder that was the size of a flash drive. Then she ran a second line so that she could listen as well. She heard Linda talk about a list that had the names of some deep cover agents. But their country or countries of origin was not mentioned. Nonetheless the stranger was very happy.

Linda's visitor went on trying to persuade her to continue working but was making no headway and finally gave up. When they decided to go to bed, Shadow Two broke down her equipment and headed back to her position.

She had been in that position for half an hour when she began to feel uneasy. She looked around with her night vision goggles but saw nothing. She took them off and decided to move. Suddenly she was attacked from behind. If she hadn't already been in motion, the projectile would have hit her. She took two quick steps to her right all the while looking towards the direction that the projectile came. There was a black figure coming at her fast!

"Ugh!" was the sound she made as a kick landed on her stomach. The blow knocked her to the ground. She rolled instinctively and popped up on her feet in a low fighting stance. This time, she saw him coming and reacted. She threw two black steel darts at the fast moving figure. The first one missed. The second landed in his right thigh causing the attacker to stumble and give her an opening. She didn't waste it. She attacked and hit her target in the sternum causing him to gasp. Then she fired a low kick at his knee. Her opponent stepped back dodging the blow and then countered with a left punch followed by a right cross. She blocked both attacks and responded with a front push kick knocking her attacker down. As she approached her advisory, she drew her blade. Her attacker recovered from her blow and decided to retreat. She watched as the dark figure faded back into the darkness. She decided not to pursue him. Instead, she made a quick sweep of the area and found her bag. Suddenly she heard footsteps approaching fast down the lane. They stopped, turned on their flashlights, and began sweeping the area. She took cover behind a large rock that had brush growing around it which gave her good cover and concealment.

They were the bodyguards; she recognized their silhouettes. Why do they have flashlights? And how did they know there was trouble? She stayed put and watched the pair search the area. She ducked down hugging the ground as their lights came her way. Suddenly, a car showed up, and the guards headed for Linda's place. She crawled around a rock until she could see the house clearly. She quickly took out her camera, started shooting video instead of stills, and watched as the mystery man briefly talked to his men.

"What-the-fuck just happened?" Who was her attacker? His fighting skills weren't very high but his stealth ability was very impressive. If it wasn't for her senses alerting her, she would be dead. And who was this fucker who commanded such security? She waited an hour before she broke cover and headed to the room. Interestingly during the entire incident, Linda never came out or went past a window. Even more, she kept the lights on.

Once home, Shadow Two examined her stomach. A nasty bruise was turning a deep blue. She took some dit da jow and liniment and rubbed it on the bruise. "I guess Paul won't be getting any for a while," she thought. She replayed the audio listening intensely to every word. What is Linda into? What was she being paid for? She remembered the two women who wore a tattoo of a globe with the Number 5 in the center. Maybe this has something to do with that? She added that in her report. Then she put away the recorder and crawled into bed.

That morning after breakfast, Shadow Two and Paul walked down the lane past Linda's rented house. The front door was open and so were the windows. She could see a cleaning woman in the house. Linda left sometime in the early morning, and she suspected the mysterious stranger was also no longer in town.

## Spain

Royce sat by the pool at a villa in Rhoda, Spain, and listened to his agent giving him the report.

"How did you let that person get the best of you?"

"She was quite skilled. She moved a split second before my blade landed. I don't know how she could have heard me; she must have sensed me," he replied.

"So you are out of commission?"

"Yes, I took a dart to my right thigh, and it's infected."

"Can you cure it?"

"Yes, I already took the antidote; it was a basic poison not meant to kill."

"What would you say her skill level is?"

"High, whoever or wherever she received her training—it's top-notch."

"When you recover, notify me. I have more work for you."

"I shall, and sir, sorry for the failure."

Royce hung up the phone without replying. "Who has a female operative that has a high level of unconventional training," he thought. Of course, that was a stupid question; it had to be the CIA. Since Linda retired, they have been watching her. He thought it was because of the Depore incident, but this shed new light on the subject. He got up from his lounge chair. As he walked to the pool, he called over the two nude Spanish beauties who were sunbathing to come swim. Two curvy bronze buxom women walked towards him, and the three of them jumped in the cool water and began to frolic.

Wilhelm read Shadow Two's report and listened to the audio in his office. He sure would like to know what was on that list but he had ordered Shadow Two home. Linda would surface; this he was sure of. He had a mission to plan and this could wait for now. He called MARs and told her to assembly the staff.

# Headaches

## *Chapter Five*

Wilhelm sat in the planning room at CIA headquarters with Rodney's two CIA deputy directors and a NSA deputy director. They were discussing Wilhelm's preliminary plan. He had informed them that he needed six people to complete the mission even though they thought he needed twice as many. Wilhelm and Rodney wondered how he was going to get into the country and what cover story would be used. It wasn't like he was unknown to the intelligence community. Part of his plan was to use his notoriety to pull a little sleight of hand. But the way this meeting was going, he might have to rework his plan.

A phone call came in for one of the CIA deputy directors. When he returned, he had a grin on his face like he had just gotten his dick sucked.

"I know how we can get Wilhelm into the country in plain sight," he said.

"Well what's your great idea?" Rodney said in a monotone voice.

"There's a trade delegation going to Angola in six weeks. Part of its mission is crop buying and selling. Wilhelm can be part of that delegation. After all, he's a farmer of sorts or at least he grows crops. So he and Sanaa can slip in with them while his team carries out the mission."

"What do you think?" Rodney asked addressing Wilhelm.

"It could work ... depending on how long they'll be there and what alternate insertion and extraction sites are available."

"I'll give you the time frame and schedule of the trade delegation. You work on the alternatives," Rodney said.

47

"I think we have covered everything, gentlemen. I'll keep you in the loop." Then Wilhelm excused himself and left the room.

He went back to his office and told his staff what he needed then left for the farm. With the new time frame, he would have to rework his plan which he could do best at home. It was 10:30 p.m. Wilhelm had been working in his library since he arrived home around 2:00 p.m.

"Got a minute?" a voice said softly. Wilhelm looked up from his work and saw Afra standing in the doorway. She was wearing a red sleeveless a-frame summer dress and was barefoot.

"Of course, for you, I'll give you two minutes," he said with a smile and a laugh. Afra walked in and headed for the bar.

"Is it one of those talks?"

"No silly, I want to have a drink with my husband. With the little one and you being so busy, a girl has to pick her openings; so here I am. Now come over here. I really do have something I want to talk about." She handed him a single malt scotch neat and poured herself one. They sat on the leather couch and talked.

The next morning, Wilhelm arose early. He looked over at Afra and watched her sleep as he entertained the idea of a morning romp. But he decided against it and got out of bed. He would let her sleep and catch her later in the day. He put on a robe and headed for his bedroom. Once there, he was careful not to wake Colleen as he cleaned up and dressed for the day. He went downstairs, stopped, and talked with the guard before he headed into the kitchen for breakfast. While he and the chef talked, Afef came in dressed in a blue cotton robe and slippers.

She sat down and poured herself a cup of coffee from the French press.

"Boy! That tastes soooo good," she said after taking a good long sip.

"Rough night?" he inquired.

"Yes, I was up late doing paperwork and checking the books. It would help if you could take a look at them."

"I don't have the time, Afef. You'll have to handle it. Now, what do you want for breakfast?"

He knew what was happening. He had been extra busy lately after just finishing one assignment. And now starting another one, he had even less time to spend with his family. They were starting to let him know it. If they all did it like Afra did last night, he would have no complaints.


*Prague*

Number 5 sat in the dining room of the Grand Hotel in Prague dining with three men.

"Mr. Cinq, we discussed your offer and the money is generous. But before I give you our answer, we have one question."

"Ask me anything. I want you and your partners to be comfortable with this arrangement," Number 5 said as he wiped his mouth with his napkin.

"You want us to eliminate Libertaire's bodyguard and not touch him even if he is around when it's done."

"That's correct; in no way is Libertaire to be harmed when you make your move on his bodyguard," he replied and then took a sip of his vodka martini.

"Then we accept your offer. This is where you can deposit the payment," he said as he slid a small piece of paper across the table.

"And here is the information on your man," Number 5 said as he handed the file to the man closest to him.

Their business concluded. The men relaxed and enjoyed the rest of their meal as they drank and talked. The three killers told him the best places to party and where the freakiest and cleanest whores could be found. Then they said their goodbyes and left. As he watched them leave he thought, "Who would have thought three Chechen killers could be so nice." But he couldn't forget even if he tried that these three men were known as the *Craftsman of Death* and that name was well earned.

Number 5 was pulling out all the stops on this one, and he was getting a little concerned. After all, Libertaire had the resources of the United States. He decided to think about that later. For now, he had to find out which CIA agent was watching Linda and if that person was even CIA.

He ordered another martini and looked over the addresses that he was given. He settled on two: one club and one whore house. He informed his driver that he was ready to leave. Then he and his two bodyguards left the dining room.

*Washington, D.C.*

Wilhelm was staying in the townhouse this week working on the operation day and night. This was not an easy mission. The country and location of the target made it very difficult to hit and get away. He didn't have enough information yet. He had plenty of conventional info. Maps of the terrain in 3-D and satellite images of the target including thermal images were on his desk. He had tide charts, weather reports. What he didn't have was an understanding of the people whom he would be dealing with, not the Chinese but the Angolans.

The state department sent over a history report. His people told him that they didn't have much Intel on the place nor did they have any assets in the area. He needed real Intel; he needed to talk to someone who knew the people and the lay of the land. He picked up the phone and dialed a number. After briefly talking to the person on the other end, he hung up. He sat back in his chair and looked at the mountain of paperwork on his desk.

"MARs!" he yelled.

"Yes, sir," she said as she entered the office.

"I want you to organize this mess into three categories and have it ready by five." She looked at her watch; she had two hours to get this done.

"Yes, sir," she replied and walked over to his desk.

Wilhelm was already out the door and headed for his next meeting. He sat in the briefing room with the operation boys listening to their latest plan. This time he liked the extraction but the insertion was still wrong. He decided to go with the first insertion plan. He returned to his office to find three neat stacks and no sign of MARs. He locked the paperwork in the safe, left the office, and headed to the townhouse.

For his dinner, he prepared lamb chops, cream spinach, and baked sweet potato with lots of butter. He liked to cook; it took his mind off things. He found that he didn't think about anything but what he was cooking. He had been away from the farm for a week now. It was about time to go home and check on things. Tomorrow, he would stop by and visit Derek on his way home. He needed an update, he thought. He plated his meal on a plain patterned china plate, opened a bottle of Spanish red wine, and sat down to eat.

After dinner, Wilhelm sat in the backyard and smoked a cigar while enjoying the evening air as he waited for his guest. An hour later, one of the guards informed him that his guest had arrived and asked if he wanted him brought outside. He instructed him to show his guest to the living room and said he would be along directly. The guard left. Wilhelm put his cigar out and headed inside.

"Hey old man, how are you?" he said as he entered the room and gave him a hug.

"I'm fine, young man. It's you I'm worried about. After your call and what you asked about ... well ... you see why I'm concerned."

"Let me take your coat and have a seat. You want a drink?" Wilhelm asked as he took the elder man's suit coat.

"Yes, a drink would be good about now. But what I really would like is something for my knees; they've been a little sore lately," he stated with a sly smile. Wilhelm knew what he meant so he brought a bottle of *Bowmore Black Ceramic* single malt scotch and two glasses. Next, he brought over a hookah and brass box.

"I think this may help your sore knees," he said as he sat down and poured the drinks.

"Is it Afghani? That works best."

"Yes, it is." Then Wilhelm filled and lit the hookah. The elder man took a long slow pull and upon exhaling said,

"Now that's good medicine." Wilhelm took a pull using his own tube.

"You're right, this is good medicine. Now that you are feeling better, tell me about Angola."

The elder man took another pull, exhaled, and began.

"I was sent to Angola in 1972. Let me tell you it was a fucked up time to be in Angola. My mission was to track the uprising everyone knew was coming—that meant the Cubans. We all knew ... well ... those of us who had any sense knew. The Cubans were the difference in this fight so I paid particular attention to them. The country hasn't quite recovered from those days but there is still a group of nationalist, a small group, but they can help you. I will put you in touch with them. Beyond that, I'm afraid I can't help you."

Wilhelm and his guest smoked and drank way into the night. The elder man answered all of Wilhelm's questions that he could. And when he left, Wilhelm had filled in most of the blanks.

Wilhelm went to bed thinking about what he just learned and how the information he just received differed from what his notes indicated. Six hours later, he awoke with different questions in his head which needed answering. He dressed in a light blue double-breasted summer suite, a pearl white French cuff shirt, pearl cufflinks, a blue and white silk tie with pin, and light blue leather Stacy Adams oxfords. He chose a dark blue summer-weight fedora then went downstairs.

Wilhelm had a light breakfast, went over the new security procedures with his men, and had his driver take him to the safe house. The car leisurely drove through the streets of the upper-middle class neighborhood that hid the safe house. Here, the houses started at eight hundred thousand dollars and went up, and the nosiness of the housewives and househusbands helped with security. His driver pulled into the garage. Wilhelm waited until the garage door closed before getting out of the car. As he entered through the side door, he was greeted by two bull mastiffs both black in color, both holding him and his driver at the entrance. The two dogs stood three feet away baring their teeth and snarling. Wilhelm and the driver stood still; his driver had his hand on his pistol.

"Calm down, you hounds," Captain America said as he approached his boss and patted the dogs on their heads. "Go play now." he told them. The dogs trotted off with their tails wagging.

"Nice choice in guard dogs," Wilhelm said and then headed into the house. "Thanks boss, I took a page from your book."

"How's he doing? Have you cracked the code?"

"Not all of it yet, but I think you'll find what we have deciphered to be quite interesting." The two of them walked into the computer room that was set up especially for this purpose. They found Derek in front of one of the many computer screens.

"What do you have for me, Derek?" Wilhelm said matter-of-factly.

"What? No! How are you doing? Have you had your cock sucked today? Nothing, but what do you have for me," he said mimicking Wilhelm's voice.

"You're a lucky man, Derek; you live in luxury, eat well. And best of all, you're not dead. What more could a man want?"

"I can think of a few things. But that's not why you come a calling. Is it? Let's see. You want to know if I'm living up my end of the deal. Well, Mr. Libertaire, I am."

"I am all ears. Tell me what you have learned."

"First, I have something I want to talk to you about," he said as he spun around in his chair. Wilhelm looked over at Captain America who hunched his shoulders as if to say he didn't know what was going on.

"Okay, tell me what's on your mind," Wilhelm said as he sat down on the leather couch.

"I want a night out ... just one night out and I like to ... no ... I really need to get laid," he said with his arms folded across his chest.

"Why would you think I'd let you go anywhere, you piece of shit slaver."

"Because, *I found* a double agent," Derek said with a big smile. Wilhelm sat there looking at him and then at Captain America.

"What-the-fuck is this all about Captain? Is he shittin' me or what? Because if he is, first it's his ass then yours."

"No, sir, he's serious about the double agent. Concerning the night out, it's the first I've heard of it."

"Let's start with the agent; then we'll talk about you getting laid."

"Fine, here," Derek said and handed Wilhelm a piece of paper. Wilhelm read it then looked at Derek.

"Have you read this?" he asked Captain America.

"Yes, sir, I have."

"And what do you think of this?"

"I checked it, sir, and it's legit."

"You two are telling me that this CIA agent is a double agent and this information came from the Stanley files."

"Yes, sir, that's what I'm telling you. The encryption that they used is about seven years old. So we worked on those files first. Granted, it has taken a bit of time. But once we cracked it, this and a lot more has been decrypted."

"How much do you have transcribed to date?"

"Seven hundred pages give or take a few."

"Where is it?" Captain America walked over to an open safe, took out a folder, and handed it to him. "Fuck, how much more have you deciphered?"

"Nothing since this batch, the Stanleys changed the encryption on this next lot, and we haven't broken it yet."

"Do you know who this double agent works for?"

"No, sir, not yet. What I do know is that she does work for our government and there are only a handful of private companies that could pull this off."

"Now that you have what you want, what about what I want," Derek said.

"You are not going out, Derek; that's not going to happen. But since you have upheld your part of the deal so far, I'll tell you what I am willing to do. I will let you have a small private party, two girls max. You can dance, drink, smoke, and fuck until dawn the next day."

"I'll take it. Hell, I didn't think I'd get that much, and Captain you owe me ten million dollars." Then he let out a hardy laugh and spun around in his chair. Wilhelm got up and signaled for the Captain to follow as he left the room.

"I'll arrange for the girls and the party favors ... and Captain good job. As for the dogs, you took the right page." Wilhelm left the safe house and headed home. On the way, he called Shadow One. Then he called Shadow Two and told her what to get for Derek's party tomorrow night and where to deliver it.

Wilhelm opened the file and began reading; it contained a wealth of information on the CIA, KGB/FSB, Mossad, and others. It also covered operations and double crosses. But what caught his attention was the information on operation *Sugar Cane*. As he read, it became clear that he and his team were the bait. Reading on, he came across a communication from Rodney to Frank; it spelled out what was going to happen.

"Damn, Frank was right; he was following orders." As he read on, he discovered why Rodney gave those orders. Then he concentrated on the double agent and who she could be working for. The Council came to mind. In fact, they were the only ones that came to mind. Since Bryda exited the scene, the private espionage business had been quiet at least the ones who could pull something like this off.

Wilhelm pulled up to the front steps of his house. He walked in and was met by a not to happy Afef.

"I need to talk to you now!!"

"By all means, Afef; let's go to the kitchen."

"No, this is not a kitchen conversation; let's go to the library." Then she headed that way. He handed his hat to one of the staff and followed her. When he entered the library, he found her sitting in front of his desk. He put his briefcase on the desk and sat down in the chair beside her.

"Now what's so important?"

"We have a house guest who I particularly do not like—it's Junior's new girlfriend. Normally, I would careless who he is seeing ... but this chick ... I don't trust or like. You need to tell him to drop her."

"Are you going to tell me who this young lady is? And what has she done to offend you? Or do I guess?"

"Her name is Heather Gil, and she hasn't done anything in particular. I have a feeling about her." Wilhelm ran her name through his memory and the only person he came up with was Senator Gil (R).

"If you could just talk to him ... . With all there is to do around here, I just don't have the time, and you're busy and gone most of the time. Now that you're home, it would *really* help if you could take care of this one little thing." Wilhelm sat there listening and reading her body language; she was tense and wound up.

"Hold that thought," he said as he got up, walked across the room, and closed the library doors. "Make us a couple of drinks," he said as he walked over to a tall wood cabinet, unlocked it, and took out a thirty-six-inch-tall glass dragon bong. It sat on a brass base. One of its outstretched claws held a glass bowl, and it had connections for four smoking tubes. He filled the bowl with a pure indica strain, brought it over to the sofa, and sat down. Afef brought over two gin martinis and sat down beside him curling her legs under her.

"What do you say to us enjoying a smoke and decompressing? I have had a very long week and it seems you have also. So let's smoke this very good indica and then I will see to Junior, okay?"

"I say, yes, my husband. Let's enjoy ourselves." Then she smiled, leaned over, and gave him a kiss.

They talked, drank, smoked, kissed, and laughed for the next hour and a half. And when they emerged, Afef was relaxed and so was he. She went off to see about dinner, and he went to find his son and his son's new sex partner. He checked all the places where he thought he would be but had no luck. So he told one of the house guards to locate him. He stood there and listened to the communications while his security force went about locating Junior. In two minutes, he had a location. Junior and Heather were out riding. Wilhelm gave orders to have them returned to the house.

When they returned, they were told that Wilhelm was in the kitchen and to go there. Wilhelm looked at the young lady dressed in blue jeans, a loose fitting blouse, and sneakers. His son was similarly dressed wearing his Georgetown University tee shirt. Wilhelm was sitting at the table drinking a beer when they walked in.

"Dad! This is Heather Gil."

"Pleased to meet you, sir" she said softly.

"Nice to meet you, Ms. Gil. Sit down, have a beer. You must be thirsty after a good ride." One of the kitchen staff brought over two frosty mugs of beer as the pair sat down. Wilhelm fed her and his son beers as he questioned them and found out all manner of information;

none of it had to do with anything important. He invited her to dinner, and laughed inwardly at how Afef will react to her presence. Now he understood why she had a problem with her.

# Who Zoomed Who

## *Chapter Six*

Early Saturday morning, Wilhelm and Shadow One sat in the library drinking coffee. He gave his assassin his orders concerning the elimination of his target.

"When will you see her again?"

"Tomorrow night, she'll be my date at the show and afterwards back to my place."

"I don't want you to compromise yourself on this job but it needs to be done ASAP. But, take all precautions."

"I'll take care of it, sir. But are you sure she won't talk under pressure?"

"I don't know if she will or not. What I want is for her handlers to think she talked. Whoever she is working for is a new player. I want to see how they react and who comes a snooping. So no torture ... a clean kill. Understand."

"Yes, sir, I understand." Then he took another bite of his toast and drank his coffee.

He and Wilhelm walked down the path to the training platform where a guard was putting weapons in a rack.

"Warm up," Wilhelm said as he walked over to the weapons rack.

"Good morning, sir," the guard said as he approached. Wilhelm returned the greeting and talked to the guard for a moment before he left. He looked up at the terrace patio and saw George having coffee with his two oldest children. Wilhelm walked up the stairs and on to the platform and stopped in the center.

"Alright, let's get started; we have a lot to cover." Shadow One walked about ten meters from the platform, turned, and began his run. First, he did a cartwheel followed by back flips using the last one to propel him up on the platform.

He landed on his feet, two meters away from Wilhelm sporting a smug smile.

"Now that you have that out of your system, we can begin," Wilhelm said. Wilhelm walked to the other end of the platform and turned to face him. "*Wudang Longhua Quan!*" (Dragon form) he yelled. Shadow One's face became serious; then he bowed and started. When he was finished, Wilhelm corrected him and had him do it again. "*Fuhu Quan,*" (Taming the Tiger form) he said, and they repeated the process. This went on as he took him through the forms. Finally, he practiced *Xuanzhen Quan* (Mystical Truth Fist) which ended the fist sets. Next, Shadow One went to the weapons rack and selected a double-edged sword and a staff then returned to the platform this time using the stairs. He started with the staff and performed *Ba Xian Gun* (Eight Immortals Stick). Then he picked up the sword and practiced *Ba Xian Jian* (Eight Immortals Sword). After a short rest, he finished with *San Feng* 108 *Taiji* form.

Wilhelm walked over the weapons rack and selected two dragon fast blade swords and returned as Shadow One was finishing the form. The blades that he chose were narrow and very sharp. The double edges would do serious damage if they hit their mark. He handed him a blade, walked to the outer edge of the bagua symbol, and unsheathed his sword. He laid its scabbard gently on the platform; Shadow One did the same. The two men stood quietly, regulating their breaths, relaxing their minds. The two-person form that they were about to practice required total concentration. Wilhelm took his ready stance; Shadow One followed. They started to circle one another moving to their right. When they stopped after one complete circle, Wilhelm ended up on the *Qian* symbol and Shadow One on the *Xun* symbol.

Shadow One attacked coming straight at him. His sword looked very thin making it hard to see. The manner in which he held it was designed to do just that. Wilhelm parried a thrust and attacked at his midsection causing him to jump back and regroup. Wilhelm didn't give him any breaks; he attacked this time sustaining the attack. He was striking at all eight gates, twisting and turning and attacking from strange angles. Shadow One was working hard to defend himself; he had not seen this attack before today; it was new and deadly. Wilhelm had upped the ante, and Shadow One was doing his best to hang in there. Most of all, he didn't want to get cut. Finally, Wilhelm slowed down and allowed him to catch up. The fencing lesson settled down, and they found a rhythm that allowed them to play for twenty minutes. Wilhelm broke contact and stepped back. The two men circled their hands over their heads and down to their waists, took a deep breath and relaxed.

"What was that technique you used to attack me? I could barely defend against it," Shadow One said as he wiped the sweat off his face.

"That was your lesson. Play it back a few times in your head, and we'll work on it next time." Wilhelm looked up at the patio and signaled for the children to come down; it was time for their lesson. Shadow One jumped down from the platform, picked up his bag, and headed for his car. When his children arrived, he told them of his change of plans and that they would be shooting against him at the skeet range instead.

Back in his library, Wilhelm was just about to go downstairs to his secret office when his cellphone rang. He answered it; Shadow Two was on the line. She told him that she had completed her task and that all was in order. Then she hung up. He leaned back in his chair and stared at the folder in front of him. He wondered what else would he find once he ran the information through the computer. He got up and walked to his secret entrance. He gave the six-foot-tall bronze statue of the African huntress a quarter turn counter-clockwise which opened the new security system panel that revealed a hand, eye, and voice recognition unit. Wilhelm went through the process; the door opened, and he walked down into his own private world of secrets.

## The Show

Dressed in a midnight blue double-breasted Christian Dior tuxedo, Shadow One was talking to a client who had just purchased from him a pair of Bugatti Veyrons for his twin girls. He looked around the room trying to spot Sally but it was a useless endeavor. Two hundred people were attending his show which was by invitation only. They had to be worth fifty million dollars or more. His merchandise was luxury toys for the super-rich spanning from airplanes to custom yachts and everything in between. Although the night had been a success and he had made a ton of money, his mind was on his assignment.

"Hello Jonathan," a voice said behind him. He turned around and there stood, Sally.

"Hello, yourself! My, don't you look good tonight," he said taking a good look at her. She was dressed in a teal-colored cocktail dress, black seamed-stockings, and three-inch, black stiletto heels. Her chocolate-colored diamond necklace and matching bracelet sparkled in the light. Her diamond pendulum earrings swung freely as she laughed and wiggled.

"I looked for you earlier. Where have you been?"

"One of your customers was trying to convince me to become his mistress," she said and then looked at her empty glass.

"I seem to be out of liquor. Would you mind joining me for a drink somewhere a little quieter?"

"Of course, let's go to the private lounge." He took her by the arm and led her to the lounge. Once inside, the room was quiet; jazz played softly. A few people sat at the bar and more spread out on couches around the room. They found an empty couch and sat down. The bartender walked over and took their order.

"When will you be done? I mean when does this event end?" she asked.

"In a couple of hours ... . You still coming back to my place afterwards or did you decide to become a mistress?" he teased.

"Don't laugh. I haven't told him no yet." Then she kissed him. "Of course, that is if you want me to." she said slyly then sipped her drink.

"Making all this money has made me horny as hell and fucking you has been on my mind all day. So you can't be anybody's mistress until I tap that ass one more time. By the way, did you drive or take a cab?"

"I drove, but I don't think I'll be driving out of here, not after this drink. What did you order me anyway?"

"It's a French 75. You like it?"

"Yeah, it tastes good but one of these is my limit. In fact, I think I'll hang out here for a while."

"You do know that I have to get back; there is still a lot of selling to be done. So hang out here. I will be back soon."

"Okay, I'll be right here," she said and then signaled to the bartender. Shadow One got up, leaned over, and kissed her. Then he left the lounge and returned to the event. Sally ordered another French 75 and relaxed on the couch. She was thinking about the best way to get the information that her *real* employer was asking for. They knew he was a world class assassin and skilled interrogator but they didn't know who he worked for. He defiantly worked for one person or organization and was loyal to them even though her boss and a few others had offered him contracts at top dollar. He turned them down; he turned them all down. Now her boss wanted to know all she could about him especially who he works for.

## Carriage House

Jonathan and Sally arrived at his carriage house in the early morning just before sun came up. They road in silence for most of the way since she was drunk and he was tired and had been thinking about the night's proceeds. Amazingly, she woke up with energy as he started up the long private driveway that he and his few neighbors shared. Sally got out of the car with shoes in hand and walked across the grass to the front door where she waited. Jonathan parked the car in the garage and walked around to the front door. They went in. He was greeted by his two Dobermans with their short tails wagging a mile a minute. But when they saw Sally they let out low growls.

"It's alright; she's with me," he said to them and they backed off following him into the kitchen.

"Your companions don't seem to like me," she said as she sat on the stool at the counter.

"It's not you, baby. They don't like anybody but me and I like it that way," he said with a smile. "Make yourself comfortable; I have to let them out," he told her. Then he and the dogs headed for the side door downstairs. He went through his routine checking the cameras before opening the door and letting the dogs out. Then he checked the kitchen camera and watched Sally as she raided his refrigerator. He returned to the kitchen five minutes later with the Dobermans close on his heel. "Find everything?" he asked to the now-munching Sally. She nodded as she chewed on a mouth full of sandwich that she made.

"You want me to make you one?" she asked after swallowing and taking a sip of beer.

"No, I'm going to take a shower and go to bed. When you're done you can join me." Then he left the room. Sally nodded in reply as she kept on eating.

She entered the bedroom just in time to watch him dry off. She stood just inside the doorway and smiled. She looked at this six-foot-two, two hundred fifteen pounds of perfectly muscular and tanned man. She suspected he was Brazilian but wasn't sure because he lightened up in the winter then took on an exotic look. His almond-shaped black eyes and dark wavy hair confused her about his ethnicity. As she watched him dry his back, she couldn't help but notice the rippled muscles in his back and shoulders. Then he turned around and faced her as he started to dry his chest and abdomen. Now he was putting on a show for her and she was enjoying every minute of it. As he dried off, he started to slowly move his hips causing his still wet cock and balls to sway. During his performance, he smiled sexily at her giving her his best boyish grin, and then he turned around. While drying his legs, he bent over just enough to let her see his cock hang and swing; then he turned around and looked at her.

"Are you enjoying the show?" he asked in a baritone voice that made her wet every time she heard it.

"You fucking better believe it," she answered as she approached him. When she reached him, she rubbed her hands first across his chest, next down to his eight-pack abs, and finally to his cock before kissing him. As they kissed, she manipulated his manhood with her fingers until she felt him getting hard. Then she backed away and gave him a show of her own as she undressed. Once naked, she stood there and looked at him. His body was devoid of hair except for his head; she also was hairless. She thought about how their bodies will feel sliding sweatily against each other. The thought made her quiver. Walking over to him, she looked into his black eyes for a moment then lowered herself until she was face to face with his cock. She began kissing and licking it until it showed signs of hardening then she took him into her mouth as she played with his balls.

They fucked in every position she could think of. Both of them were high on the night and each other. When Sally awoke, she found herself alone in bed. She reached over and felt for her cellphone on the night stand.  It wasn't there.  So she got up to look for it and found it hidden under her dress.  She checked for messages, noticed the time, and headed for the bathroom.  After showering, she put on an oversized t-shirt that read, "420 Everyday."  Then she went looking for Jonathan.  She found him in the living room on the phone.  He smiled at her and motioned for her to sit down.  She curled up in the large wicker chair that was suspended from the ceiling.  The chair filled with pillows looked like a bird's nest as it hung.

"I thought you were going to sleep the day away," he said after hanging up.

"Still doing business?  Don't you take off on Sundays, at least?" she replied.

"I will take off this Sunday for you; I promise from now on no more business.  And you know you look like a giant bird in that chair," he commented laughing as he sat up and reached for the low table in front of him.  He opened a glass box, took out a bud, and placed it in his grinder.  "Are you hungry or would you like to smoke a joint with me?"

"First the joint, then maybe some more of that loving, and then I'll see about eating," she said as she climbed out of the chair and sat next to him.

He rolled the joint and told her to put on some music.  Sally maneuvered her way around the two dogs and over to shelves that held his collection of LPs.  She picked one, placed it on the turn table, and began to sway to the music.  Turning to face him, she began to dance her way towards the couch.  Shadow One lit the joint, took a deep pull, and watched her dance.

"Give me some of that!" she said with her hand already reaching for the joint. "You know what I just realized?" she said then coughed.

"What?"

"Your dogs didn't growl at me; I think they are getting use to me being around."

"Stranger things have happened like you passing that joint." Sally took another pull and passed it. The rest of the day was spent listening to music, having sex, smoking joint, and talking. He made dinner for her, and they talked about nothing important. But he made sure not go outside. He didn't want any of his neighbors to see him or her today. As far as they knew, he wasn't home.

Shadow One made a phone call after dinner and made sure that Sally could hear him. He was making arrangements to kennel the dogs at Freddie's Working Dog Kennels. Then he pretended to place a second call making travel arrangements. All the while, he was hoping that Sally would take the bait. After he finished, he sat down on one of the three high chairs at the kitchen island.

"Leaving," she said.

"Yes, I'm afraid so."

"When are you going?"

"Tomorrow, after I drop off the boys."

"When will you be back?"

"In a couple of days—Wednesday at the latest." Sally looked at him for a moment from across the kitchen island.

"When are you taking me home?"

"Are you in a rush to leave?"

"Just answer the question, please."

"I'll take you when you're ready to go. I do realize you have to go to work in the morning. So you tell me when you're ready to leave."

"Perfect answer, because I want to stay awhile longer. I like hanging out with you and your killer dogs," she said as she looked over at them lying at his feet.

Sally had someone watching Jonathan's place. That person would be in place before he took her home on Monday. Once home, she sent her report to her controller. From there, she didn't know where the information went unlike at the agency. The way that she was taught to handle intelligence information for the organization was very complex and compartmentalized, totally different than at the agency. Next she called the kennel and confirmed that the dogs had been dropped off. After that, she contacted the person watching Jonathan's house. She received a report that he had returned home then left an hour ago with one suitcase. He also informed her that he would stay on station until she arrived. Sally waited for the call from the airport. When it came, her contact confirmed that Jonathan had made his flight. Now all she had to do was to wait until dark. Systematically, she laid out her equipment and began her check.

Shadow One went through his routine after dropping Sally off. He took the Dobermans to Freddie's. Afterwards, he went straight home, pulled out a medium hard-cased suitcase, changed clothes, and pulled the car around front. He had a feeling that he was being watched and not just by one of his nosy neighbors/ He wanted that person to believe what he was observing. So, he set his house alarm but put one on a timer. Then he left, put the empty suitcase in the back seat, and drove off. He parked in the airport's short-term parking garage and caught his flight. Later, he returned on the very next flight, changed cars, and then drove to the suburbs to a private club and spa where he settled in for the day.

At dusk, Jonathan left the club and headed for home. He arrived at the park located on the other side of the woods that bordered his house. He changed into all-black treadless rubber slipped-on sneakers. He knew if the house was being watched, they would have someone watching the front and side doors and maybe another was watching the back. Although there was no visible back door, there was an entrance. "That door should unlock in precisely twenty minutes," he thought as he looked at his watch. He looked at the sky then at the woods and headed off in the direction of his home. He worked his way silently through the woods which he knew very well. When he got close, he began his search. First, he went to his right about fifty meters until he could see his side door. Next, he doubled back and went fifty meters to his left. Having found no signs of someone being in the area, he decided to go for the door. He looked at his watch; four minutes remained before the alarm would shut off for one minute and then reset and rearm.

Shadow One sat back to wait but didn't like his location, so he decided to move. As he began to move, he saw movement on his left side and froze in place. He slowly turned his head and focused his eyes into the darkness in the direction of the movement. He spotted a man sitting with his back to a tree not more than ten meters away. He slowly backed up all the while keeping an eye on his target. When he had reached the angle that he wanted, he stopped. He took out his pistol, screwed on a silencer, and started his stalk. When he was in range, he aimed the green laser beam on the man's temple and pulled the trigger. The man fell over never making a sound. He went over to the body and conducted a quick search. He took the man's communication set and black nylon bag; then he headed for the secret door; he had seconds to make it. Once inside, he took a deep breath and headed for his security room and night vision cameras. Fortified in his security room, he searched the woods around the house. Next, he located the second man who was close to where he thought he would be which was positioned to watch the front and side entrances.

ℙ

Sally conducted one last check of her equipment before packing her action bag; then she put on her coat and left. When she arrived at the park, she noticed several cars parked. From what she could tell, this park doubled as a lover's lane after dark. She put on her black rubber ankle boots, strapped on the action pack, and slipped into the woods unnoticed. When she was close to the house, she contacted the man on surveillance then approached him.

"Any changes?" she whispered.

"No, nobody in or out, all clear," he answered. "Do you need me?"

"Yes, stay here until I return." He nodded in response.

Sally cautiously circled to the side of the house while staying in the shadows and using the terrain to cover her approach. When she was in position, she headed for the side door. Shadow One watched her from the time she arrived on site. He admired her field craft and the way she worked. He observed as she pulled out the equipment she needed to defeat his alarm system. He didn't think she had enough time to study his system. Obviously, he was wrong. Sally worked quickly and silently. Within three minutes, she rerouted the alarm current and now was working on the door locks. "Smart girl not breaking the current; that would have activated the backup, very smart girl," he thought.

A minute later, she was in. Closing the door softly behind her, she paused and listened. Then she reached into her bag and pulled out a head lamp. She put it on and started for the stairs. The light from the lamp was just enough for her to see a few feet ahead at a time while hiding her presence from anyone outside.

Shadow One watched as she went through his house room by room sometimes taking pictures. He left his security room and waited for her by the side door. He didn't have to wait long before he saw her light coming down the stairs. He waited until she was in the center of the room before he turned on the lights.

"Shit, where-the-fuck did you come from?" she said as she looked at him and the gun which was pointed at her.

"I must say, you are impressive. The way you breached my security system ... and that fantastic performance playing the lover," he said as he walked towards her.

"Are you going to torture me before you killing me? I know you are a skilled torturer," she said.

"No, I'm not going to torture you," he replied. Then he shot her twice in the chest and once in the head with the silenced 32 caliber pistol. Satisfied that she was dead, he went outside and eliminated the last man.

# Council's Special Resources
## *Chapter Seven*

*Council Headquarters*

Number 2 was reading the report on the deaths of Sally and her team. She knew all too well about the circumstances of their deaths. Their eliminator was Jonathan the world class asshole. He had demonstrated his skill once again, and she had lost her best and only agent inside Department 2. She needed to replace her as soon as possible but for now she would use another agent who is close to that department. Number 2 sat back and stared at Jonathan's picture.

"I'm going to kill you in the most horrible manner possible. This, I promise you," she murmured in a low menacing voice.

She got up from her desk and began to prepare for today's meeting. Number 1 was an information freak; he was always calling for meetings. He wanted to know what was going on all the time but he did run a tight ship. She liked that about him most of all. She could guess what today's meeting would be like which pretty much followed the same routine. First, he would ask for each report even though only he, she, and Number 3 were attending these meetings. The other two were out completing their assignments. Number 5 was hiring and checking on killers as well as spies. Number 4 was in Africa putting together the space age resource machines that she doubted would work. This water-earth thing had to be a hoax, something he came up with to con money out of some poor African leader whom he would sell a bill of goods to, not that she minded. Finance was at the forefront of everyone's mind and was one of the main reasons anybody got into this business. She showered, dressed, and headed for the meeting room. She walked into the room and noticed Number 1 and Number 3 laughing while holding drinks and standing near the huge bay window on the other side of the room.

"What's so funny?" she asked as she approached them.

"He was just telling me a dirty joke," Number 3 said as they turned to face her.

"I see. Care to share it?"

"No, I don't think so," Number 1 said. "But I can offer you a drink; you're about three behind at this point."

"Yes, I think I'll have Sherry, if you please." Then she walked over to the window and looked out.

Number 1 brought her the Sherry. They sat down around the small round stone table in oversized chairs that gave them a great view of the canyon.

"I have great news!" Number 1 said. "We are going to Africa to demonstrate our new product. I've set up meetings with three leaders. We'll leave in three days. So I want you, my dear, to get me as much information on *these* men." Then he handed her a file. "Number 3, I want you to look over these figures and contracts and give me your report and recommendations in two days. This goes for you as well, Number 2." Number 2 and Number 3 began to look over their packets and files as Number 1 got up and refilled their glasses.

*The Farm*

Wilhelm sat in the kitchen having breakfast and reading the overnight reports. It was 5:00 a.m., and the house wasn't up yet on this Saturday morning. Just he and the chef were awake, and all was quiet—a rarity in the house. In a few hours, that will all change. He came across the report that confirmed the death of Sally; he glanced at it and moved on. Today was going to be a busy day. The material for the replica building had been delivered a few hours ago, and the building crew would be there at sunrise. The team that he picked would arrive at 8:00 a.m. except for Tommy. Just then, George walked in and broke his concentration.

"Sit down and have a cup," Wilhelm said to him. George sat down. The chef brought him a mug and filled it, said good morning, and went back to his duties.

"Everything is ready. We can start whenever you're ready, sir," George said; then he took a sip of his coffee.

"Fine, had breakfast yet?"

"No, sir."

"Chef! Fix our friend one of your special omelets; he as a long morning ahead of him."

"Yes, sir. What do you want in it, George?"

The two of them sat and talked about the farm. While he ate, Wilhelm realized just how much he knew about its operations. By the time Wilhelm was ready to go, he had a new appreciation for his trusted bodyguard and friend.

"Let's go before you get fat from Chef's cooking," Wilhelm said jokingly as he rose from the table. He looked down and saw his two French mastiffs lying underfoot.

"Don't just lie there; let's go, guys," he said to them. The dogs got up, shook their bodies, and fell into step with him as he headed to the library. There, he picked up his tablet and a memory stick and left. George was waiting for him out front in the wrangler with one guard. Wilhelm climbed in and sat in the back.

"Are we taking the dogs, sir? I'm sure they would like to hang out," George said looking over his shoulder at his boss. Wilhelm looked over at the two dogs being held back by another guard.

"Let'em go!" he ordered, and the two dogs jumped into the jeep.

As George drove, Wilhelm plugged in the memory stick and looked at the operators whom he had chosen for this mission. He had decided to use contractors for this operation because chances were good that they all wouldn't get out. When it came to the environment, the area in which they had to work was not the friendliest. Also their enemy was ruthless and well trained. They needed to assault a building located on top of Bei plateau in the middle of the jungle in Angola then make the rendezvous. These guys are not going to be happy once they find out what they signed up for. Then again, this is what they do for a living. The jeep pulled up in front of the training house. George and the guard got out. He said something to the guard who afterwards headed off towards the rear of the house. The guard ran back and reported to George.

"Sanaa is around back with her gear, and the materials are a half mile to the east."

"What-the-fuck is she doing around back?" Wilhelm questioned.

"She says that's where she was dropped off at around 5:00 a.m., sir," the guard replied.

"Let's pick her up; then head to the construction crew and maybe the rest of the team are there," Wilhelm told George.

"Good morning, Ms. Amina. Could you get in and tell me why you're not with the rest of the team?" Wilhelm said. She climbed in, gave the dogs a cautious look, and then sat down.

"Well, sir, the helicopter landed not far from the back porch and with all the gear; it was the first place I landed so to speak," she explained.

"An hour later, another helicopter landed in the direction where we're headed now, sir." Then she was quiet. Wilhelm listened to her but he didn't acknowledge her report even though she had answered his question. The jeep pulled up in front of a stack of two by fours and stopped. Sitting in front of the lumber about twenty-five meters away sat four black men dressed in civilian clothes.

They got out of the jeep, and George and the guard spread out. They did this by habit; there was no need to be told. His guard eyed the four men as he took a casual combat stance and took his assault rifle off of safe with a flick of his thumb. George was closer to Wilhelm but still between him and the men. Sanaa had taken a few steps to her right and found herself standing behind the jeep. The two mastiffs milled around. The male pissed on the wood as Wilhelm stood there putting faces to bodies. Then he turned the tablet off.

"So that's him," Lee said.

"Yeah, that's him," Daniel replied.

"I like his dogs. What are they? They're fucking huge," Jhon said.

"Did you get a look at how his security team set up?" Paul added.

"Yeah, I caught that. The three of them spread out just right, and the one in the tactical gear is trying hard to look relaxed," Lee said.

"I bet that sidearm is a 10mm, and that AR he's carrying is chambered in 30.06," Daniel said.

"How do you now that?" Paul asked.

"Because I did my homework and I know a guy who worked with him. Everything his security team packs is custom and deadly," Daniel continued.

"Well, he's not going to walk over and invite us for drinks; let's get off our asses and report in, shall we," Lee said. The four men got up and walked towards him. As they got close, the two mastiffs closed ranks in front of Wilhelm and gave one loud menacing bark.

"It's okay, guys. They won't hurt you," he said to the dogs.

"Good morning, sir, my name is Lee and this is Daniel, Paul, and Jhon. We are your team, sir."

"Good morning, gentlemen, I want you to get your gear and meet me at the training house. You will find it about a half mile west," Wilhelm said. Then he signaled to George, called the dogs, and walked away. The four men headed back to their gear. Sanaa stood there while the guard watched everything in silence.

When Wilhelm arrived at the house, he found the four men sitting at the table drinking coffee and talking. He introduced Sanaa, and told them there was one more operator whom they would meet later. Then he introduced the trainers and the chef, had the men shown to their rooms, and told them training would start in fifteen minutes. The team returned dressed in black cargo pants, black t-shirts, and black boots. One of the trainers ordered them outside and the five of them filed out.

"Back to the house," Wilhelm said to George as he headed for the door. George followed his boss to the jeep while thinking this was a strange meeting and beginning of a mission.

*South Sudan*

Number 1 was pleased with what he saw when they arrived at the research center. The plane had circled the area twice before landing. From the air, the center looked like five ordinary buildings. But once on the ground, it was a different story. Five buildings in all included the living/business quarters, research building, communications center, staff/security quarters, and a well-stocked warehouse. Their living area was lavish. Every luxury that was needed or thought to be needed was in there. Each of their personal living areas was set up for each member's personal tastes and was staffed to fulfill their every request. After the tour, Number 1 let Number 4 know that he was very pleased.

"Tonight we have our first meeting with the three leaders who accepted our invitation. The festivities will begin at 8:00 p.m. tonight," Number 4 told them.

"Good, that gives me some time to relax and unwind; that flight was taxing to say the least," Number 2 said.

"Then by all means, go and rest. Someone will notify you in plenty of time," Number 1 said. "Now tell me how are we situated here and don't leave anything out. Also what's the entertainment going to be like? You know these African leaders like lots of everything and pretty white girls. You did get the white girls, didn't you?" Number 1 asked.

"Yes, I did, and I have enough liquor, food, and women for them. But do you want to see the lab and the demonstration that I have prepared for them?" Number 4 asked.

"Yes, I do. So take me to the lab and along the way bring me up to speed on what all this is costing."

While Number 1 and Number 3 were looking over the lab and paperwork, Number 2 was checking the reports concerning Jonathan. She was having him followed. And when the time was right, she would kill him. She stripped down and sat in the hot tube that gave her a view of the private garden. "He really did think of everything," she thought. Then she pressed the service button and laid back.

The private planes of the three African leaders and their entourage had all landed by 7:30 p.m. Meanwhile, Number 4 was preparing for the demonstration. He inspected the room while Number 1 watched the leaders from Nigeria, Mali, and South Sudan. They talked and drank amongst themselves as their aides stood to the side and held their own mini-summit.

"Where in the hell is Number 2! Why does she have to be late all the time?" Number 1 said as he looked at his watch.

"We have time. Let them finish their drinks. I sent for her," Number 4 replied.

Number 2 glided into the room as if on cue. She was wearing an open-back black silk haltered-style evening gown that caressed her body. She wore her hair up, and her makeup made her look ten years younger. Adorned in a ruby necklace, earrings, and bracelet, she was ravenous. She walked into the middle of the room, took a glass of champagne from the waiter, and stood there sipping it. The room slowly quieted as the men started to notice her. When the room was completely quiet, she spoke.

"Gentlemen, thank you for coming. I know some of you have traveled a great distance to be here. But be assured, you have not made the trip for nothing. What you will see this evening is the future and the power to make nations like yours respected, prosperous, and powerful. So I will now turn your attention to my colleagues ... but first, a toast to those who see the future and seize it. Salute!" They all raised their glasses and drank. Then she looked over at Number 1 and winked.

"Gentlemen, if you would follow me, I will escort you to our research facility," Number 4 said. The leaders walked into the state-of-the-art facility and were impressed. "These are an example of the crops that can be raised in your regions; crops that couldn't grow there before. With these genetically enhanced seeds, you can grow in any area you choose. Please gentlemen, ask any questions and feel free to handle the seeds." Number 1 hung back; he was watching intensely looking for any sign of trouble and observing the clients' reactions. He was surprised at Number 2's performance. He hadn't expected it. But he was more concerned with her power over men after watching their reaction to her. He watched as the leaders' experts examined the grain and received their samples. "Now gentlemen, what you are really interested in ... . If you will, follow me please," Number 4 said.

He led them to a 500 liter tank of water and stopped. Number 1 knew this was it. If they didn't get the formula right, he would look like a fool and all was for not.

"In front of you is water from our own well. I invite your experts to test its purity," he said. Number 4 showed them where the testing kits were, and each man took one. They picked up a beaker from the table and filled it halfway from the spout on the tank. "First, I want you to test it for minerals and any other standard contaminant that you would find in water and is not fit to drink." He stepped back from the table and let the men work. The African leaders talked to their advisers while they waited. Number 1 lit a cigar, and Number 4 talked with his technicians.

"We are ready," one of the men said. Number 4 walked over to them.

"Now tell us what you found," he said.

"We find this water to be undrinkable, and it contains the following contaminants." The man read the seventeen contaminants to the group.

"Now I am going to add dirt to the mix just enough to color it a deep brown." He climbed a step ladder and poured dirt into the tank. When he thought he had enough, he stopped and stepped down. Next, he pressed a red button and the tank water started to swirl. He waited a minute then pressed the button again turning it off. After the water settled a bit, he told one of the guards to bring him the box.

"Gentlemen, please gather around. In this box, I have a pill; it's not magic; it's science." He waited until they gathered before continuing. Then he opened the box and showed them the six white pills that were a little larger than a marble. He passed the pills around and let the men examine them up close. When they returned them to him, he began. "Now your experts have tested the water, and you witnessed the dirt being added. Watch what happens when I add this white pill to the mix." He climbed the ladder and dropped it in. They waited for what seemed to be an hour to Number 1 but actually was only three minutes. The water started to clear up. Ten minutes later, he told the same men to retest the water. They filled new beakers and reran the test.

"I don't believe it! But I saw it with my own eyes. The science is true and correct. This water is drinkable," the expert from Nigeria stated.

The other experts all made similar statements. All asked how this was done. Number 1 smiled broadly and joined the conversation.

"This is why I invited you here. With this technology, you can not only feed your people but you can use land that was not available to you before. You can turn deserts into productive land and sustain life anywhere in your country," Number 1 told them.

"Now if you would, follow me back to the meeting area. We will begin the festivities," Number 4 told them. When they returned, the room had been transformed. The men found it full of women, all tall, shapely, and buxom, some blond, some brunette. Two women were available for each man, and three very handsome, well-built, tall men were added to the mix as well.

"Well done, Number 4. You didn't forget the white women, and the setup is superb. Your presentation was perfect. It's times like this that reminds me of your genius for organization and administration." Number 2 walked up and addressed them.

"I take it, all went well," she commented.

"Yes, quite well. And your speech was well timed too," Number 4 replied.

"Are those three gorgeous men for me?" she asked.

"Of course, my dear, I very well couldn't leave you out of the fun, this evening. And how are your quarters? I hope they are to your liking."

"If your taste in men is as good as your decorating skills, I'll be in heaven, tonight. Now if you will excuse me; I think I'll start on those delicious darlings," she said and then headed for the men. Number 4 stood there and watched as the waiters weaved in and out of the crowd offering drinks, hors d'oeuvres, and desserts. The men talked to each other and to the women. Number 2 was surrounded by the three men who were laughing and having a good time. But he couldn't have fun just yet. There was still a ton of shit to do. "It was okay if they had a good time. But I have work to do," Number 1 thought.

*The Farm*

When Wilhelm arrived back at the house, he found Tommy talking to one of the guards.

"What are you doing here? And who's watching asshole?" he said as he got out of the jeep.

"I have Daryl watching him while I'm gone. Everything is fine, boss. I'm here because you need to see this." Then he held up a folder.

"Come on and show me what you got. Sanaa, I want you to go with this young man. He will show you where you'll be staying and where to put your gear." Then he, Tommy, and the dogs headed up the stairs to the house. George had the guard take Sanaa to the security quarters.

Wilhelm went straight to his library, pressed the kitchen button, and told the chef to send in a pot of tea.

"Okay, Tommy, what do you have that's so important that you had to leave the apartment?"

"This batch of Intel, if I'm not mistaken, has information about double agents and agents from a yet unknown organization. We began decoding this batch when Derek ran across the information. So far, I've identified seven agents who work for MI6 and us. I still have about hundred pages to go." Just then, the tea arrived. He and Tommy stopped talking.

"Thank you. I'll pour, and please close the doors on your way out," he said to the server. "Are you sure about this information? You didn't misread it?"

"No, sir. I triple checked it, and I still can't believe it. I have no idea who this other organization is either. But they are mentioned throughout these papers."

"What is their name? How are they identified?"

"They're called the Council or the Council of Five. I've never heard of them; maybe it's a code name. I'm just not sure, sir," Tommy said then poured himself a cup of tea.

Wilhelm sat and listened; he could hardly believe what he was hearing—the Stanleys those sneaky Stanleys. He wondered how long they had been collecting data on the Council and what else Tommy and Derek might find in those documents.

"Sir, when do I start training?" Tommy asked.

"Tomorrow, be at the training house at 6:00 a.m."

"Yes, sir. Do you want me to continue with this? Or should I turn it over to Daryl, sir?"

"Turn it over to Daryl. I'll call him and fill him in. I need you to be focused 100 percent on this mission. Now is there anything else I should know about?"

"Yes, sir, there are several mentions of Spain and North Africa. But there's no connection that I could find to anything in this batch."

"All right, I'll look into it. But I want you to clean out your stuff from the apartment and get your mind around this assignment. I'm counting on you on this one, and I need you to be 100 percent and then some. So take the rest of the day off. I'll see you in the morning." Tommy got up and headed for the door. "And Captain, you did good on this one," Wilhelm said to him as he left.

Wilhelm picked up his desk phone and pressed George's extension.

"Yes, sir," he said.

"Put a man on the door," was all he said and then hung up. A moment later, a guard knocked on the door. "Come in!" he bellowed. The right side of the pocket door opened up, the guard stepped in, and stood there. "Do not let anyone in until I tell you to, understand, no one," he said to the guard.

"Yes, sir, I understand; no one is to be admitted." Then he stepped back through the door and closed it. Wilhelm gathered up the papers and walked to the entrance of his secret work area, went through the protocols, and descended into his cavern. He walked to his computer station, placed the papers into the document feeder, adjusted the tray, then walked up to the terminal, and sat down in his command chair.

"Computer, on!" The 60-inch transparent screen came alive.

"Good morning, sir," a female voice responded.

"Computer, scan, and organize the papers in the tray by country, city, location, and name. Display on screen." He listened to the computer begin its work; it was extracting papers at a high rate. He sat back and waited. Then the information started to appear on the screen; he viewed the pages on the screen as they were being arranged. He saw a pattern first in Germany, then in Spain, next in Ukraine. The list kept building. He sat and watched in amazement. Then he started to worry.

Wilhelm sat there looking at the screen. His eyes scanned from one section to the next all the while giving the computer instructions. When he finished, he sent a note to Wendy.

Will be in your area. Will notify you of my arrival.

He instructed the computer to code and send the message to her. Then he looked at his watch; he had been down here for six hours. Wilhelm shut down the center and went upstairs. He relieved the guard and called George into the library. George walked in and stood in front of the desk.

"Sit down, George. In fact, before you do that, would you fix me a scotch? And you one? Also I have orders for you." George poured two stiff drinks, brought them over, and sat down after handing Wilhelm his drink. Wilhelm took a sip then began. "I'm going to Spain in a few days and I'm going alone. While I'm gone, I need you to supervise the training." Wilhelm paused and took another sip of his drink.

"That's never a good idea, boss. If you're not going to take me, take one of the other guys. There are a dozen men and women who you can choose from. Why go alone?" George protested.

"I'm taking this trip alone. I have my reasons and none of them include me getting killed. I'll be gone a few days, a week at the most. And you're to do what I ask you to do. It would save both of us a lot of time and energy," he said and downed his drink. He held his glass towards George who took it and refilled both of their glasses, this time making them a triple. "What are you trying to do, George, get me drunk," he said when he saw the glass.

"No, but whatever is making you take such a risk ... you might as well get drunk," he replied. Then he took a good sip downing half the glass of scotch.

# Hunting Shadows

## *Chapter Eight*

Wilhelm sat in his office looking over the plans for his latest assignment and was trying to figure out how to minimize causalities. As it stood now, their extraction was the most vulnerable part, more so than usual. And he didn't trust the underground group that he had been put in touch with. Yes, they had provided valuable information on the target and the personnel as well as information on certain political figures. But he couldn't count on them to help the team if they needed it. At least, that's the smart play.

"MARs!" he yelled.

"Yes, sir," she said as she entered the office.

"Book me on a flight to Madrid tomorrow, and tell the boys upstairs to come to my office." She turned and left going back to her desk and getting on the phone. MARs had worked out better than he had thought. Gladys had good instincts.

After his meeting, he left the office and headed to the townhouse. On the way, he sent Shadows One and Two a text message. An hour after he arrived home, Shadow One appeared on his front door step. One of his guards escorted him to where Wilhelm was waiting.

"Want a drink?" he asked.

"I'd rather have a spliff and a juice," he replied.

"You have to roll your own; you'll find what you need in that wooden box over there," Wilhelm said as he pointed to it. "I'll have the juice brought to you. Now let's get to it," Wilhelm said as he sat on the couch in his living room. Shadow One finished rolling his spliff of Sour Diesel just as the pitcher of mango-pineapple juice arrived. "These are your targets. All three can be found in either Ukraine or the Czech Republic—two men, one woman. I need you to find out who they are spying for as double agents and you need to record your interrogation. I need these people alive; you are not to harm them. As for this person, I need this target eliminated," he said as he handed him a picture of a man.

"This is one of China's best assassins. His name is Yu Yuen; he's responsible for the removal of three agents working in Tajikistan. The last report has him headed back to the area for reasons yet to be ascertained. I need you to stop this guy; he's become a big problem." He handed him his file. "Do you have any questions?"

"Yes, after the recording session, do you want me to clean up afterwards?"

"No, absolutely no, I want the information they possess and make sure you are not identified. I don't want you to have any excuses to kill these targets."

"I understand, Sifu, no harm will come to them," he said as he took a long pull of the spliff.

94

They sat and talked for the next hour with Wilhelm giving him more instructions and his exit and contact points. Shadow One went over the file of the man whom he was tasked to kill. He asked questions that a killer would ask, and Wilhelm answered them. He proved to him, once again, his expertise and experience. Wilhelm offered suggestions and gave advice on how best to kill his target. Shadow One listened and then left.

Wilhelm went to the kitchen. A few of the guards were playing dominos and drinking coffee.

"Please continue playing," he told the men as he passed by headed to the cupboard. He took out a plain white kitchen apron and tied it around his waist wrapping the long string around his body and tying it in the front. He walked to other side of the kitchen and turned on the radio. His guards were accustomed to their boss cooking. Sometimes he cooked a meal just for them. They had come to the conclusion that cooking helped him think, and he cooked the best meals when he had a tough assignment. Wilhelm pulled out his ingredients, some pots and pans, and a chopping board, lit a joint, and began to prepare a meal for two. A moment later, Shadow Two entered the kitchen.

"Hmmm, that smells good," she said as she stood in the doorway with a hand on her hip looking at him and the men at the table. Wilhelm looked over at the table. The men got up and left leaving the dominos where they lie.

"Have a seat; dinner is almost done. I thought we would have a bite to eat as we talk," he said as he kept cooking. She sat down at the table collected up the dominos, put them away, and asked for some wine. Wilhelm pointed to the wine cooler; she got up and went to it.

"I had no idea you knew wine. I thought you were strictly a scotch man," she said as she looked at his selection of wines.

"I keep a few bottles for guests and freeloaders like you."

"Oh, so you got jokes as well. Just for that, I'm going to open this one," she replied holding the fifty dollar bottle of Spanish wine.

"Don't get drunk. We have a lot to go over tonight. Have you healed from your last mission?"

"Yes, sir, I have; I am 100 percent."

"Are you back to full training?"

"Yes, I'm back to full health and fitness. Stop worrying; I can do the assignment," she said seriously.

"That's good to hear because you will be doing some traveling and I need you in top form," he said without looking around at her.

"I hope you're hungry because I am. We're having bison steaks, sweet potatoes fries, and a three green medley with sour dough bread. Now help me set the table." She set the table and opened another bottle of wine. They sat down to a comforting meal and talked about everything but the mission. He laughed at her jokes and listened to her rambled about her friends and boyfriends. After dinner, he cleared the table, and they went to the living room to discuss her mission. They sat on the couch and Wilhelm began his briefing. He handed her a file that contained four pictures.

"The first two targets are to be interrogated; it is to be recorded and sent to me. You are not to harm these targets. If at all possible, they are to remain alive. As for your last two targets, you are to eliminate this man; his name is Roberto at least that's what he is calling himself. Now he is a freelance hitter. This one is to be tagged and she can't know she has been. I'll leave it up to you on how to accomplish that. Roberto can be found in Milan. Your other targets are in London and Germany respectively. You will be leaving tomorrow night. These are your exits if you need them, and here are the addresses of safe houses. These are your contacts; they will provide you with the equipment you'll need. Also in your packet is information on your last target. Bring your A-game; he's good at what he does."

She sat there quietly studying the information that she had been given. "This must be an important job, first the dinner, then the special orders," she thought.

"Now do you have any questions?" he asked breaking her concentration.

"No, I pretty much get it. You didn't give a girl much time to study but I can handle it."

"I told you not to drink too much," he said as he poked her in the side making her laugh like a little girl.

"After that dinner, who's drunk? I have to go home and exercise as it is," she replied as she stood up. She bent over and gave him a kiss on his forehead, said goodnight, and left. It was 11:00 p.m. and all of his business was done for the night. He put on some jazz, rolled a joint, and slipped into the night.

*Madrid, Spain*

Wendy was waiting for Wilhelm as he cleared customs. She watched as he walked towards her and wondered why he was here.

"Wilhelm, nice to see you. This is a surprise I'm going to regret," she said giving him a hard look.

"No, it's not, and it's nice to see you also. I take it, you are still a little mad at me."

"A little is an understatement, but let's not do this now. Why are you here?"

"I'll tell you about it on the way to your office," he said then walked off. Wendy and her guard followed. When she caught up to him, they were on the escalator.

"You did that on purpose you son-of-a-bitch," she said through clenched teeth.

"Did what?"

"Walking fast knowing I couldn't keep up with these damn heels on."

"You need to relax, Wendy. I didn't do it on purpose. I guess this promotion and posting agrees with your fashion sense. I won't ask for a thank you," he said with a shitty smile as he looked down at her shoes. Wendy knew he was fucking with her, and it made her madder than she's been in ages. But she couldn't blow her cool. She had to stay calm; there was plenty of time to pay him back for what he did.

On the ride to the embassy, Wilhelm engaged her in small talk forcing her to interact with him. By the time they reached the embassy, she had relaxed and her mind was back on why he was there. As they walked to her office, she could hear the whispers:

"That's Libertaire," they were saying. They entered her office. She closed the door and offered him a drink before sitting down behind her desk.

"Why are you here, Wilhelm? You send me a message you're coming but you neglected to add the reason."

"I know I should have let you know more about my visit, but I have my reasons. There's a man here who I need to talk to. He may have information on a case I'm working on. I'm here to meet with him," he explained.

"Bullshit! You're telling me that you've come all this way without George, I may add, to meet a guy. That's bullshit,

Wilhelm, and you know it. Next you'll ask me for personnel to help you carry out your plan," she said laughing. Wilhelm sat there and looked at her with a blank expression and watched her laugh.

"The person I'm going to meet says he has information on the organization that was responsible for the elimination of your strike team. This is the same organization that Frank was working for, and he is here in your backyard. So here I am." Wendy stopped laughing, and a serious mood took over her as she stared at him. "Would you like that drink now?" he said with a smile.

"Yeah, I'll get them." Wendy got up and went to the bar. When she returned, she sat in the chair opposite him. "What is the name of this man?"

"He goes by the name of Royce. I've never heard of him, but that's his claim," he said then took a sip of his scotch.

"Do you have a picture of this man?"

"No, I don't, but my information has a person that fits his description who's leasing an apartment here in Madrid. So I need your help in identifying him. After all, this is your area of responsibility."

"I'll help you only if I can be there when you meet this Royce fellow."

"Okay, I figure you have just as much invested in this as I do."

"Then it's settled. I'll have some of my people get right on it," she said then raised her glass and drank her shot in one gulp. "Where are you staying?"

"At the Ritz."

"I'll have a couple of my people provide security while you're here. I don't want you killed if I can help it."

"Don't put yourself out on my account. I came without security for a reason so have them keep their distance," he said then stood up. "And on that note, I'll be in touch. And remember, have them keep their distance. I don't want this guy scared away." Then he left her office. Looking at her computer screen, she watched him as he cleared the floor. She walked to her office door, opened it, looked around the room at several agents, and then pointed to two of them. A man and woman got up from their desks, entered her office, and stood in front of her desk.

"I am about to give you a career making assignment. Sit down," she said to the agents standing in front of her. "Yes, that was Libertaire in the flesh, and you two are going to guard him. You're not to let him out of your sight. You're to follow him wherever he goes. And be inconspicuous. Of course, he will know you're there, but you'll act like he doesn't know you are there. Is that understood?" The two agents answered her in unison. "He's staying in the penthouse suite at the Madrid Ritz. You two will be across the hall. By the time you get there, it will be all arranged. Your cover name is Cortez. A team will bring you your equipment. Now get going and keep me posted with 12-hour reports."

The two agents left her office and headed for the hotel. Wendy sat there thinking about this Royce fellow and what could possibly make Wilhelm travel without security. She could bet Langley and Rodney didn't know about this little trip, and she wondered how they would feel if they found out. Then she picked up the phone and began making calls to contacts who she thought could help her locate and identify Royce.

*Washington, D.C.*

The men known as the *Craftsmen of Death* stepped off the Air France plane at Reagan International Airport. After clearing customs, they took a cab to a home located in a comfortable middle-class neighborhood. A tall statuesque blond answered the door and welcomed them in.

"My friends, it's good to see you. How long has it been?" a tall slim man said in his Russian-American accent. "Come, sit, and eat. My wife has prepared a wonderful meal for us. We will eat and drink, and you can rest from your journey. Afterwards, we do business. So relax. You are safe here," he said.

"Thank you, my friend. We could use a good meal and the sharing of some good vodka with an old friend," one of the Chechens said. Their contact showed three men to their rooms.

After they had cleaned up and changed, they came down for dinner. The five of them ate and drank. The men asked about old friends and enemies and laughed and talked for hours. Later the four men went to Nikolai's office for business.

"Here are the weapons and communications gear you ordered. And here is the tracking equipment. Do you know who this man works for? If you're not quite sure, this information will spell it out for you. This is the latest intelligence on your man," Nikolai said as he handed him the file. The tall Chechen took the file and began reading it while his colleagues went over the equipment.

"Now that I know a little more about my target or in this case I should say my opponent, he should make this an interesting hunt," he said then revealed a most evil smile. The men finished their business, stored away the equipment, and then went back out to the living room. As they were having a drink, they heard a knock at the door. The three men grabbed their guns and made ready.

"It is okay," Nikolai's wife said as she headed for the door. "It is only my girlfriends. I thought you might want some company tonight." She went to the door and opened it. In walk three Ukrainian women. All three women were stunning. They were six feet tall, curvy with ample breasts, and milky-white skin and dressed to accentuate those assets. One woman was a redhead; another was a brunette, and the last one had coal black hair.

Nikolai's wife introduced the women to the men using the names they had given her. She had selected each woman for the sexual preference of each man as per her husband's instructions. She also had outfitted each room with the toys they would need. Next, she rolled out a small steel table. Cocaine, an assortment of pills, hash, opium, and marijuana lay on top of the table. Liquor, bongs, and other instruments for enjoying themselves sat on the bottom shelf. She put on some party music and joined her husband and guests in the living room.

His wife had matched the black-haired woman with the leader of the Chechen killers. She was dressed in a dark miniskirt, a sheer blouse, high heels, black fishnet stockings, and garters. As his wife watched them interact, she knew she had made the right choice. "Tonight should be interesting," she thought. They partied late into the night drinking and laughing and dancing. Then the men took the women to their rooms.

The dark-haired woman walked into his room and stood at the foot of the bed facing him.

"What's your name?" he asked her after closing the door.

"Tattia," she answered. He walked to the armoire and opened it. Then he turned and slapped her hard across the face causing her to stumble. When she looked back at him, she was smiling. She looked past him into the armoire and saw the assortment of leather paddles, whips, restraints, and a few things that she didn't recognize. As she began to undress, she said, "Let's party, baby. I hope you know how to use those toys." He didn't answer her. He just started to take his clothes off with that evil grin on his face.

## Mission Training

The sun was rising and George was standing on the front porch of the training house drinking a cup coffee when Tommy drove up.

"Where's everybody?" he asked George while sitting in the jeep.

"On a run, park around back; meet me at the pistol range. They should be back any minute now," he said. Tommy drove to the back of the house and parked. Then he and an instructor walked to the range. They were talking and joking around when he saw George coming. He was carrying a plastic bag.

"What's he up to now?" Tommy said to the instructor as they looked on.

"It looks like a candy bag," the instructor said as he stared at the bag.

"I believe you're right. What's he going to do? Give us candy when we do something right," Tommy said.

"Whatcha got there, George?" Tommy asked when he walked up.

"Lollypops. Tommy, me, and you are going to have a rematch."

"How much this time? You know you have yet to beat me at this game," Tommy said.

"How about three hundred and we use the new guns," George said then headed down range. Tommy and the instructor watched as George setup the lollypops, twenty in all. Then he returned. "Now we're going to the fifteen meter line. Each of us has ten shots. The one with the least left wins. Agreed?" George said.

"Agreed," Tommy replied. "I can use and extra three hundred," he continued.

"Can I get in on this?" the instructor asked.

"Hell yeah, you can. Who do you like?"

"I'll take George for three hundred. Can you cover it." he said.

"Put your money where your mouth is," Tommy said. Then he reached in his pocket and began counting out bills.

The instructor loaded two PPX tactical navy pistols in 9 mm and handed the weapons to them. George looked in the direction the team should be coming from and saw them in the distance. Then he walked to the firing line.

"Let's give it a minute, Tommy. There's some people who should see this."

"Sure, I'm in no rush to take your money," he said jokingly. In a few minutes, the team ran up. As they stretched and caught their breath, the two men began. The team stopped what they were doing and watched as Tommy and George shot the lollypops.

"Fuck!" George said when he missed his last shot.

"Better luck next time, and you know there will be a next time," Tommy said as he took the magazine out and cleared the weapon.

"Team, this is Captain America. He is the sixth member and will be training with you for now on. As you can see, he's a hell of a shot and he has other talents as well. I'm sure you all will get acquainted as you train. Now the instructor will get you familiar with the PPX what we were just shooting, the M416 CQB in 7.62x39, and the DP 12 gauge shotgun. So pay attention. I'll see you later at the explosives briefing," he said. Then he paid Tommy and left.

# Mission Madrid

*Chapter Nine*

*South Sudan*

Number 2 walked out into the garden where Number 1 was sitting and sat down.

"What's on your mind?" he said.

"I just received word that Libertaire is in Madrid at the Ritz."

"Fantastic!"

"Why is this good news? We have no idea why he's there and alone without his bodyguard?"

"You're sure he's there without George?" he said as he leaned forward in his chair and looked at her with renewed interest. "Who has he had contact with since he's been there?"

"The usual, he was picked up by the station chief, had a short visit to the embassy, and then off to his hotel. He has a security team watching over him, of course. How many, I don't know yet. Other than that, he's been hanging around the hotel as if he's waiting for someone."

"Do nothing. Just keep an eye on him. I have a feeling Mr. Libertaire is setting a trap," he said as he sat back with a thoughtful look on his face.

"A trap? Why do you think he is setting a trap?" she said puzzled.

"I have an agent in Spain. I hadn't figured he would locate him so quickly. The fact that he is alone is what's causing me to pause. I don't believe the CIA would allow this behavior. He has to be setting a trap of some kind. So have your agents report on his movements, and see if they can sniff it out. Do not interfere or make contact."

"Alright, if that's your orders," was all she said. Then she left the garden.

He sat in the garden for the next two hours thinking about Libertaire and what he could be up to. He pondered the possibilities, the many reasons why he was making this move. But when it came to dealing with Libertaire caution was advised. He got up, went to his office, and placed a call.

"Hello Royce, how's Spain?"

"Fine, why are you calling? I thought we weren't to communicate until after?"

"I'm aware of that but a problem has appeared in your area."

"What problem?" he said seriously.

"Libertaire is in Madrid."

"What do you want me to do about that? He doesn't know I'm in Spain does he?"

"Not that I'm aware of, but I'm working on it. For the meantime, sit tight; do nothing. I just wanted to keep you informed."

"Thank you," Royce said and then hung up.

Royce sat smoking a cigar. "So he's here; that can't be a coincidence, that bastard with his courtesy call. Well, here's my opportunity," he thought. He picked up his cellphone and sent a text. He waited for the reply, sent a second text, and then took out the SIM card. He picked up a second cellphone and hit the speed dial. "We're going to Madrid. See you in an hour," he said and then hung up. He told one of the young women to pack his suitcase and what to put in it. Royce and one of his female companions boarded the train in Barcelona for Madrid. The man he called also boarded.

Wilhelm changed for dinner and went down to the hotel's restaurant. After he was seated, he told the waiter to tell the couple at the table across from him that their meal was on his tab. As the waiter told the security team what he said, they looked over at him embarrassed and smiled. Wilhelm nodded in reply and smiled to himself. He remembered when he was a young operative tasked to follow someone like him. But he was looking for the one that was a little better than these two yahoos. He knew Wendy had put someone much better on him. He just had to spot the son-of-bitch.

He settled down to dinner and had a simple four-course meal with some very good wine. Afterwards, he took a walk and smoked a cigar. All the while, he was checking to see who was following him. When he didn't spot a tail other than Wendy's people after he had walked two blocks, he hailed a cab and headed to Madrid's Chinatown. He got out of the cab and headed down an ally for thirty meters. Then he turned left and went down another ally for ten meters. He opened a wrought iron gate, went through a short tunnel, and then opened and closed the gate on the other side. He turn left again, went a few meters, and stopped and listened. When he didn't hear anyone following him, he proceeded down the narrow street until he came to an unmarked door with no handle. He knocked and waited. The door opened and he stepped inside.

"Nin hao ma," he said to the old man behind a high desk.

"I am doing fine, Mr. Libertaire. Long time no see," he said in Chinese half smiling and showing yellow teeth while biting down on a cigar in the left corner of his mouth. "You here for a game?" he asked.

"Yes," Wilhelm replied. The old man stepped down from his perch and beckoned him to follow. The man weaved his way around the crowded floor full of tables with Chinese men and women gambling and took him to a backroom. When they entered, Wilhelm saw five men sitting around a table with their suitcoats hung on the back of their chairs. The men looked up. When they saw who the old man had with him, they broke out in Cantonese and greeted him. Wilhelm responded in kind. He walked to his chair, hung his coat on the back, sat down, and then lit a fresh cigar as a man shuffled mahjong pieces.

112

He left the parlor a little after sunrise. When he reached the street, he saw his tail waiting on him. He hailed a cab and returned to the hotel. Wilhelm repeated this pattern for the next three days; he only varied his times and entry and exit points. He knew Wendy's people were puzzled by his behavior, and he was sure Wendy was keeping a close eye on him. But he had a method to his perceived madness. Every night that he played mahjong, he learned more and more about the major players in Spain. It turns out these old men had eyes and ears everywhere, and with the help of Mr. Wong, the old man who owned the place, he learned about Spain's underground.

P

Royce hadn't been idle either since he arrived. The first thing that he did was locate Wilhelm. Then he put a tail on him. After the reports kept coming back the same, he decided to put his plan into action. He went to the North African part of town and met with a man who could provide the men and weapons that he needed. He gave the man special instructions and received his assurances that he would have everything ready in time. Royce paid him and left. He went to a café where he met a young Spanish woman. They sat, drank sangria, and flirted with each other. Across the street in a nondescript car sat one of Wendy's agents who was taking pictures of the pair. The agent watched the pair until they left the café and went to the young lady's apartment.P

Wendy paid a visit to Wilhelm's hotel room that afternoon.

"Come in," he said.

"You always answer the door that way?" she asked as she walked in. "Of course, I do when I have security across the hall."

"I have some information for you. I believe we have located the man you're looking for." She handed him a manila envelope and headed to the bar. Wilhelm opened the envelope and took out the pictures as he stood in the middle of the room. He looked at a close up picture of Royce. Now that he saw him, there was something about him, he thought. He searched his memory to place him. Next, he looked at the woman in the picture who was with him. Then he looked at the picture of the North African.

"Who's this man?" he asked as he held up the picture for Wendy.

"That is Bakari, a mid-level player. He deals in arms, hash, and other stuff, anything to make a buck."

"So is this your man or not?"

"From the description I have, this is him"

"You mean, you never laid eyes on him till now?"

"That's what I'm saying."

"How did you get onto this guy?"

"I can't tell you that, Wendy, not just yet. But I need you to find out about this woman."

"She's just a fucking local working girl. I doubt she has anything to do with this."

"All the same, get me a work up on her. I want to know about everybody who he comes in contact with."

"Alright, I'll give you whatever you need. Wilhelm, I hope you know what you are doing," she said before she left.

P

Royce sat at the desk in the apartment that he was using and wrote a short note. Then he called to his companion.

"Yes, my love," she said as she walked into the room.

"I need you to run and errand for me; so get dressed," he told her.

"Yes, my love. Give me a minute," she replied as she left. When she returned, she was dressed in a light blue sundress, large brimmed straw hat, sandals, and handbag. He looked here over. "Good," he thought, "she looks perfect. His security won't suspect a thing."

"Here, sweetie, take this over to the Ritz and give it to the desk clerk. And sweetie, don't open it."

"I wouldn't dare, and I resent you saying so," she said as she pouted.

"I know you wouldn't. I shouldn't have said that. Now get going and hurry back." He kissed her, patted her on the ass, and watched her leave. The cab took her to the hotel. She asked the driver to wait for her. Then she went to the front desk, gave the note to the clerk, and left.

Wendy answered her cellphone. A voice informed her of the note that was just dropped off. It was the clerk at the hotel—one of her agents. She opened the email and looked at the pictures of the woman whom she didn't recognize. So she ran her through the system. While she waited for the results, she called Wilhelm.

"Hello."

"You have a message waiting for you at the desk. Would you like it delivered?"

"No, I'll get it. Did your agent get any pics?"

"Of course, just because they aren't handpicked by you, doesn't mean they don't know how to do their job," she said with attitude.

"Has she been identified?" he said ignoring her outburst.

"No, I'm running her now. It will take a few minutes. I'll let you know when I know." Then she hung up.

Wilhelm hung up, picked up his room key, and headed down to the lobby. He went straight to the front desk. The clerk handed him the note without him having to ask. He stood there and opened it.

*I have information on the Council I think you will be interested in. I'll be in touch. Royce.*

Wilhelm read the note then went back to his room. "Finally, he's made contact. I was starting to think this was a false lead," he thought. Then he dialed Mr. Wong.

"Hello Mr. Wong, the players are gathering, and I need a stage for the play," he said in Cantonese.

"I have the perfect venue for your production; it awaits your arrival," he responded and then hung up. Wilhelm hung up and went to his laptop where he started to do research on the surrounding area around the place where he would meet Royce. He called Wendy and brought her up-to-date. In turn, she told him what she had found out.

"You should have received a package for me by now. Would you bring it with you?" Wilhelm said.

"Yes, and you will be very interested in what I found and a little disappointed, I'm glad to say. I'll leave as soon as I hang up, so goodbye," she said. Wilhelm could hear her laughing in the background before the phone went silent.

Wendy arrived at his room an hour later with a black hard plastic gun case. She handed it to him as she headed to the bar.

"You been drinking a little heavy, anything wrong?" he asked.

"No, nothing's wrong, everything's just fine. It's you being here. When you show up especially unannounced, death and destruction follows closely," she said. Then she took a sip of her drink and sat on the bar stool crossing her legs. "Why do you like cannons? How come you can't use regulation fire arms? They kill just as well." Wilhelm didn't answer her. He was busy unlocking the gun case that he had George send him.

"To answer your questions about firepower, take a look at these." Then he held up the two guns, one in each hand.

In his left hand, he held a P239 SAS. In his right hand, he held a Coonan classic with compensator. Both were in 357 auto mag.

"This is what I need for this job. The energy transferred to the body through body armor will not just knock a man down but will keep him there a while. And if he is not wearing armor, I only have to hit him once. So which one do you think I should carry?" he asked her while smiling and laughing.

"Fuck you, Wilhelm," she said joining him in laughter.

"Now that's the Wendy I know. You were once a happy killer for Uncle Sam. What happened?"

"This fucking post is what happened. Don't get me wrong, I love the perks but the paperwork and boredom..."

"Well, we're going to have a little excitement in the next day or two, and you're going to catch some heat from this. Are you okay with that?" "Yeah, I'm okay with that if this guy can answer some questions and point us in the right direction. Right now, we're running blind, and this guy is all we have. As for the woman who delivered the message, she's the girlfriend of this guy Royce. Sometimes, he travels with more than one companion, but she's the main one from what we can tell."

"Could you send a couple of agents to deliver a message?"

"Yeah."

"Good, do we know where he's staying?"

"He rented an apartment near the museum."

"What have you found out about him so far other than where he's staying?"

"Not much, he seems to be a nobody—not connected to any government, and I can't find any connection to any major or minor criminal organization."

"Well keep at it; I won't meet with him till tomorrow night; he will assume rightly so that he's being watched. He should do nothing until the meeting but keep a close eye on him. Now this is the message I want your agents to deliver," he said. He gave her the message and instructions on how he wanted it delivered. They talked for a while longer; then she left.

The two agents whom Wendy sent to deliver the message were waiting in the dark apartment for Royce and his company to return. They had learned from his companion whom he had left home for the night that he was out partying and would probably return with a playmate for the evening. They tied her up and placed her in the closet while they waited for him. At 4:20 a.m., Royce returned laughing and fondling the woman who accompanied him. They both were drunk. The agents could smell the liquor. The woman saw them first when he turned on the lights and got his attention.

"Who-the-fuck are those guys?" she said just as the bullet slammed into her forehead killing her instantly. Royce looked down at the woman's body and then back at the two men standing ten meters in front of him.

"Did you kill the woman that was here?" he asked.

"No, she's in the closet, but she might have a bit of a headache when she wakes up," one of the agents answered.

"Mr. Libertaire will meet you at the exotic circus tomorrow night at 10:00 p.m. I don't have to remind you that this is a private meeting. Do I?" the agent said as he pointed his pistol at his head.

"No, by all means, you don't have to remind me. You can tell Mr. Libertaire that I will be there."

"Now if you would be so kind as to sit over there," the agent said pointing to a chair on the far side of the room. Royce walked over to chair careful not to step in the blood that was pooling on the floor and sat down. The agents walked around the dead hooker and left. He reached down the side of the chair but didn't feel the gun he had hidden. It was gone. He got up, went to the closet, got his companion out, untied her, and placed her on the couch.

As he revived her, he spoke softly to her, and stroked her hair. "He's as brutal as I expected him to be. Killing him tomorrow night will be sweeter than I ever imagined," he thought.

Wilhelm was playing mahjong when his phone rang. He answered it and listened to the report from the agent. He hung up and went back to playing. As he was leaving, he bid Mr. Wong a good morning and said,

"I look forward to tonight's entertainment."

"The meal should be quite good as well," was Wong's reply.

Wilhelm sat at the table looking at the stripped down P239 lying on the towel in front of him. He looked at his watch then he picked up the hotel phone and called the room across the hall.

"Come over here; the door is open," he said then hung up. After a short knock at the door, it opened. The two agents who had been shadowing him for a week walked in. "Come over here and have a seat," he said. They walked over and sat down looking nervous.

"You're not in trouble so relax. You two are wound up too tight. If you're ever going to make it in this company, you have to learn to *relax*. Now which one of you has that fantastic hash I've been smelling for the last two days?" They looked at him in disbelief; neither said a word. "Come, come now. I know it's one of you so out with it," he pressed. Then the sandy blond-haired one raised his hand. "Ah, so it's you, the loud one," he said with a smile. "Do you have any on you now?" The agent shook his head. "What are your names?" They told him; then he told the guy to go get it. He returned with two grams of Afghani hash. He unwrapped it from its wax paper and showed it to him. "Now that's what I'm talking about. Young lady, if you would pass me that ash tray behind you, I will roll you the perfect

Jamaican spliff." The female agent handed him the ash tray. The two agents watched in amazement while Wilhelm rolled the spliff laced with the hash and lit it.

As they passed the joint around, Wilhelm questioned them and learned among other things that the girlfriend of the male agent supplied him with hash. But what he really wanted to know was about this Bakari character and how Wendy was running her post. By the end of the joint, he found out all he wanted to know; then he turned his attention to them. He looked at the clock and started to put his weapon back together. When he had done that, he addressed them. "I suggest you go back to your room, clean your weapons, and rest up. Tonight might be a little taxing on a tired body." With that bit of advice, the agents got up, left the room, and returned to theirs across the hall.

Wendy picked him up. They were at the restaurant theater an hour ahead of schedule so they had dinner and watched the show. The exotic circus was better than he thought it would be. Because anything Wong had a hand in, one had to be skeptical. The performers executed complex routines while semi-nude, jumping, rolling, and swinging on ropes with no animals involved. The performance lasted an hour or so and was winding down when Royce walked in. He and the woman who delivered the message walked towards the table where Wilhelm and Wendy were seated.

Wilhelm watched his approach while simultaneously watching Wong's men get into position. Wendy had brought two extra agents whom he stationed outside. His bodyguards were by the door.

"Mr. Libertaire," Royce said as he stood in front of him.

"Yes, Mr. Royce. Please sit down. Would you like a drink or shall we get down to business?"

"I think I'll have a drink. There's plenty of time to talk. The night is young. I think you have a few questions for me. I do remember much better with a drink in my hand," he said smiling like he had the upper hand which he thought he had. Wilhelm signaled to a waiter who took Royce's and his lady friend's order.

"You know, there's something I have wanted to ask you if you don't mind. It's off the subject but it is a curiosity," Royce said then took another sip of his drink.

"Of course, Mr. Royce," he replied. Wendy was looking across the table at Royce's companion and thought, "She's way too cool; she has to be a pro; be sure to kill her first." Then she smiled at her.

"Well I would like to know how a Black American with a German first name and a French last name became so important in the CIA. You do pronounce your first name with a V is it not?"

"Yes, it is. And to answer your question, the CIA doesn't care what my name is or how it is pronounced as long as I kill scum like you."

"Ah, yes, killing people like me…but you're not here for that. Are you? Because if you are, I 'm at a disadvantage. I came to talk," Royce said and then signaled the waiter.

"Now that you've satisfied your curiosity, tell me about the Council," Wilhelm said turning the conversation to seriousness. Royce downed his drink and ordered another while his companion was still on her first. Wilhelm noticed this and so did Wendy.

"The Council consists of five people. Nobody knows who they are or if they are all male, female, or a combination. What I do know is that they have their hands in everything from intelligence gathering to suppling tooth paste to third world countries and everything in between," Royce told him.

"What's your connection to them?" Wendy asked.

"I did a few jobs for them but then we had a parting of the ways. You understand," Royce replied smiling.

"Why talk now?" Wilhelm said leaning forward slightly and looking at Royce in the eyes.

"To tell you the truth, after I heard what happened to Frank Depore and the Council may have had a hand in it, I decided it was in my best interest to separate myself from them. You do have a reputation Mr. Libertaire. The way your agents delivered your invitation early this morning shows you live up to it very well," he said then paused and looked for a reaction to what he just said.

"You haven't told me anything new Mr. Royce. So why did you contact me? And why shouldn't I kill you?" Wilhelm said breaking the silence. Royce's eyes darted back and forth between Wendy and Wilhelm which made Wendy uneasy. She adjusted in her chair to give herself a better shot at the woman if it came to that, and she was thinking it would come to that.

"The Council is somewhere in Africa selling a new technology which it recently acquired. It's rumored to give a lot of countries true independence. This new found freedom will cause countries like yours billions of dollars."

"Do you know what this technology is or what it does?" Wilhelm asked.

"No, but I might know someone who does," he replied.

"Who?"

"A man that goes by the name Talaus, have you heard of him?"

"Yes, I have. That's a little out of his line of work. What does he have to do with that project?"

"That I am afraid, I do not have an answer to. It has been interesting meeting you, Mr. Libertaire. But I'm afraid I have run out of time. I have another pressing engagement. You will excuse me, won't you?"

Royce and his companion got up from the table and made their way through the crowd to the door. But before they could exit, a shot rang out. Wilhelm and Wendy looked around the room but couldn't locate where it came from. A second later, the room erupted in gunfire. Wilhelm turned over the table. He and Wendy pulled their weapons. To his right, Wilhelm spotted a man firing an automatic weapon. He fired twice. The 357 rounds slammed into the man's chest propelling him backwards into the running crowd and causing the people to trip and fall over his body.

Wendy located a target: A man firing a pistol was coming towards them. She leveled her 40 caliber pistol at him and fired twice hitting him in the head. His brains sprayed all over the face of the man who was behind him which gave her time to take him out also. Next she got up and moved towards the bar where three of Wong's men were firing. When she reached the bar, she realized there was firing outside. Her security team was engaged in their own firefight with a half dozen men.

"Wilhelm!" she yelled. As he looked over, she pointed outside. He saw what was going on. He motioned to the door. Then he was up and moving. She followed. Wilhelm fired his pistol as he sprinted to the door and aimed at his targets' center mass as they presented themselves.

When they emerged from the building, Wilhelm noticed that Wendy's two agents were down. Six men were advancing

126

towards them and were firing as they came. Wilhelm moved to his left and Wendy to her right splitting the fire coming at them. He grabbed one of the downed agents by the collar and dragged him behind the car. Wilhelm took the agent's M4 carbine and remaining magazines, changed to a fresh magazine, and began firing. By laying down a base of fire, he allowed Wendy to move up and get a better firing position. Once there, she picked off the assailants. Two of them went down immediately before the others could react.

Wilhelm took two more out as they started to retreat. The remaining two pulled back but kept up their firing. Wilhelm, Wendy, and a few of Wong's men pursued them until they jumped into a van and took off. Next they turned their attention to the wounded and dead. He found that of their four agents, one was dead and two were seriously wounded. He and Wendy along with the help of the remaining agent gathered their dead and wounded and headed for the embassy.

After he had changed clothes, filled out an action report, and smoothed things over with the local police, a he and Wendy headed back to his hotel.

"Where are you keeping your stash?" Wendy said as she walked into his room. "I could sure use a joint right about now."

"Over there on the bar. I guess you need something to take the edge off."

"Take the edge off, my ass. I want this feeling to last as long as it can. This is what I have been missing, a good shoot out. When you showed up, I knew it was only a matter of time," she said as she lit the joint, took a deep pull, and then danced her way to the bar.

"Let me put on some music to aid you in your dancing," he said. Then he hit the play button on the disc player and a Timbaland mix resonated in the room.

"Ah, this is my jam," she said as she began singing along. "Luv 2 Luv U."

Wilhelm lit a joint, sat down on the couch, and watched Wendy lip-sync to the song. He was replaying the night's events in slow motion in his head. What impressed him was how those guys fought. And more importantly was how the remaining two conducted their retreat. They were pros. He doubted Royce's boy Bakari had access to such skilled labor.

"How long will it take to ID them?" Wendy didn't hear him. She was still lip-syncing in her own world. She was happy probably happier than she had been in a long time. She had been in a gunfight and nothing pleased her more than firing her weapon preferably at people like she did tonight. Wilhelm sat there thinking and smoking his joint. He would have to wait for the information.

# Back to Work

*Chapter Ten*

Sanaa watched Tommy as he field striped his rifle for cleaning. They had just finished practicing, and she was dying to ask him a question.

"Why are you staring at me, Sanaa?" he said without looking away from what he was doing. The other men looked up at her and waited to hear what she had to say.

"Well, I'm curious about your nickname," she said slowly.

"Here it comes; watch out everybody," Lee said laughing.

"Yeah, every time he tells it, he usually ends up punching the person," Daniel chimed in.

"Don't listen to these assholes, Sanaa. Tommy loves telling this story. Don't cha, Captain America?" Paul said as he fell over laughing.

Tommy cleaned his rifle while his teammates teased him. He just smiled and gave them a look, but he didn't mind the ribbing. He knew it was a matter of time before she asked. And they were right; someone always asks.

"Okay, Sanaa, ask the question," he said as he looked over smiling slightly.

"Alright then, why do they? I mean Mr. Libertaire and those guys, call you Captain America."

"Now that wasn't so hard, was it? After I tell you, I'm going to punch you like he said." Then he laughed and the guys joined in. "Well it's quite simple really; my last name is America. It seems that a few grandfathers back decided it was a good name to have. Of course, this was just after the Civil War ended and nobody saw fit to change it all this time. As for the Captain part, I was a captain in the army. As you can imagine, I've heard it all. After the army, I came to work for Mr. Libertaire. He used it as a code name. There, now you know the story."

"Aw, that was so sweet. I've never heard him tell it like that before. That was touching, I tell you just touching," Jhon said with his hands on his chest.

"The story isn't finished yet; you haven't punched her," Paul half yelled. Tommy leaned over, punched her lightly on the thigh, and then winked at her.

"If you all are done with your warm and fuzzy life stories, get those rifles cleaned and get that 13k run done," the head instructor said as he walked by. The team quieted down and watched him as he passed by. Afterwards they resumed cleaning their rifles.

℘

The three Chechen killers got up early despite their late night of partying. Their partners were still asleep as was their host's wife. They sat at the kitchen table wearing trousers and wife beaters, drinking strong coffee, and looking over pictures of their target. In front of them was a picture of George. Also on the table was the latest Intel on him and any associates or acquaintances he had. The men drank coffee and talked while planning out how they would kill him. The only thing they could expect with this target was he would prove difficult. If they missed, he had the skills and the resources to come after them. So they were being extra cautious and took their time.

Just then the leader's cellphone rang. He answered it and listened to the voice on the other end. When he was done, he hung up without saying a word. Then he addressed his colleagues.

"It seems that Libertaire has survived yet another attempt on his life in Spain. It looks like he will be there for a week or so my source thinks. That means we have been given a gift. Let's not waste it. With Libertaire gone, maybe our boy will venture out from the manor." The two men nodded in agreement and went back to studying the information in front of them.

## *Hamburg, Germany*

Shadow Two landed in Germany, reached out to her contact, and made arrangements for a meet. She would meet the woman who would be helping her at her favorite restaurant in Hamburg. It was the perfect place for such a meeting. This restaurant catered to the jet setters. The waiters were accustomed to eccentric patrons and tended to mind their business. She sat in a booth where she could see the patrons' comings and goings. She ordered a lemon drop martini and waited. Then she focused on a young woman dressed in a blue cocktail dress and watched her as she approached. The woman spotted her, causally walked over, and sat down.

"Libertaire said you were a looker; he wasn't lying. I'm Amelia. If you need anything, contact me. I'm available to you and you alone. The boss was adamant about that. You must be special," she said with a smile.

"I don't know how special I am but thanks any way. Do you have what I requested?"

"Yes, everything you ordered you'll find at this address. Here is the information you requested." She slid a set of keys and a flash drive across the table to her. "The blue Mercedes 300SL is yours. It's parked in the garage down the street, space 22. Anything else I can do for you ... just reach out." Then she slid out the booth and melted into the crowd. Shadow Two finished her drink and then left. She went to the garage, picked up the car, and headed for the safe house.

She arrived at the safe house, pulled the car into the garage, and waited until the door closed before getting out. She took out the pistol that was provided with the car and entered the house. She went through each room and opened every door. When she was satisfied, she took out her bug hunter and checked for listening devices. After sweeping the house and finding no bugs, she unpacked her equipment and checked it. She had audiovisual and communication equipment as well as weapons. Her arsenal contained a sniper rifle, a 9 mm pistol with two 17-round magazines and a suppressor, a set of six throwing knives, and a small vial of poison. She repacked all of it and put her special suitcase away. Next she checked her phone for messages. Finding none, she undressed and took a shower.

*Kiev, Ukraine*

Jonathan arrived at the Premier Palace Hotel in Kiev and walked into the lobby. Before he could make his way to the front desk, he was waylaid by Lydia.

"Before you check in, you should know that a woman has been asking about you. And she doesn't strike me as your usual fuck'em and leave them type," she said as she smiled while looking around the room.

"Thank you, Lydia, for that bit of information. Now if you could point her out, I will make a real effort to avoid her," he responded.

"She isn't in the hotel at the moment. But I'll let you know the minute she gets back." Then she walked away.

Shadow One checked in, went to his room, took a shower, changed clothes, and headed to the hotel bar. There, he spotted his contact, a young man in his mid-twenties, tall, and a little out of shape with long hair pulled back in a man bun. He was dressed in a gray pinstriped tailored Armani suit. His gray brimmed hat sat on the chair next to him. Jonathan walked over and addressed him.

"It's nice to see you in person," he said as he sat down at the table.

"I think you have me mixed up with somebody else and you should go," Sam said.

"Alright, I'm a traveler from the West yet I head East," Jonathan said then smirked. "Well, what's the reply?" he continued.

"Oh, it's you. I like it when you say those stupid sayings," Sam said laughing.

"It's protocol."

"You acted like an ass the last time I worked with you, and it was a nightmare."

"Well this will be a cake walk; it's an Intel gathering job; so relax."

"Don't be a prick; I'm the guy who gets you the shit you need, and you sit here and blow smoke up my ass about an easy job. But it's good to see you. Now, I know I'll see some action. Look at me, Jonathan. I'm wasting away," he said while patting his belly. Jonathan laughed and then signaled to the waiter.

"It's nice to see you, Sam. How's the family?"

"Fine, I have a new little one, a girl. My wife says she's done having children," he said just as the waiter arrived. They talked about old times, asked about people, and had a few drinks before getting down to business.

Then Lydia came by and pointed out the woman who had been asking about him. He asked Sam to identify her and then rose and approached her. As he closed in on her, he looked her over as she sat at the bar. She looked to be 5'10", 160 lbs. with dark hair and fair skin and looked like she worked out. She was dressed for a day on the town. She wore six thousand dollars in clothing alone. Then add in her modest pieces of jewelry which cost another four thousand dollars. Who is this woman? She's obviously wealthy but her face didn't ring a bell with him.

"Hi, I'm Jonathan. I hear you've been looking for me," he said flashing his sexiest smile. The woman half turned around on the bar stool and smiled.

"Yes, I have. It's nice to finally meet you," she said and extended her hand. He took it lightly in his hand and shook it; then he sat down on the stool beside her and ordered bourbon.

"You have me at a disadvantage. You know my name, but I do not know who you are."

"Forgive my manners; I'm Janice Strums. You actually know my sister, Debbie. She bought an airplane from you." She smiled and took a sip of her drink.

"Her name escapes me, but I meet a lot of people. So how can I be of service to you?" All the while, Sam was taking the pictures that Jonathan needed and ran her on the known persons database and face recognition software.

"That's right; keep her talking. I need fifteen more minutes or so," Sam was thinking as he waited for the results. Meanwhile, Shadow One was keeping her busy as Sam watched him work.

He watched in amazement as Jonathan went from hello to the touching part when he lightly touched her knee while running his hand up and down her arm. She was doing the same thing on different parts of his body. Both wore phony smiles as they were going full blast. At that moment, Sam was glad he was married. To have to play the game they were playing was not only exhausting but dangerous. But Jonathan made it look easy. For him it was easy. He loved this life; he was born to do this work; he was one of the rare ones. The information that Sam was waiting for came in. As he read the results, he looked up at Jonathan. Then he sent him a text:

*She's a hired killer. Information attached.*

Then he sat back and watched. Jonathan's phone buzzed, and he looked at it.

"Excuse me a moment, will you?" He skimmed over the information and looked at the pictures. He glanced at Sam then turned his attention back to her with renewed interests. "So what type of plane did I sell your sister?" he asked her and then signaled to the bartender.

"I think it is a custom gulf stream; she had it done in all pink," she responded. Just then, the bartender showed up. He ordered another round and looked around for Lydia. He saw her and waved her over.

"Would you join me for dinner, Ms. Strums? I was just about to have a bite," he said just as Lydia showed up.

"Yes, it would be an honor and maybe we can discuss a bit of business," she said as she reached out and touched his leg. Jonathan spoke to Lydia. Afterwards, she left. When she returned, she informed him that his table was ready and the chef would honor his request. As he and Ms. Strums were shown to their table, he passed by Sam and winked. Sam shook his head in amazement. They enjoyed a five course dinner and then went dancing. Upon their return, she invited him to her room. They started kissing and feeling each other's bodies before the door to her suite closed. Soon after, they both were naked on the king-sized bed in a sixty-nine position enjoying each other's juices. Jonathan changed position and entered her. It would be the first of many positions to come in this early morning fuck-fest. "Oh, yeah," she half moaned as he entered her. The fuck session marathon had begun.

Jonathan lay there listening to Janice's steady breathing as she lay on her right side. The sun was up. Its beams of light were trying to break though the heavy drapes as they highlighted the swirls of dust that the ceiling fan had stirred up.

He got up and did a quick, quiet search of her room and found her pistol in 32 caliber along with a suppressor. He laid the weapon on the table by the chaise lounge, removed the clip, and cleared the weapon. Then he covered it up with a magazine and took a shower. When he returned, he found her awake and sitting up in bed.

"I thought you had left then I heard the shower. I'm glad you stayed," she said. He looked over at the magazine and saw it hadn't been disturbed; then he started to get dress. Janice climbed out of bed and headed to the bathroom. When she returned, she found Jonathan standing in the bedroom holding her gun.

"When did you know?" she said matter-of-factly as she stood in the bathroom doorway naked looking him in the eyes.

"You shouldn't ask about a person days before he arrives. It might tip him off," he replied not answering her question.

"Are you going to kill me while I'm naked? I would like to put something on, if you don't mind."

"I do mind. I like you just the way you are. Now if you would sit over there, if you please," he said as he pointed with the gun to the chaise lounge. Janice walked over to the lounge, sat down, and then put her legs up and posed.

"Is this okay or do you prefer me with my legs open?" she asked sarcastically opening her legs then closing them. Jonathan pulled up a chair and sat down.

"Who are you working for?" he said seriously. He had crossed over to his work mind, and all emotion had been removed. She looked into his eyes and saw the change. He was a killer, and she had been caught. Her mind raced. She had to think of an answer to keep him talking. The longer he talked, the longer she stayed alive.

"I don't know. I was hired by proxy. I just took a contract; that's all," she said in the most convincing tone that she could muster. Jonathan looked at her. He leaned forward and slapped her across the face with the pistol.

"Fuck! That hurt. Did you have to do that?" she said as she held the side of her face and felt the blood from the cut on her cheek.

"I'm going to hit you every time you lie to me. So once again, who are you working for?"

"I told you I do not know. You know how this works. You're a professional killer for hire. I honestly don't know whose paying for this." She waited for the next hit, but it didn't come. He just sat there and stared at her.

"Then there's nothing useful you can tell me."

"No, I'm afraid not. But that's not a good reason to kill me. If you let me go, I'll be out of the country in two hours and you'll never see me again. What do you say to that, Jonathan?" she said as she swung her legs down and sat on the edge of the lounge. Jonathan raised the pistol and shot her twice in the chest killing her. As he headed back to his room, he pulled out his cellphone and called Sam.

*Aachen, Germany*

Stephanie, also known as Shadow Two, was looking over the latest intelligence on her first target. Amelia had found her first target who was residing in the village of Aachen. She sat on the floor, spread out the pictures, and looked over the report. After several hours of studying the maps and pictures along with the psychology report and other shit that Amelia provided, she started planning her mission. When she finished, the sun was up. She made breakfast, sent Amelia a text, and went to sleep. Six hours later, her cellphone woke her up with a message from Amelia:

*All arranged. Will meet you at final destination.*

Stephanie got up and began to make ready her equipment for travel. Then she showered, dressed, and left the safe house. She went straight to the airport. There, she made contact with the baggage handler who would make sure her equipment got through. Next, she picked up her boarding pass and headed to the gate. After she cleared the check point, she sent a text informing Wilhelm of her progress. Shadow Two arrived in Bonn, picked up her luggage, and went to the train station where she caught a train to Aachen. Once there, she got into the car that was provided, drove to the new safe house, and set up for the operation. She headed into town for a bite to eat and to observe her target.

It was Thursday night. According to her intelligence, her target met her husband for drinks and dinner at their favorite pub every Thursday. The target is a Caucasian woman, 35 years old, and 5'8" tall with brown hair, brown eyes, and a birthmark high on her inner left thigh. She had been married to an administrator in the border patrol for ten years—the length of her time as an undercover agent. The company had placed her here to monitor the border with Belgium. The little city of Aachen was perfect. As she sat drinking the biggest beer she ever had and eating an equally large pretzel, they walked in. She recognized her from the pictures. Her husband waved to some friends and smiled while she took stock of who was in the room. Her eyes briefly stopped on Stephanie.

"This may be tougher than was planned. This bitch is still on her game," Shadow Two thought as she watched them. By chance, a cute young man approached her and started flirting. She invited him to sit down. He was her perfect cover.

Stephanie spent the next week watching and clocking her target's movements as well as her husband's. He was easy and boring. He went to work and came home. He didn't even return the flirts that the redhead with the big bosoms who worked in his office gave him daily. In contrast, her target was a housewife whose routine was sporadic. She jogged daily at 8:00 a.m.

Afterwards, she lounged until she went out either to go shopping or on some days disappeared until 3:30 p.m. Always, she made sure to be home before her husband got in precisely at 5:00 p.m., Monday through Friday.

Shadow Two had Amelia helping her track her target's movements. But today, Amelia was playing lookout while she broke into her target's home. This was the ninth day of observing her, and she thought it was time to see how her target lived. Amelia parked across the street a little ways from the house. Shadow Two got out. She walked casually down the street and then up to the front door of the house. There, she took out her lock pick tool, selected the right pick, inserted it into the lock, and squeezed the small trigger. The door lock clicked, and she listened to the tumblers set. She tried the door, and it opened. She looked around one last time checking her surroundings and then entered. Once inside, she found a nicely furnished home not cluttered and very neat.

This was the day that her target disappeared so she had a few hours to look around. Stephanie started in the living room and went though it thoroughly. She looked in all the places that she was trained to look and in the place she had learned to look. Finally she found her stash that included her go bag. In it were money, a gun, and three passports—one from Belgium, one from the United Kingdom, and the last one from France. Hiding it in the laundry was a good move; her husband wouldn't stumble over it there. She put everything back and checked her watch; she had been in the house for two hours. One more time, she went through the house making sure she didn't leave anything out of place. Satisfied, she left the house locking the door behind her. She walked back to car, and they drove away.

"I have to find out where this woman disappears to," Shadow Two said.

"I keep losing her on the south end of town down around the walking trail. I'm going to have to find a way to follow her when she's on the walking trail. Won't I?" Amelia said smiling.

Shadow Two set up on the trail in different locations on three different days. On the fourth day, her target strolled by. She followed her for a mile or so staying in the foliage and out of sight. Then her target stepped off the trail to a side one and went another half mile until she came to a small clearing. There, she sat down on the grass and looked at the trees and sky. Just when Shadow Two thought this was just another nature hike, a man appeared. Her target smiled at him as he walked over and joined her. They talked for a while; then they stood up and took their clothes off. She took out her camera and snapped some pictures. After a few choice photos that she knew her husband would not appreciate, she sat back and watched the fuck session. When they finished, they smoked a joint and talked for a while. Then he rose, got dressed, and left the same way he came; she did the same.

Shadow Two waited until she was sure they had a good head start before she followed the man. She found a hidden trail a few meters in from the opening. At the end of it was a house. She squatted and watched the house for a short while. Not seeing any movement, she decided to take a look. Using the deep afternoon shadow that was cast on the east side of the house for cover, she made her way to the side window. When she peered in, she saw the man talking to another man.

They looked as if the subject of their discussion was a serious one. The second man got up and left the room. When he returned, he had a map. He rolled it out and was telling the other man something about why he needed the map. She knew there was no way to find out what area the map represented but her curiosity was killing her. She knew not to take the risk so she took his picture, withdrew, and returned to the car. She drove to the safe house and downloaded the pictures that she had taken. Later, she called Amelia and told her the plan.

Shadow Two continued to watch her target for a few more days before putting her plan into action on that Thursday. At 4:00 p.m., a problem arose with the paperwork about a truck carrying machine parts from Belgium at the border crossing where her husband worked. Her target didn't get the message that he would be very late and for her to go home. Later, he would meet her there. As routine, she went to the pub, waited for him, and had a drink. Since he didn't show up, she headed home unaware that Shadow Two was waiting for her. When she walked through the door, she saw Shadow Two standing in the living room. As soon as she reacted, Amelia put her gun at the back of her head. So Amelia used her foot to close the door keeping the gun in place.

"Come have a seat, Renee. I just want to talk to you." Amelia gave her a nudge, and she started across the room.

Shadow Two directed her to the chair in front of a video camera setup and had her sit.

"Who are you? Are you with the company?" she asked.

"Which companies are you referring to, Renee? You see, I have information that you are playing both sides. I like to know all about it. So if you'll just speak clearly and look at the camera, it will be over in a jiffy." Shadow Two sat down across from her and crossed her legs as Amelia aimed her gun at Renee's chest.

"I don't know what you're talking about? What companies are you talking about? I'm a house wife; I live a boring life with my husband," she said convincingly looking back and forth between her and Amelia.

"I almost believe you, very good performance, Renee. While you're lying, would you mind telling me who this is?" Shadow Two said as she tossed her a folder of pictures of her and the mystery man. Renee opened the folder and slowly looked through the photos. She looked up at Shadow Two. "I think your husband would like to know that his wife is a world class cocksucker and nature lover. Wouldn't you?" she said smiling. "I tell you what, Renee. You answer my questions and all of your secrets stay that way. If you don't tell me, I'm going to shoot you up with some shit that will make you tell then kill you. If you take option one, you'll get a head start at least before they come for you."

Shadow Two sat silently for a moment letting what she just said sink in. She took the gun from Amelia and motioned towards the silver case. Renee watched as Amelia opened the case, took out a syringe, and filled it. When she returned and stood beside her, Renee spoke.

"How much of a head start?" she said in a quiet voice.

"At least a week, a girl with your training can be long gone in a week, I'm sure," she said sarcastically. The fact was Shadow Two didn't know what her boss had in mind. He could string her along or she could be dead tonight. That wasn't her concern; she needed specific information.

"Okay, I'll tell you what you want to know. Ask your questions," she said looking deflated and defeated.

"Good choice, the chemicals are so harsh," Shadow Two replied. For the next ninety minutes, Renee told her everything that she knew about the intelligence organization that she worked for. She also filled in the blanks concerning the mystery man whom she was seeing. When she was finished, Shadow Two checked the recording and had Amelia pack it up while she held the gun on Renee.

"What about the pictures? Renee asked.

"I have copies. You can keep those," Shadow Two said as she stood up. "I suggest you get your affairs in order fast and get lost even faster. My boss isn't the type to sit idly for long. After he views this, well sugar, just don't waste any time." She and Amelia were out the door leaving the woman sitting there. Before they could get to the car, they heard a gunshot.

"Well, I guess she made her choice," Amelia said. They got in the car and drove away.

*The Farm*

"Tonight, you'll be transported to an army base for a HAHO (high altitude high open) refresher course so you don't kill yourself doing the operation. We prefer you kill yourself in training," George said smiling with the men laughing. "So pack your shit; your ride leaves in an hour." The men got up from the table and headed down the hall to their rooms.

"Not you, Sanaa. You have a different training program to attend." So she sat back at the table, poured herself another cup of coffee, and watched her teammates stage their equipment. After they loaded up and left, George put her in the jeep and drove her to the security personnel quarters. Once there, he took her to her room and introduced her to Sandy who was sitting on the bed looking gorgeous.

Sandy was a fashion model before she came to work for the agency. Her job was teaching what she called "the lost art of feminine wilds." The tall, dark-skinned woman sat before her dressed in an expensive summer dress that Sanaa had no idea who was the designer.

"I will leave you two ladies to get acquainted. Sanaa, pay attention. There's a test on the subject later," George said; then he was gone. The woman introduce herself and the two of them talked about what was expected and what she would be teaching her in the coming weeks. As Sandy was leaving, one of the security personnel stuck his head in her room and announced dinner.

Sanaa followed the crowd and her nose to the dining hall. She was surprised at what she saw. To her right was a rifle rack that was filling up fast as personnel were filing in. To her left was the beginning of the chow line. She walked over, got into line, and pick up a tray, plate, coffee cup, drinking glass, and silverware. As she went through, she was amazed at the variety and amount of food that was offered. Steamed and fried bass and perch, roast beef and mutton, au gratin, mashed, and sweet potatoes, seven different vegetables, hot and cold coffee, and tea, and a variety of juices were part of the selection. When she arrived at the desert table, her sweet tooth began to ache. After passing on desert, she looked for a place to sit. Everywhere she looked, she saw men and women talking and eating. Then she felt a tap on her shoulder and looked around.

"You Sanaa?" a woman asked. "Follow me," she continued before Sanaa could reply. The woman led her to a table and they sat down.

"Hi, I'm Lucy," she said and then extended her hand. Sanaa accepted it and the two shook hands.

"Have you meet Sandy yet?" Sanaa nodded. "Good, pay close attention to her. That woman will teach you shit about men you had no idea existed. I still use the shit she taught me but that's another story. Any way, I'll be your instructor for the fast kill course," she said and then paused to eat as she looked at Sanaa and waited for her reply. Sanaa didn't say a word. She just ate and observed the goings on around her. When they or more accurately Lucy was finally finished, they put away their trays and walked outside. "Let's take a walk, shall we?" Lucy said to her and she headed towards a large grassy area.

"What are you going to teach me, Lucy? And what is Sandy going to teach me about men I don't already know?"

"I'm going to teach you the fast kill amongst other things including the handling of the MP7 sub-machine gun. As for the rest, you just pay close attention and do as you are told. That lady can be a real bitch. Don't let the smile fool you," Lucy said seriously. They walked a while in silence further into the grassy area before Lucy stopped and sat down. Sanaa did the same.

"Now what?" Sanaa said as she looked around.

"Look, my job is to teach you and look out for you for the next two weeks. We're going to train hard and the days will be long, split between me and the dragon lady. So you have one job, one concern. Learn it all and learn it fast. I'll teach you all I can, and don't talk too much. Most of us don't have your sense of humor." Sanaa sat there looking at Lucy. This Puerto Rican woman looked lethal and tough but was very pretty.

Lucy was going to teach her some wild shit she never heard of but had no doubt of its existence, and another woman was going to teach her a new way to seduced men. When she joined the CIA, she knew there would be some weird shit going on but she didn't see this one coming. Working for Libertaire has taken her to a whole new level, and she was unsure if she could make the grade. Libertaire didn't take failure well. Rodney would have her head if she didn't complete this mission. So she would take Lucy's advice and learn this shit fast.

*House of the Flying Snakes*

*Il est Képi Blanc*
*Loyal first mate with secrets*
*Warrior bachelor*
By Claire L. Hand

# Chechen Shoot Out

*Chapter Eleven*

*George's World*

At the training house, George sat in his office going over the schedule. The men were off practicing their jumps. Sanaa had started her special training for the next two weeks which meant he had a breather while they were busy training elsewhere. He thought he would call a friend, take in a movie and dinner tonight, and enjoy his first night off in weeks. He finished up, said goodnight to the staff, and drove back to the house. Once there, he went straight to his room and undressed. Then he picked up his electronic appointment/phonebook and browsed through the names and information of the women filed in it. He selected a beautiful dark-skinned woman who enjoyed the same genre of movies as he did and shared other similar interests. He called her. After he hung up, he called Cee's and made reservations.

He showered, shaved, and dressed. He chose cream-colored deep-pleated summer cotton pants, a loose-fitting turquoise silk shirt, and cream-colored Italian leather loafers. He checked his compact 9 mm pistol making sure it was loaded and then placed it in a concealed holster on his right side. He took one last look in the mirror checking to make sure his weapon made no outline. Satisfied, he left. He selected the jaguar from the garage and headed into town. As he passed the strip mall, a man in an awaiting car pulled out and followed him. The man in the car made a phone call, talked briefly to a man on the other end, and then hung up.

"I just heard from one of our people; your target is on the move," the Russian said to the Chechen killer.

"Have him follow him and don't lose him. Soon as he settles down at a location, have him notify us," the leader said.

"He already knows to do that," he replied matter-of-factly. At that point, the men stopped playing cards and got up from the table. It was time to get ready. This might be their only chance to kill him so they had to be ready to move at a moment's notice.

George picked up his date and they headed to the movies. His tail called it in and the Chechens headed to the location. Because their target moved a lot, they settled on handguns and sub-machine guns. They planned to ambush him. The three men waited in the parking lot of the movie theater. But when the movie let out, the crowd was too big to start shooting. So they followed him to Cee's and set up there. Patiently and quietly, they waited two and a half hours while George and his date enjoyed a leisurely dinner. As soon as they saw he was ready to leave, they got into position. One stayed in the car; the other went across the street and stood in the shadows; the third one stood by another car which was parked on the opposite corner.

The killers readied their weapons and waited. George and his date walked out of Cee's and turned right heading up the street towards his car. Just then, George saw movement from across the street and zeroed in on it. He saw the Chechen stepping out from his shadow hideout and raising his sub-machine gun. George reached for his gun as he pushed his date down yelling,

"Gun, get down!"

George and his assailant began firing at the same time. Fortunately, he was saved from that first blast by the fact he was moving. As he dashed for the car, he fired at the man across the street causing him to take cover. Next, the second assailant began to fire as he crossed the street. He shot out car windows and flattened tires as he tried to hit George. As he approached, George pushed the car remote and opened the trunk of the car. When he reached the car under heavy fire from both assailants, he pulled out a M4 carbine loaded with a thirty round twin magazine. He began to return fire. George alternated between the two men using the three-round burst setting forcing them to take cover. Then he started his assault. He knew he couldn't win this fight staying behind cover. They would quickly out flank him and kill him. So he attacked them starting with the man across the street. He put his weapon on automatic fire and began moving. He kept the fire up on his target as he zigzagged towards him.

For a split second pause in his firing, George changed magazines. That's when his assailant stood up and opened fire hitting him in the left shoulder. As he was falling, he squeezed the trigger stitching the man across the chest. The bullets caused him to fall backwards as his sub-machine gun fired into the air. As George landed, he rolled to his right. The rounds from the second hitter impacted in front of him. He looked in the direction of the shots trying to get a fix on the man. He heard the distinct sound of a shotgun being fired. Then he saw the man lying in the street. The right side of his head was missing. Cee headed towards him in a flat out sprint. As George started to get up, he saw a car coming at them. A man was firing a sub-machine gun from the driver's side window. Cee stopped, turned, and fired at the car. George did the same. The car suddenly veered and slammed into some parked cars. The man inside was dead.

"How bad are you hit?" Cee asked him.

"Not bad, it's my left shoulder," George replied looking up at the big man.

"Can you walk?"

"Yeah, if you help me up." Cee helped him up, and they went over to check the car. The driver was shot up pretty good. His body slumped over towards the passenger seat. They checked the other two men.

"Hey, have you seen my date?" George asked Cee.

"Yeah, she's over there; she didn't make it," Cee said as he pointed towards the sidewalk. George walked over to where she was lying. He kneeled down and closed her eyes. One neat hole in the center of her chest killed her instantly. "She must have been hit just as I pushed her down," he thought. He stood up and looked at the crowd that was gathering.

"Let's go back to my place and get off the street," Cee advised.

"That's a great idea; the cops will be on edge when they get here. I have to make a call," George said as he cradled his shoulder. Then they headed for the restaurant.

Once in the restaurant, George pulled out his cellphone and pressed the number 4 button and waited.

"Help line," a male voice stated.

"This is George; I have a situation," he began. Then he told the man on the other end about what had happened. He listened for a few minutes and then hung up.

"Everything taken care of?" Cee asked.

"Yeah, my bigger problem is who wants me dead, and what-the-fuck is my boss going to say about all this attention." Cee handed him a large scotch and said,

"I'm glad I'm not you in so many ways tonight. You're right about Wilhelm; he's not going to like this shit."

Number 1 and Number 2 had returned to headquarters soon after the demonstrations in the Sudan. They left Number 3 to oversee the project and handle the day-to-day running of the facility. Number 2 was reading intelligence reports in her apartment when she came across the report informing her of the death of her agent in Prague.

"Fuck!" she shouted. "That bastard! That son-of-a-bitch! I'll get you and it's not going to be a pretty death," she swore. When she regained her composer, she left her apartment and went to Number 1's office.

"Well, what can I do for you," he said as she walked in and sat down.

"I need a problem taken care of. I thought you could help with it."

"Tell me about it," he said as he became serious and leaned forward on his desk to listen to her.

"My problem is named Jonathan; he's an independent contract killer. Although, I suspect he works for someone exclusively. He killed an agent that I planted in the CIA and ran for six years. Then he eliminated the hitter I sent after him in Prague this week; that's two good assets gone. What I want is for this guy to be removed. He's becoming a painful thorn in my side."

"You should talk to Number 5 about this. He handles all of our removals. I'm sure he'll be most cooperative. This will give you two a chance to work together."

"Good, I'll do just that; this guy has to be killed. Now for another piece of business..." They continued to talk for the next hour as she informed him about the various projects she was working on. Later, she returned to her apartment and began to pack.

*Spain*

Wilhelm sat in his hotel room looking in disbelief at the message that he had just received. How could Rodney give such an order after receiving the information he had sent him? But there it was. The orders were to eliminate the double agents, not bring them in but silence them. Something was seriously wrong here; he was missing something; something he has overlooked. He thought this can't be right. Just then, his laptop buzzed alerting him that a message was coming in. He walked over to where it was sitting on the bar, opened it, and typed in his code. He waited as the message was decoded and displayed on the screen. The message read:

*Assassination attempt on your man George.*

*Wounded but not fatal.*

*Return to station immediately.*

"What has George done now?" he thought as he reread the message before erasing it. He called Wendy and had her arrange for his flight home and for Pam to stop by his hotel room. When Pam arrived, he gave her a special mission. He handed her the information she needed and the name of a contractor if she needed assistance. The room phone rang; he answered it; it was the front desk informing him that his car had arrived. He waited a few minutes allowing Pam a head start before leaving the room. When he reached the lobby and headed for the car, he noticed three men converging on him. They were dressed in dark blue suits and plain black shoes. They kept their hands in sight. The three men stopped him in the middle of the lobby.

"Mr. Libertaire, we mean you no harm. My boss would like to speak to you before you leave," the man said in a thick Russian accent.

"Where is your boss?" Wilhelm asked as he looked past the men towards his driver. He gave his driver the signal to stay put thus stopping his approach and having him put away his gun.

"He is in car outside; he will be happy to give you a lift to airport. Your man can follow, no problem," the Russian stated with a broad smile.

"And if I refuse your kind invitation, comrade."

"Then we would be forced to use violence, and I have my orders of no violence. Are you trying to get me in trouble?"

"No, no, I wouldn't want to do that. I will accept your offer. Lead on my good man," Wilhelm said sarcastically. As they passed his car, he told his driver to follow him. Then he got in the Russian's car, a typical black sedan.

"Hello Wilhelm. Thank you for accepting my invitation on such short notice," the man said.

"Radoslav, I should have known you were behind this taxi service; these guys are just your type," Wilhelm replied.

"So what do you want, Radoslav?"

"It is not what I want, Wilhelm. It is what I am about to do for you. A favor of sorts and the best part is you don't have to do one in return." Then he handed him a large manila envelope. "In there is information about Mr. Royce I think you will find most interesting."

"Why the gift?"

"Once you read the information inside, I think you will agree we should work together on this one."

"Bullshit, Radoslav! You are not known for generosity, and you never give a favor for nothing in return," Wilhelm said as he stared at him with a deadly serious demeanor.

"Alright, I told my superiors you wouldn't go for it so here it is in a nutshell as you Americans say. When my bosses found out you were after Royce, they were confident that he would cease being among the living soon. Then he survived the shoot out and disappeared. Needless to say, we were disappointed. At that time, we decided to aid you in your quest. Besides if you the great Libertaire kill him, our mutual friends in the community will say very little about it. But if we do it, well, the fallout could be embarrassing. You understand?" Radoslav sat back and waited for his response. As he did so, the car pulled up to the terminal. Wilhelm looked over at the entrance and saw three agents waiting, his driver and his two assigned bodyguards.

"I'll look this over. If it has any value, I'll act on it. That's all I can promise you. And Radoslav, if you decided to ask for my help in this manner again, I will send your men back in a box. Thanks for the ride; it was most informative and give my best to the misses." Then he got out and walked over to his agents.

"Who was the Russian, sir? I didn't know whether to take a defensive stance or just wait, sir. Sorry I didn't catch them earlier," the driver said looking very nervously not taking his eyes off the Russian car until it was out of sight.

"It's alright. Radoslav was just repaying a ride I gave him last year. You two did a good job. I'll put that in my report. The next time I'm in town, I'll ask for you," he told the two agents who had watched over him. They smiled broadly and said,

"Yes, sir, and thank you, sir," almost simultaneously. Wilhelm shook his head and walked into the airport with his driver right beside him.

Wilhelm settled into his private first class compartment on the super airbus. He told the stewardess to bring him a double scotch and to close the curtain all before taking off. As the plane began its ascent, Wilhelm was reading the information that Radoslav had given him. The information the Russians had passed on was indeed valuable; it contained evidence of Royce's dealings in the bio-chemical warfare trade. No wonder the Russians are eager to see him dead. Royce also had ties with the Chechen resistance movement and the Russians didn't want him selling anything to them. He thought Radoslav had a good reason for paying him a personal visit. He was right. This guy had to go and quickly. He took out his phone and sent Pam a message:

*Find and observe. Do not engage or capture. Wait for further instructions.*

Next he sent another message to Scott in MI6:

*"You will know what to do with this,"*

was all it read. He attached the file and pressed send.


*The Farm*

Wilhelm told his helicopter pilot not to fly over the training grounds on the way to the helipad. When he landed, Anthony met him.

"Where's George?"

"He's at the firing range, sir." Anthony knew his boss wasn't happy with what had happened. He and the staff had standing orders to stay on the premises when they were in training for a mission. He knew George was in serious trouble for breaking the rule and getting himself shot in the process. He also knew there was nothing he could do to help his friend.

When they arrived at the range, the men were going through a multi-person shooting drill. George was yelling at them for fucking up.

"You motherfuckers can't shoot for shit! Get your act together before I shoot you cocksuckers! Hell, you should be able to shoot a target ten feet wide. What's the matter? Jumping out of planes has affected your aim, fucked up your eyes. You've shot this drill a thousand times yet you are acting as if this is the first time you've done this. Now do it again and this time do it right! Or your asses will be on the firing range until your dicks dry up! You hear me?" The men answered him. As they began reloading their magazines, they noticed Libertaire standing behind George. One of the men told him to turn around.

"Why? Will it make you shoot better if I turn around? I don't think anything will get you fuckups to shot better but I'll try anything at this point." He never finished the sentence because when he turned around, he saw Wilhelm standing there.

"Boss, I didn't know you were back. I would've met you personally," he said nervously.

"No need. I had Anthony do that because I was under the impression you were shot and seriously hurt. But I see my information was wrong." He walked over to George and took a look at his shoulder. "It looks like you'll live. Tell you what, have Anthony take over. You come back to the house and tell me how this happened." His mannerism said he was concerned about his friend. Wilhelm realized he wasn't nearly as angry at him as he thought he would be. They got into the jeep. As they drove away, they could hear Anthony barking out orders and the firing began again.

Back at the house, they went to the library. Wilhelm closed the door. Once he was behind his desk, he pressed the button that turned on a red light that assured them privacy and let the guard know that he was not to be disturbed.

"Fill a bong; I'll get us a drink," Wilhelm said as he walked over to the bar and started to make two scotches. George opened the wooden box on the table in front of the couch where he was sitting and took out a bud. He placed the bud in a two-foot-tall glass bong and lit it filling its inner chamber with thick white smoke. Wilhelm brought him his drink and sat in the chair across from him. He waited until George had filled his lungs, held the smoke for a moment, and then exhaled.

"Now tell me how you got shot and managed to get your date killed. I've heard the official version and I've heard Cee's version. By the way, he thinks you're some kind of badass. Now I want to hear it from you." Wilhelm sat back in his chair and stared at him. George took another hit and began. A half-hour later, he finished. Afterwards he took another hit from the bong.

"The I.D. on those men came back as Chechen hit men known as the *Craftsmen of Death*. Someone thought enough of you to hire the best. They just underestimated their target. That being said, if you had stayed on the grounds and obeyed the policy, maybe just maybe you wouldn't be wounded, a young woman would be alive, and the best chef in the city wouldn't have to take a forced two-week vacation.

"What-the-fuck were you thinking? Or is it, you weren't thinking? I have that rule of no one leaves the farm when training for a mission for this very reason. I know you thought you could slip out, get fucked, and slip back—no harm, no foul. You have plenty of ass right here. What happened to Lucy and that other chick? I left you in charge; I thought you would take care of things here while I was away. What if this was a snatch job and not a hit? What if you caught one the right way? Then we wouldn't be having this talk. If you cross the line again, I'll have your head and they won't be able to find the rest of you. Do we understand each other?"

"Yes, sir. We understand each other. But it doesn't make sense why someone or some agency would want me dead. Removing me wouldn't compromise security. So why the hit?" George asked then took another pull on the bong.

"I'm looking into that. In the meantime, you're to stay on this side of the road. Anthony will finish the training. You'll rest and heal. Now bring me up to date on the training." For the next two hours, George brought his boss up to date on everything to do with the program. He included the team's weaknesses, Sanaa's progress, and what he thought of the mission's chances of success. Then he was gone, and Wilhelm prepared to face his family. He had been gone for two weeks and was sure they had a lot to tell him. He stepped out of the library and into the kitchen where he found them gathered. He smiled and was glad to be home.

*Brussels*

Upon arrival at her penthouse, Number 2 was greeted by her female butler.

"Welcome home, madam. I trust your trip was successful."

"Yes, it was, Katherine. Is my bath ready?"

"Yes, madam. It is."

"Get Brian on the phone and tell him to get his ass over here," she said as she headed up the stairs. In her room, she began to strip and headed to the bathroom. She slipped into the tub and closed her eyes. When she re-opened them, Brian was standing there naked with his flaccid cock in her face. Brain is a well-known model in Europe and was climbing the fashion ladder fast thanks to her. She had taken an interest in him two years ago. Besides, the sex she was getting was a good return on her investment.

She reached out with her wet, warm hand and cupped his balls. Then she took his soft cock in her mouth and began to suck on it. She enjoyed the feeling of his soft cock in her mouth. As he grew to full length, she began to jerk him off while keeping him in her mouth. She looked up at him and watched as he made faces of pleasure twisting his mouth into a funny shape. Then his hips started to spasm. She heard him say, "Oh fuck!" Immediately, she felt him explode into her mouth. She continued to suck and lick his cock for a few moments longer. Then said,

"Now that we have the cobwebs out, let's get down to some serious fucking."

Brian helped her out of the tub and into the bed where for the next three hours she worked out all of her frustrations. Afterwards, she rose from the bed, looked over at the still-sleeping Brian, and headed for the shower. She dried off, put on an oversized cotton robe, went downstairs to her office, and closed the door. It was time to implement phase two of Number 1's plan to kill Wilhelm. She would be adding one more name to that list.

# Nikkei

## *Chapter Twelve*

*Final Stage*

Wilhelm sat in the meeting with Rodney and his staff of five. He half listened to what was going on.

"Do you think this approach will work, Wilhelm?" Rodney asked.

"No I don't. To have me and my team in the area for two extra days will cause complications that I don't have the time to address."

"So what do you have in mind?" one of the deputy directors asked. Wilhelm looked at him and took a deep breath before answering.

"This is why. First, the Chinese run patrols up to five miles from the site. My team cannot wait two extra days at the six mile line and make it to the site on time through that type of terrain. Second, if we go with my time frame–the night before the gala—, there is no way the minister of trade is going to call it off. That way, while their agents are busy investigating who has done this and focus on the delegates who decide to leave, my guys will have the time they need to get out and deliver the package."

Rodney listened to his plan and had to agree with it. "After all, it was his neck on the line," he thought. Then he spoke,

"We will go with a combination of Wilhelm's plan and yours," he said pointing to the man from the State Department. "You will get Wilhelm in. Once there, Wilhelm will take operational control. This should satisfy everyone. If it doesn't, too fucking bad." Wilhelm got up and left the conference room.

He went back to his office, sent a few official communications, and went over the modifications to his exit plan. Then he reviewed the maps and latest intelligence reports on Angola with Bob from operations. Satisfied, he headed back to the farm by helicopter. He still had a lot a work to do. He wanted to be around for the final training exercises since live fire exercises were pending, not to mention Sanaa's field test. He decided to move Sanaa's field test up by two days; he needed to know if she could kill. He knew Rodney had an alternative motive and a specific plan in place and wondered what part Sanaa was playing.

He would move Sanaa's test to two nights before the annual carnival and dinner dance that his wives sponsored for charity. This would be perfect for such a test. He thought about how his special agents were fairing. Since their last reports, they both were on the move to their next targets. He also wondered what Scott was doing about the information which he sent. Just sending it could end his career or worst. But he didn't have time to worry about that now. He had four weeks to pull this all together. If nothing else went wrong and no hiccups arose in the training, he'll be fine. But that was wishful thinking. With George out of commission, he will have to take over the kill house training in the mockup building for their assault. Anthony was a doing a good job so far but without combat experience the members of the team wouldn't take him seriously. They needed to take this phase of training seriously, and they needed to be pushed hard.

*London*

Shadow Two was at a London dance club deciding which one of these fine young men she was going to take home and ride until dawn. She spotted Linda. "It can't be," she thought as she moved closer for a better look.

"Well fuck me," she said out loud then she headed for the bar. She took out her phone and texted Wilhelm.

*"Linda Banally is in London, have eyes on, will keep contact until further orders,"* she typed. She waited for a reply and kept her eyes on Linda. She knew her boss would reply. He never slept so she didn't worry about the time difference. Besides it was early just a little past midnight. So she sat at the bar and flirted while she waited.

Wilhelm's phone buzzed. He picked it up, saw who it was, and then read the message. "Well I'll be damn; so she's in London—smart girl, hiding in plain sight. Well played Linda, well played," he thought. He typed, *"Tag and release."* and pressed send.

Shadow Two looked at her phone and read the message. "Shit no dick tonight," she thought. Then she turned her attention back to Linda. She followed Linda back to her flat on a quiet tree lined street. She watched Linda get out of her car and enter the house. Then she looked for security. She scanned the street and found no one. The street was empty at 3:00 a.m.

Just as Shadow Two was preparing to leave, a door opened across the street. A man in a dark suit stepped out. He walked up the street to the corner, crossed, and went down the other side. He crossed again and started back up. She ducked down in the car seat and watched as he passed by. She sat up in time to watch him go back into the house. "So your security is directly across the street, clever girl. Or is it your benefactor that's watching out for you?" she thought. She started the car and quietly drove away. She turned on her headlights when she reached the corner. She went straight back to her hotel room, sent the information, showered, and went to bed.

℘

Wilhelm sat in the library thinking. "What was Linda up to in London? How long has she been there? Does Rodney know she's there? This and a many other questions were running through his mind. Labor Day was almost here, and the farm was about to be overrun with children and adults. The upcoming charity and dinner dance was his wives' fundraising event to help various charities that they supported. And the team would be running their live fire practices and assault routines this whole month. This was going to be an intense month for the team, not to mention for himself. He still had to finalize his exit plans, and Bob still had his doubts about the extraction. He got up from his chair, walked to the window, and looked out at the early morning sun rising. As he enjoyed the view of the dawn, his eyes caught movement to his left. He focused on the shape and determined it was George. He had been working hard these last few weeks to get back in shape. And having nothing to do and nobody to yell at was driving him crazy. Wilhelm decided to release him for duty and let him take over the training. Besides, he would need Anthony to run the security for the event anyway plus free him from that duty.

P

Stephanie awoke and checked her phone for messages. As she suspected, Wilhelm sent instructions.

*"Proceed to Milan immediately. Must capture and secure target. Use whatever resources necessary. Success of this mission most important."*

"Hmmm, first I'm to eliminate the target. Now I'm supposed to capture and baby sit the target. I wish he'd make up his fucking mind," she screamed as she headed to the bathroom.

*Milan, Italy*

Stephanie landed in Milan midday. She picked up the rental car that was arranged for her and drove to the apartment that would be her base of operation. She swept the apartment for listening devices. Once she was satisfied the place was secure, she sent word that she was in place and waited. During her wait, she went out and picked up some food and wine and returned to the apartment. While preparing her lunch, she heard a knock at the door. She checked the monitor as she chambered a round in her pistol. She looked at the man who was standing there and looking at the camera. Stephanie pressed the intercom button and spoke.

"Can I help you"?

"Yes, maybe you can. Is your car for sale?"

"It sure is for the right price."

"I think I can match your offer." Then she hit the buzzer and he walked in.

Stephanie pointed her pistol at him and said,

"Check in." The man went through the proper protocol and gave the recognition sign. Then she put her gun down on the counter where she was chopping vegetables and made sure it was within easy reach.

"I'm here to back you up. I just got my orders a few hours ago. They pulled me off another case to help you. It must be important. They never do this shit at this station. And who is

174

this Libertaire guy. I've never heard of him before today. He must have a lot of pull for the station to rearrange like this."

"Yeah, he must. You hungry?"

"A little, I could eat."

"Great, a newbie that doesn't even know who Libertaire is. I'm going to be stuck with the heavy lifting again," she thought as she smiled at him and kept chopping the carrots. They ate lunch, drank a bottle of wine, and talked. She found out that Doug wasn't all that green; this was his fourth snatch job. The six-foot, two-hundred-ten-pound, brown haired, hazel-eyed agent was a pleasant sort. One would never have guessed that he had been in the field for six years. He still was happy and didn't seem to mind the work even when it was boring as hell and he felt like shooting himself. Her jet lag was catching up with her; the wine and big lunch didn't help either. So she took a nap; it was intended to be a short one—an hour or two. But when she awoke, she found that she had slept for five hours.

She walked out to the living room and found Doug sitting near the window that faced the street. He was drinking a cup of coffee.

"Had a nice nap?"

"Is that coffee I smell?"

"Yes, it is. Want a cup?"

"After I clean up, see you in a minute." She took a quick shower, changed, and reemerged as a new person. "If you would join me at the counter, I'll fill you in on this mission," she said. Then she poured herself a cup of coffee and started her computer. Doug walked over and sat in the high chair opposite her and held out his cup. She refilled it pouring a little on his hand.

"Holly shit! That's hot," he said putting his cup down and shaking his hand. "I suppose that wasn't an accident," he said with anger showing on his face.

"What-the-fuck you think. The next time you want coffee ask for it nicely," she retorted staring hard into his eyes. Doug smirked and nodded in agreement. "Now let's get started," Stephanie said and then took a sip of her coffee. "This is Nikkei; she's a double agent. Our job is simple: Find the bitch. Snatch the bitch and bring her back here. Once that has been accomplished and before we procced any further, we will await orders from that man you never heard of." Doug looked at the pictures of Nikkei. He studied her face and body shape and memorized her walk. He watched the video of her a few times then turned to Stephanie.

"What if the other side tries to take her?" he asked.

"We kill them, Doug. She is to come with us or nobody. Understood!" He nodded in agreement and she continued. "Like all well-paid double agents, she enjoys the finer things in life. Here is a list of her known hang outs." Doug looked at the list and then at her. "What's the matter, Doug?

"The horses ... I don't ride that good; in fact, I'm a lousy rider," he said with a smile.

"You can try praying she doesn't go riding. But if she does, we do."

For the next week, they looked for her. They checked and rechecked places she was known to frequent. Shadow Two was beginning to think that she had gotten wind of them and moved on. Doug thought she had left town as a matter of protocol. Stephanie decided to check out a lingerie fashion show and maybe pick up a few things. She had Doug hangout outside and keep a watchful eye. When she picked up the lingerie that she had ordered during the show, she spotted Nikkei. Nikkei was in the next line talking to another woman and was acting very normal. Stephanie paid for her things and hurried out ahead of Nikkei.

"Come on! She's close behind me," she said to Doug as she passed him by. Doug went ahead and got the car while Stephanie kept a look out for Nikkei. Doug pulled up and she got in.

"Has she come out yet? How do you want to handle this?" he asked.

"There she is. But I don't know who that woman is she's with," she said as she pulled out the camera and started to take pictures. "We won't make a move on her here, too many people. Follow her; let's see where she goes," she stated as she took pictures. They followed her to a restaurant and then to a villa forty minutes out of town. As they sat on a hill overlooking the villa, Stephanie took pictures of the place and sent them off. "Now that we have a location, let's head back to the hide and wait for the information I requested to come in. Then I can plan how we are going to snatch this bitch," she said.

"How come the bad ones live so good? It never ceases to amaze me," Doug said as he started the car. Stephanie read the information on the woman who was with her target and shook her head.

"This chick is a piece of work, a real pro," she said out loud. "Listen to this; she worked a case here three years ago. Her cover was a governess to the children of this lady she's hiding out with. She worked there for fifteen months then left to get married leaving the woman no wiser and becoming good friends in the process."

"What's the woman's name?" Doug asked.

"Not important, Doug, we're not after her," she said with a smirk. "Now that I'm armed with information, this is how we are going to get this chick," she said swinging her legs off the couch and heading to the kitchen.

They watched and followed Nikkei for three days. Stephanie decided that if she followed the same routine again during the next day, they would take her. She and Doug were in place before dawn. They watched the sun come up. At sunrise, they turned their binoculars and attention on the house. They watched

Nikkei walk to the stables and ride out for her morning exercise. If she kept to schedule, she won't be back for two hours. So they settled in and had a breakfast of sausage, cheese, and coffee while they waited.

Nikkei returned a half-hour later than usual and went into the house.

"Let's get ready," Stephanie said to Doug.

She got up and walked to the car. She changed her blouse but left her cargo pants on. Next, she checked her weapons.

"I thought we were going to snatch her?" Doug said as he watched her go through her paces.

"We are. Why do ask?"

"Watching you load that rifle gave me the thought. If we're going to snatch her, why the rifle?"

"She's acting funny this morning. I have a hunch it's better to have it ready just in case." She went back to checking the equipment, and Doug joined her. They took turns watching the house while the other enjoyed the comforts of the car.

"She's leaving the house and heading for the garage," Doug said.

"Let's get into position," Stephanie said as she took out her pistol and started to screw on a silencer. Doug jumped into the car and headed down to the intercept point at the bottom of the hill behind a stand of trees.

In a few minutes, they heard the sound of a motor changing gear. "That bitch is really moving," she thought. Then she yelled at Doug,

"Put the fucking car in the road now!" Doug stepped on the gas and the car lurched forward. The rear wheels were spinning and trying to get enough traction. Finally the wheels caught a grip and caused the car to leap into the middle of the street. A loud squealing noise was heard to their left. As they looked over, they saw Nikkei's car swerving from side to side as her tires smoked trying to stop. She slid off the road into a pasture and took part of the fence with her for the next fifty meters before she stopped.

Stephanie and Doug were out of the car and running towards her before her car stopped. But Nikkei was ready. She stepped out the car on the passenger's side and opened up on them with a silenced assault rifle. They hit the ground and Shadow Two started firing back aiming at the car just to the right of Nikkei making it too hot for her to stay there. Nikkei took off running and grabbed a small black satchel as she did. She and Doug followed. The chase turned into a running gun battle.

Nikkei would stop and fight for short periods of time then resumed moving. All the while, Stephanie and Doug kept her in sight and stayed in gun range. Returning fire with their silenced pistols, the three of them were having a quiet death match so as not to bother the neighbors. Nikkei found a small stand of trees and dug in. She held them at bay with her rifle fire. Stephanie called Doug over to the rocks where she had taken cover behind and said,

"She doesn't know I have a rifle and she has to be low on ammo. So I want you to use the terrain. Work yourself around the left side of those trees. When you get there, I'll let her know she's out gunned."

"I was wondering what you were waiting for ... carrying a rifle on your back and not using it," he said.

"Watch and learn, junior. Now go. Time is not on our side so be quick about it," she said with a smile as she readied her rifle. Doug started off as Stephanie laid out magazines. Then she heard Nikkei yell out.

"Who the-fuck are you? And what-the-fuck do you want?"

"I'm here to save your fucked-up life in case you aren't aware, you stupid double-crossing bitch. There is a kill order on you and judging by your response, you were kind of expecting this."

"Yeah sort of, who are you with FSB, the Chinese, or the Council?" Nikkei yelled back.

"Neither I'm with the company, the same one you used to work for. Now why don't you give up? You can't win?"

"What? Are you crazy? Give up and be tortured? I'd rather be dead. But I'm not going alone, bitch. You can bank on that shit," Nikkei replied. She resumed firing, this time with careful well-aimed shots that kept Stephanie pinned down.

"I'm in place," Doug said over his radio earpiece.

"Good! When you hear me fire, you start firing and don't shoot her. As much as I like to, we need her alive, over."

"Roger that," he said.

When Nikkei slowed her firing, Stephanie opened up on her position firing three-round bursts into the trees on either side of her.

"Fucking bitch! You had a rifle all along, you sneaky cunt!" Nikkei yelled. She noticed the dirt by her feet kicking up. So she tucked them under her and looked for where the firing was coming. In short order, she found him. "Shit, I'm trapped and almost out of bullets," she thought. She just couldn't bring herself to kill herself so she gave up. "Alright you win! I give up!" she shouted. She threw out her rifle and handgun and stood up. Doug was the first one to reach her. He was searching her when Stephanie walked up. "Nice blouse," Nikkei said.

"Shut the-fuck up. I don't want to talk to you," Stephanie replied then punched her in the face.

"Huh! I take it you don't like me; maybe we got off on the wrong foot," Nikkei said as she spit out blood from her mouth. Doug pulled her hands behind her back, restrained her with quick cuffs, and tightened them. As he did, Stephanie went through her

182

satchel. She found a compact pistol, some money in euros and U.S. dollars, and a file along with five passports.

"Let's get out of here," Stephanie said. The trio headed off in the direction of the car. When they arrived, a few of the farm workers had gathered around the car in the road and were talking and smoking. They ducked down. Doug peered over the small rise and watched them for a minute before speaking.

"I'll go down, get the car, and meet you just around that bend."

"You sure you can handle them?" Stephanie said.

"Yes, I'm sure.

How's your Italian? Can you talk to them?"

He shot back, "Just relax. I'll take care of it. See you down the road." He stood up and walked away. As he approached the men, he smiled and pulled out a cigarette. After lighting it, he began to talk to the men who had gathered around. They talked and pointed to Nikkei's car wondering who it belonged to. Then Doug looked at his watch, said his goodbyes, got in the car, and drove off. Once he turned the bend, he stopped the car, and Stephanie and Nikkei stepped out from the trees.

Stephanie gagged Nikkei and put her in the trunk. They headed to the safe house. There, she had Nikkei strip and put on a robe. Stephanie went to her room and told Doug to watch Nikkei and feed her if she got hungry. In her room, she went through Nikkei's bag and dumped the contents on a small table.

She itemized the contents before putting them back. Then she sat down and started to read the file. An hour later, she came out. Doug and Nikkei were talking as they drank a glass of wine. They watched Stephanie as she walked over to the counter, poured herself a glass, and then sat down on a stool across from them.

"Tell me, Nikkei, how do you know Frank Depore?" Nikkei gave her a hard look then said,

"So you read the file but you don't quite understand it. Do you?"

"No, not really but you didn't answer the question. How do you know Frank?"

"He was my boss and lover, a long time ago."

"Refill, Doug," she said sliding her glass towards him. "And who are the Council of Five? Some kind of terrorist group?"

"Now that's above your pay grade. I think I'll wait and talk with someone who has a little more clout than you do," Nikkei said with a smile.

"Okay, have it your way," she said as she got up and went back to her room.

"Well that was pleasant," Nikkei said.

"Yeah, that's the problem. She's not the warm and fuzzy type," he said.

Stephanie got on her computer, began to type, and waited. A minute later, a message appeared; she read it and replied. She took pictures of the files, uploaded them, and hit send. She received a conformation and more instructions. She read them, deleted the file, and ran a cleanup program.

"Here, put this on. You'll be picked up soon. This is your traveling clothes," Stephanie said as she threw the coveralls at her. Later, Doug made dinner. They watched a movie that he and Nikkei had to explain to her. There was a knock at the door. Stephanie checked the monitor and told Doug to open it. Two men entered and talked to her. Afterwards, she gave them the satchel.

"Miss Nikkei, would you come with us, please?" one of the men said in a very British accent.

"You bitch! You cunt! You're turning me over to the Brits, the fucking Brits! You bitch, I'll get you for this!" she screamed as the two men took her from the safe house.

℗

Wilhelm sat in his communications room and read the message:

*"I'll let you know what I shake out of her. Scott."*

He smiled, instructed the computer to shut down, and headed up the stairs.

# House Party

*Chapter Thirteen*

*Carnival Weekend*

Labor Day weekend was a big deal at the farm. It was the time for the annual charity fundraising carnival and picnic. For one hundred fifty kids, it would be a day of endless fun and food—a chance to run wild in the great outdoors, ride horses, go fishing, play games, and receive all sorts of gifts and prizes. In fact, this was his wives' project—part of their grand scheme to give back to the universe. Personally, he didn't buy into all of that. Maybe, it was his job and all the shit he'd seen, let alone done. Fuck the universe. It will take care of itself; he had his own set of problems. In a few short weeks, his mission would begin, and he still had a few loose ends to tie up. This and a million other things were running through his head. As he walked around the grounds, his two mastiffs and guard were close on his heels. He spotted Colleen who was headed straight for him with an intense look on her face. Her look said he had forgotten something.

"Dianna just suggested to me that we may have an out-of-town guest coming to dinner tonight. Anything I should know?" she asked as she fell in step with him.

"Not that I'm aware of. I have no plans for the evening that concerns work. So tell Dianna not to spread rumors especially to you," he said.

After their talk, he headed for his library. In about four hours, one hundred couples and a few singles would be eating, drinking, and dancing at the dinner dance. . So if he was to have a surprise guest, it would happen then. Wilhelm poured himself a Hendricks double and sat on the couch to drink it.

"Are you ready for her, sir?" George asked as he walked in.

"Ready for whom, George?"

"Lucy and Sanaa, sir, tonight's test," George said.

"Yes, send them in, and you should attend also," he said as he walked to his desk and sat down.

George left and returned with the two women. They stood in front of his desk and waited for him to speak. Wilhelm waited until George closed the pocket doors to the library and turned on the red light above the outer door which signaled to the guard he was not to be disturbed.

"Over there on the coffee table are two laptops. Have a seat and open them, please." Lucy and Sanaa did as he told them. A white male face appeared on their screens.

"That is Gregory; he's your target tonight. Sanaa, you are to seduce Mr. Gregory then kill him." Sanaa looked up from the screen at Wilhelm then looked back down. Lucy looked over at her and winked. "Hit the enter button, ladies," he said. "That is the club where you will find your target; it's one the hottest in the D.C. area at the moment. It's his favorite hunting ground for sex, and note he likes a lot of sex. That may be you're in. You should know that his favorite type of women at the moment is Asian and Indian.

"So I hope you learned all of the tricks that Ms. Sandy taught you over the last two weeks. Tonight's the night you put them to use. Your mission is simple: Find him. Seduce him. Then kill him quietly, very quietly, and try not to make a mess. All of the information you need on your target is on that laptop so study it carefully. Your jump off time is 2200 hours. Lucy, I want you to back her up even if he wants a threesome, but this is her kill. You are not to help her out unless she fails. Then you take out the target. George, assign a security team to go with them; three men should cover it. Now are there any questions?" When no one said anything, he dismissed them and went back to his drink.

Sanaa sat at a small desk in her room and read the information about her target. "This Gregory guy is a piece of work but there's nothing in here to explain why he has been targeted," she thought. She turned her attention back to his file and wondered what Lucy was doing.

Lucy was in her room checking three pistols which she had laid out on her bed. She was wondering if she should take a knife or garrote or both. Then she decided to take her small five shot 32 caliber pistol along with the garrote; they would be easy to hide. Next, she turned to her closet, looked through her clothes, and tried to find something sexy for the club.

Wilhelm was standing with Rodney, the ambassador from Turkey, and two businessmen. As they drank and talked shit, George walked up.

"Boss, you have a special guest waiting for you in the kitchen," he whispered in Wilhelm's ear. Wilhelm looked at him and then excused himself. The two of them headed to the house.

"Who's in the kitchen?"

"MI6. It's Scott, sir. We thought it might be better for them to meet with you there first before the other guests found out he is here." When Wilhelm entered the kitchen, he found Scott drinking a cup of tea and a guard standing watch on the other side of the kitchen with his rifle held casually.

"Is this necessary, Wilhelm?" Scott said pointing at the guard.

"You are a spy. Aren't you? And a very good one from all accounts, you should be glad my security didn't shoot first," Wilhelm said with a smile. "What are you doing here, Scott?"

"The last time I was in town, Rodney invited me to this little gathering so I thought I would take him up on it. I had no idea it would be this big and you would have so many VIPs. I feel privileged to be here," he said jokingly.

"At least, you're dressed for the occasion. The next time you want to crash one of my parties, call first." Scott looked up at him and was about to crack wise until he saw his face and thought better of it.

"Oh, I will; I promise. I thought they were going to shoot me this time if it hadn't been for George here. Now where's the booze and food in that order please?" he said as he got up from the table. As he walked out to the ballroom where the dinner dance had commenced, he said to Wilhelm in a low voice and smile, "I have some information from that bird you sent me that you need to hear."

"After the party, Scott," was all he said. Then they joined Rodney and the others.

The event went off without a hitch, and his wives raised a lot of money for their cause. Most of the guests had gone by now. Only a fraction remained in the west garden. They were mostly friends of Colleen, Afra, and Afef. A helicopter flew overhead, circled, and then landed at the helipad. Rodney was sitting in the garden talking with his wife and Colleen when he heard the helicopter. He noticed three or four jeeps racing towards the south end of the property where the runway and main helipad are located. But he didn't move neither did Colleen. As Wilhelm's security force responded to the threat, Wilhelm was in the library with Scott. He was listening to the information that Scott had extracted from his interrogation of Nikkei.

The helicopter landed and four secret service agents stepped out to be greeted by fourteen security personnel with their rifles trained on them. George stepped forward into the flood lights and spoke.

"Why have you landed here?" he asked matter-of-factly.

"We have the president on board. Can't you see the insignia? Have your men lower their weapons," one of the agents said.

"I think your men should lower their weapons, and you tell me why-the-fuck you are landing on my helipad at 11:13 p.m. without permission. You have exactly thirty seconds to tell me or die," George said. Then he backed away into the darkness.

"Tell the men to lower their weapons," a voice said from inside the helicopter. Slowly, the agents lowered their weapons.

A woman appeared in the doorway. She walked down the steps and over to where the agents stood.

"Hi my name is Paula Giglia. I'm the president's aid. The president is really on board, sir."

"Well that's more like it. Now what does the president require? And I'll see if I can accommodate him."

"The president would like to speak to Mr. Libertaire. He apologizes for the unannounced visit. For security reasons, I'm sure you understand." George didn't reply instead he started to talk on his cellphone. When he hung up, he said,

"I'm having a more comfortable car come for the president. It will be here in a moment. Lower your weapons, men, and give them some room." Then he walked away.

Back at the house there was a flurry of activity going on. A server approached and whispered something to Colleen. She excused herself and left. When she entered the living room, she found Afef and Afra waiting.

"What's going on, Colleen? Who's the special guest?" Afra asked.

"I don't know, Afra. We'll just have to wait and see. Now take a seat and try not to show your excitement too much," Colleen told her. "Where's Wilhelm, Afef?" Colleen asked.

"George went to get him. He just said to wait here; then he left," Afef replied.

"Okay, we wait," Colleen said and sat down on the couch with Afra and Afef doing the same.

George went to the library and informed Wilhelm of what was happening. Wilhelm instructed him to let the president be entertained by the women for a while and not to let Rodney near that room or allow him to leave. George nodded and left. Wilhelm and Scott continued their conversation. George sent the Rolls Royce to pick up the president and waited by the east entrance for his arrival. When the president arrived, George escorted him to the living room where Colleen, Afef, and Afra were waiting. He posted a guard with each of the secret service men and headed to the library.

"Good evening, Mr. President," Colleen's greeting began. "May I welcome you to Libertaire Manor," she said in her best lady-like voice trying hard not to let her excitement show. "May I introduce Afef and Afra Libertaire," she said as she motioned to each one. Both women smiled, did a short curtsey, and said good evening.

"It's very nice to meet you, ladies. I have heard about you and the manor since I've been in office. I'm glad I finally get to see it," he said as he looked around the room.

President Obama was admiring the large space that was decorated in an art deco design. It was not at all what he imagined. A massive fireplace faced a comfortable seating area in front of it. Life-size African statutes cast in bronze and carved from alabaster and wood stood throughout the room. Oil paintings by African-American masters and family pictures hung across the walls above large hand carved wood furniture upholstered in leather and cloth. Persian, Turkish, and Egyptian rugs lay on highly polished wood floors set the theme for the different areas of the living room. The space looked very inviting. He walked around the room with Colleen and listened as she pointed out items of interest. They returned to the others and all sat down.

"May I offer you a drink, Mr. President?"

"I thought you would never ask, Mrs. Libertaire."

"Please, call me Colleen. And what can I get you, sir?" she asked as she rose from her chair opposite from where he was seated on the couch with his aide.

"I hear your husband is a connoisseur of fine whiskey. Do you think he would mind if I sampled a bit?" he said with a big smile.

"Not at all, I'm sure my husband won't mind," she said as she headed to the small wooden bar next to the fireplace.

She returned carrying five crystal lowball glasses filled with double shots of eighty year old Bowman Single Malt Scotch on a silver tray. She gave everyone a glass, made a toast, and took a sip.

"Hmmm, what is this, may I ask?"

"Eighty year old Bowman," Afra said.

"Write that down, Paula. We should have some of this around the house," he said and then took another sip. Meanwhile, George called the library from the kitchen.

"Yes," Wilhelm answered.

"Fifteen minutes, sir."

"Go and get Rodney and bring him to the living room. I'll meet you there," he told him and hung up. "You need to stay here while I see what this is all about. The president just doesn't drop in to say hi," Wilhelm said to Scott.

"I'll be glad to hang out here and drink your gin until your return," Scott replied holding up his glass.

Wilhelm laughed as he left and headed for the living room. As he went down the hall, he saw the eight guards that were posted, one of his for one of theirs. This arrangement was pissing somebody off. He knew it was George's way of fucking with the president's men. When he walked in, he found his three wives laughing and talking with the president all with drinks in hand.

"This is an honor, Mr. President, to have you in my home," Wilhelm said. Obama stood up and extended his hand, and when Wilhelm accepted it he spoke.

"The honor is mine, Mr. Libertaire. Your wives are charming and your whiskey is exceptional. Accept my apology for dropping in on you like this." Wilhelm felt like he genuinely meant it. "Now where is Rodney? I know he's here drinking somewhere," he continued.

"He'll be along any moment now, sir," Wilhelm replied. At that moment, Colleen cut in.

"If you will excuse us, Mr. President, we have guests to attend to. It has been a pleasure meeting you," Colleen said with Afef and Afra expressing the same sentiments. Then they were gone. As they left, Rodney walked in.

"If you will excuse us, Paula," Obama said.

"Where should I go, sir," she replied.

"Come with me, Paula," Wilhelm said. As he escorted her out of the room, he told her how to get to the kitchen. "And tell the chef to make you something to eat," he continued as she walked down the hall.

"Let's get right to it, shall we?" Obama said. "Wilhelm, we need you to add on to your mission. I know it's late in the game, but Rodney assures me you can pull it off."

"Pull what off, sir?"

"Rodney, you want to answer that."

"Yes, sir. You see, Wilhelm, it's come to our attention that one of the delegates to the trade conference is a spy for the Chinese. Problem is he's high up in the Angolan government. So we can't snatch him or remove him for that matter. Therefore we need you to come up with a way to get the information and leave him in tack, so to speak," Rodney explained, and then sat back in his chair, and waited for Wilhelm's reaction.

### The Club

Sanaa and Lucy pulled up to the club a little after eleven and saw it was crowded. The line to the club had snaked its way down the street. Lucy drove by the club slowly then headed to a prearranged parking spot. On the way, she passed by her backup team. She parked and looked over at Sanaa.

"You ready? Got your plan together, girl?

"Yeah, I'm ready. I got my shit together. Find him. Fuck him. Kill'em. And if Ms. Sandy's techniques work as good as she thinks, I got this," Sanaa said with confidence. They got out of the car and walked towards the club.

Sanaa was dressed in a shiny gold form-fitting dress that stopped six inches above her knees. It had a scallop neckline and a low-cut back almost to the crack of her ass. The dress hugged her ass and body caressing it as she walked. Her hair was long, straight, and shiny and stopped at her shoulder blades. She wore a crystal-beaded choker and matching pendant earrings both caught the light and glittered. Her two-inch heels matched her dress and clutch. Her black stockings had a gold devil on the ankle. Black and gold garter belts completed her ensemble. Lucy was dressed the same way except in silver. As they walked, they listened to the cat calls from both men and women and smiled.

They walked up to the doorman. Lucy said something to him. Afterwards he looked at his clipboard then removed the red velvet rope.

"Bruce! Two for the VIP area!" he yelled. The man motioned for them to follow and led them to their table. The club was packed; the music was banging and loud; and the crowd was loving it.

"How-the-fuck am I even going to find this guy in this place?" Sanaa thought as they maneuvered through the crowd towards the VIP area. At their table, she discovered that from her vantage point she could see most of the dance floor and a good portion of the tables around it.

"I'm going to look around and see if I can locate him. You stay here, have a drink, and act like you're looking for a good time," Lucy said talking directly into her ear. Sanaa nodded her head and watched Lucy slide out of the booth. Sanaa ordered a bottle of champagne. She could drink this stuff all night and not get drunk. Soon after, it was brought to her table. That was the beginning of an endless stream of people male and female who stopped by trying to pick her up. An hour went by before Lucy returned.

"About time," Sanaa said.

"I found our man; he is on the far right sitting with two ugly bitches compared to us." Then she filled a glass with champagne and drank it down in one shot. "I shouldn't be drinking this shit. Not only will it get me drunk, I'll want to fuck half the guys in here," Lucy said laughing. "What's your next move now that you know he's here?"

"I'm going to dance, Lucy. Maybe my dancing will get his attention since he's with two ugly bitches as you put it. If he takes the bait, I'll use you to land him since he's in a doubles mood," she explained.

She slid out of the booth, smoothed her dress, and headed for the dance floor. She picked a tall good looking dark-skinned man and started to dance. He was a good dancer and she was enjoying herself. To get a better look, she moved closer to where her target was sitting. He wasn't a bad looking man. He was dressed in a light colored suit and was sitting with two women. One woman was Asian and the other looked to be bi-racial. Nonetheless, they were ugly. She stopped dancing and made her way to the bar. There, she accepted a drink from a guy whom she pretended to listen to even though she couldn't hear him over the music.

She watched her target as he got up from his table with his dates and started to dance. "Finally, a break," she thought. She looked up at the balcony for Lucy. She spotted her, got her attention, and then signaled for her to come down.

"What's up?" she said upon arrival.

"What do you usually do after drinking and dancing?" Sanaa asked as they watched the target.

"Pee, of course," Lucy said.

"Exactly, did you bring anything that can be used to separate him from them?"

"I think I did, girl."

"In that case, when our lady friends go to the powder room, you take care of them and I'll make my move on him," Sanaa told her.

"Just say when," was Lucy's reply. While they waited, they flirted with men at the bar and kept an eye on him.

After three songs, the women left for the ladies room, and he returned to his table.

"You're on," Lucy said then headed for the restroom. Lucy entered the bathroom and looked for the women. She found the Asian one at the sink and saw the other one in a stall. The restroom was crowed but not packed so she was able to slide up next to her at the sinks. She put her clutch down and took out her makeup and a small spray bottle. She pretended to check her makeup and started to play with her hair.

As she looked in the mirror, she saw the woman's friend coming out of the stall. At that moment, she picked up the spray bottle. She continued to play with her hair and raised the bottle in front of her as if to spray her bangs. With two quick squirts, the mist went pass her head and into the face of the Asian woman who coughed and gave her an evil look.

"Sorry," she said. Then she went back to fixing her hair. A minute later, the woman started to vomit violently in the sink. Lucy smirked and backed away to make room for her friend who was at her side asking her what was the problem.

Lucy left the bathroom and searched for Sanaa on the dance floor. She found her quickly by spotting her sparkling gold dress. Sanaa was dancing with a guy and a woman in front of the target's table. She was definitely putting on an erotic show for him and his eyes were glued on her. Lucy walked over, cut in dancing with Sanaa, and fell into step with her sexual dance. A waiter came over and said something to him; the man nodded and the waiter left. Her target returned his attention to them and watched this sensual show. Sanaa's hips were conveying an undeniable message of sex; her mouth and tongue reinforced that message. She and Lucy put on a well-choreographed dance routine of seduction. As she watched him, she knew it was working. He signaled for them to join him, but they danced a few more minutes before doing so. They both knew they had him.

The rest of the night went as planned. When the club was closing, they had no doubt of where the trio was going.

"Shall we take my car back to the hotel, ladies?" he said as the limo pulled up. The driver got out and opened the door for them.

"Oh yeah, baby, act two is about to begin," Sanaa said as she and Lucy got into the car. The backup team observed this as they started their car and prepared to follow them. Twenty minutes later, the limo pulled up to a five-star hotel and dropped off its cargo.

One of the backup team members followed them into the hotel and then broke off to find the best alternate escape route. Their target took them to his suite on the fifteenth floor.

"Relax, ladies. The best part of the night is about to begin," he said. Sanaa and Lucy looked around the room as they entered. So far, tonight they hadn't seen any security around this guy. So they both were extra careful; they knew their target was dangerous. "Anyone for a drink?" he said.

202

The women replied, "No." But Lucy continued.

"I could sure use a joint about now," she said smiling.

"That I can help you with," he said and headed for the bar across the room.

"How long you in town for?" Sanaa asked.

"I don't know, a week maybe longer," he replied looking up at her while pouring his drink.

"I love hotels. I'd live in one if I could afford it and only use room service," Lucy said as she sat down in a chair. He went back to making his drink but his reaction to Sanaa's statement didn't go unnoticed by the both of them.

He finished making his drink and walked over to the sitting area were the women where. In his right hand, he held a small box which he handed to Lucy.

"You'll find everything you need in there," he said. Then he sat down in the chair across from Sanaa. Lucy opened the box and found a grinder, paper, filters, and some great smelling bud.

"What's this?" she said to him.

"Afghan Kush," he replied.

"Shit yeah!" Lucy said. They were quiet as they watched Lucy roll a perfect joint—fat at one end and tapering down as it reached the filtered end. "Anyone have a light?" she asked. He reached into his pocket and tossed her his gold lighter. Lucy lit the joint and took a long slow drag. When she released the smoke, she smiled. "Now this is some first grade smoke. You gotta take a hit of this," Lucy said as she handed the joint to Sanaa. Sanaa took the joint but took shorter more frequent hits of it. Lucy was right this was some kick ass shit. She was so glad that her body didn't react to champagne. For some good reason, it just didn't get her drunk. If it did, this joint would have put her over the edge. If she wasn't careful, this Afghan Kush would put her over the limit. She could not fail this mission.

Sanaa passed the joint to him and watched him enjoyed it as he took long slow deep pulls of the pungent bud. He passed the now half smoked joint back to Lucy.

"Put on some music. This bud is making me horny and want to dance," Lucy said.

"By all means, I love watching you dance. I can hardly wait to fuck you," he said as he got up to turn on the radio. Lucy told him what she wanted to hear, and he found it for her. Then she began a slow gyrating motion with her hips. Then she let the rest of body into the act. Before he knew it, the two of them were dancing together.

Sanaa sat and watched Lucy work and was amazed at how well she was seducing their target. She got up and joined them and the three of them swayed and grinded and shared the joint. A short time later, they were naked on the bed playing with each other's bodies. He was taking turns entering both women. While he was in one, the other was making sure he was working much harder than he had to. The idea was if they delayed his nut for as long as possible, he would try harder to achieve it. Thus, when he finally comes, he would be exhausted and easier to handle and easier to kill.

They managed to delay him long enough for the two of them to have at least one orgasm. While he was busy fucking Lucy missionary style, Sanaa had time to get the small vial of poison out of her clutch unnoticed. She gave Lucy the signal and started massaging his balls. Lucy encouraged him to come by talking dirty to him.

"Come on, daddy! Bust that nut deep inside me. Let me feel how powerful you can come," she said in a breathy voice.

"Huh, huh, oh fuck!" he said as he began to come. Afterwards he rolled off Lucy and laid there panting. That's when Sanaa made her move. She jumped on his chest pinning his arms down. Then Lucy quickly squeezed her thumb and middle finger into the hinge of his jaws forcing his mouth open and allowing Sanaa to empty the vial down his throat. She closed his mouth before he had a chance to react. It all happened in a matter of seconds not giving him a chance to fight. They held him down while he bucked and rolled trying to get free. Then he was still and stopped breathing. They held their positions a moment longer just to make sure he was dead.

Sanaa got off of his chest and off the bed.

"I was wondering when you were going to make your move. But I'm glad you waited until I had that last orgasm. I wasn't kidding when I said I was horny," Lucy said breaking the silence.

"Where's that bud; I could use a joint about now," Sanaa replied. Then she walked back to the couch, sat down, and began to roll a joint.

"How do feel?" Lucy asked.

"Fine, right now. Who knows how I'll feel an hour from now."

"First kill?"

"First one up close and personal," Sanaa said. She lit the joint, took a deep pull, and held it in her lungs for as long as she could.

"Well, you did good, real good ... had me going there for a while but your plan not only worked out you got a girl laid. I'll go on missions with you anytime," Lucy said as she walked towards her and took the joint.

"Tell you what, let's finish the joint, search the place, and go home. This was a successful mission and you should be proud of yourself. I know the boss will be happy. When he's happy, good things happen. You know what I mean, girl," Lucy said smiling. Then she took a pull of the joint. They got dressed, searched the place, let their backup team know they were on their way out, and left.

## Libertaire Manor

The meeting with the president lasted a little over an hour. Then he was gone and soon after was Rodney. When Wilhelm returned to the library, he found Scott asleep on the couch. The guard whom he posted was standing by watching him. So he took the time to grab something to eat and headed for the kitchen where he found George and his wives. As he ate, he listened to their excitement about meeting the president and how they thought this year's carnival was one of the best yet. Afterwards, he returned to the library, woke Scott up, and watched the interrogation videos of Nikkei.

Around 5:15 in the morning, George called him to inform him that the ladies had returned and that the mission was successful. Wilhelm told him to have them in his office at eleven this morning. Then he hung up. He and Scott went back to work. It was seven in the morning when they stopped. He went upstairs to bed and Scott was shown to his room. At 11:00 a.m., he was sitting behind his desk listening to Sanaa and Lucy report.

"Good job, ladies! The death of your target has been reported as a heart attack. There is now one less arms dealer who should have known better than to cross the very people who let him operate in the first place," he said with a slight smile looking straight at Sanaa. "That will be all, Lucy," he added. Lucy got up, said good morning, winked at Sanaa, and left the room. "Now that I know you can think on your feet and I'm satisfied you can kill, let me update you on the upcoming mission. It has changed a bit." Wilhelm spent the next couple of hours discussing the mission and what he had in mind. As he listened to her suggestions, he found that she had a knack for planning. Afterwards, he was glad he talked to her. He intended to incorporate an idea or two of hers but that could wait right now. He had a guest to attend to.

*House of the Flying Snakes*

*Addictive danger*
*Seduces talented recruits*
*Shadows, agents, hires*
By Claire L. Hand

# Pam's Mission

## *Chapter Fourteen*

*Safe House*

Pam had been surveilling Talaus and Royce in South Africa for six weeks now. Until this morning, it had been a cushy assignment but Wilhelm called. When she heard from him, it was never good. This time would be no different. So she got herself together and headed for the meet. When she arrived at the private airfield, she was greeted by a six-member kill team—one woman whom she was surprised to see and five guys. She knew they were a kill team from their look: The men were fit but not overly muscled with clean shaven faces. The woman was lean, fit, curvy, and very pretty. They were just the type that Wilhelm would send. She also knew they were contractors not agency. She walked up and addressed them. The only white team member turned and faced her.

"First, we don't mention names. Second, I am taking you to the safe house where you'll wait. Follow me," she said. The team looked at her strangely then at each other. They picked up their bags and followed her out to the van without saying a word.

They rode in silence except for the music coming from the CD player. Their two-hour ride ended when she pulled onto a dirt road and finally parked in front of a farm house.

"This is it," Pam said as she turned the van off and got out. She unlocked the door and walked in. She did a walk-through and made sure everything was alright. Afterwards, she returned to the living room and addressed them.

"You have everything you need for now—food, drink, and two ounces of Durban Poison, very good bud by the way. I didn't stock anything for a woman, wasn't expecting one. So if you need something, let me know." Pam said and headed for the door.

"How long are we here for," one of the men asked.

"I have no fucking idea. Just hang out and wait. I'll be doing the same," she replied and then left. As she turned onto the blacktop road and started the long drive back, she thought about what was going to happen. She had a pretty good idea who it was going to happen to.

*Libertaire Manor*

Wilhelm went through the protocol of entering his underground office and walked down the sloping stairs.

"Computer, bring up the photos from P1895V1220 in order of day and time."

"Bringing up photos now, sir," the computer replied. Wilhelm sat down and studied the photos. As he was looking through them for the third time, it hit him. One man was seen in every picture taken when Talaus was throwing one of his special parties.

"Computer, isolate the man on the left of this picture."

"Isolating image." Wilhelm waited as the computer found the subject and enlarged the photo automatically.

"Computer, find all the information available on subject."

"Yes, sir, this may take some time. I have to access several databases to accomplish this task."

"Noted, now bring up today's reports." He spent the next two hours reading reports, making notes about them, and sending out replies before the computer informed him that it had finished with its task. "Computer, bring up the information," he said as he turned his chair to face the screen. The computer displayed the information which he began to read:

*Andikan Rekening: thirty-two years old, six feet, one inch tall, two hundred twenty pounds, black hair, brown eyes, South African citizen. Occupation: playboy. Family owns one of the largest law and accounting firms in South Africa named Rekening Legal and Financial Company. Also has ties and family members in both houses of government. Is a member of an elite international BDSM club. Is a major player in the underground sex scene. Assets are two homes in South Africa: one in Durban near the coast, one just outside of Johannesburg. Owns a yacht and private plane, both capable of international travel. Estimated worth: one billion dollars US.*


Wilhelm looked at the information in front of him and then at his photo. He wondered how this man came to know Talaus.

"Computer, show me Talaus' travel pattern for the last year."

"Showing pattern on screen three."

"Now show me the travel pattern for Andikan."

"Showing on screen two."

Wilhelm compared the patterns and only found two incidents showing their paths had crossed.

"Computer, send this message to P1895V1220." He dictated a message, shut down the computer, and walked up the stairs to the library. He still had the problem of the added mission objective to solve and he couldn't spend any more time on Royce. It was already September, and he had three weeks until this mission jumps off. That also meant, he had to sit on the information that Scott had shared. Even though it was actionable Intel, it had to keep for now.


*Durban, South Africa*

Sitting in front of her laptop, Pam read a message she just received. "Here we go again," she thought. She walked over to the wine rack, selected a bottle, opened it, got a glass, and sat down again. Now she had to put together a mission, which she had never done before. She only followed orders. "I guess this is what I get for asking for more responsibilities," she thought. "This isn't what I had in mind. Now he drops this right in my lap, a major operation like this." A kill team and the two agents whom she already was working with made her team eight strong. He did say study their files and use their talents according to their strengths.

Pam crossed her legs in the chair, poured another glass of wine, and opened the first file. After reading for hours and only covering two of the six files, she took a break. Unfolding her legs and standing up to stretch, she was glad that she brought her favorite house dress. She was even happier that she was wearing it now. This red cotton dress hung off her shoulders barely covering her breasts, was too short for public viewing, and was covered with the words "lick me all over." It was so comfortable and it helped her think. In fact, it was her lucky dress even if she only wore it around the house. As she walked through the living room, she thought about her college boyfriend who bought it for her and wondered what he was doing at this moment. She knew he would never guess what she was doing about now. Pam sat down on the oversized cloth chair by the front window and looked out. She could see the neighbor's children playing: Girls were playing with dolls and laughing. Boys were playing a futball game and bragging among themselves as one was trying to outdo the other.

It was a clear sunny day but not hot. A light steady breeze that barely blew moved the branches on that old tree in the front yard. She watched the goings on outside as she rolled a joint and lit it. Then she slumped back in her comfortable chair and thought about the two files she had just read. She owed the ladies in Bulgaria for turning her on to the "plant" as they referred to it. Now she had become an experience smoker, and to think that before the Bulgaria mission, she never thought of bud. She got up, went back to her laptop, and picked up where she left off with the joint hanging out the side of her mouth like a cigarette.

Many hours and a few joints later, she finished. She sat there thinking not looking at the screen but in its direction. Then it hit her; her boss had sent her a team of specialists. Not only were they good at killing, but also they had other special talents. One thing was becoming clear to her. Her boss was not only a ruthless man but also was very cunning as well. She was just beginning to understand the rules of this game, a spy agency within a spy agency. And now she was caught right in the middle. She had a feeling Langley had no knowledge of this operation. But then Wilhelm had such broad powers. She realized Langley must know about it. She shut down her computer and prepared for bed. All of this would keep until morning when she would begin to put her plan together.

Pam got up early, completed her workout, and was cooking breakfast when Steve and Cal arrived for the morning meeting.

"What's cooking? Smells good," Cal said as he sat down at the kitchen table.

"A full breakfast, fellas, I thought you deserved one after all the hard work you've put in," Pam said.

"Sounds like a last meal to me. What's going on Miss Homemaker?" Steve asked as he poured a cup of coffee. Pam ignored his comment and put the food on the table. She placed a platter of scrambled cheese eggs with onion, green pepper, and mushrooms and plates of sweet sausages and toast with orange marmalade and butter.

"Okay Pam, now I'm starting to feel like there's a last meal thing going on here. Is there something you're trying to tell us?" Cal said as he started to fix a plate.

"Yes, but after we eat," she said.

"Why wait," Steve chimed in between bites of sausage.

"Because as my father always said, 'Facing the day on a full stomach makes the day's problems easier to handle.' After I fixed such a great meal, I'm not going to spoil it with shop talk." Then she went back to eating and the trio talked about things that made them happy and enjoyed each other's company. Afterwards they sat around the table drinking coffee. Pam filled them in on the mission at hand.

"Well I'm not surprised. This job was going too smoothly, no excitement. I knew it wouldn't last long," Cal said.

"Oh, stop being you, Cal. You haven't even heard the plan yet," Steve said. Cal got up from the table and was looking around the living room.

"What are you looking for?" Pam asked.

"Where do you keep the plant?" he said.

"By the big chair." she replied. Cal walked over to the chair, picked up the wooden box, and walked back to the table. He sat down, opened the box, and took out what he needed to roll his joint.

"Anyone joining me?" he asked with a smile. Pam and Steve said,

"No." Cal kept rolling and then lit the joint.

"Oh, is that good. Nothing like a good smoke after a good meal," he said after he exhaled. "Do you know how you are going to pull this off and how trustworthy are these contractor fucks."

"I'm not concerned about them; they will do their jobs. That's why he picked me to run this mission and not one of you. Steve, you have at least twelve years on me and Cal has nine. So why pick a person like me with so little experience?"

"Cal and I are surveillance men; we watch people; we don't kill people. So when Libertaire picks someone to do something, he probably has a good reason for it and an alternative motive. Besides don't sell yourself short. You can pull this off, Pam. Just concentrate on the mission at hand." She was glad she had these two. They were some of the best at what they did, and he did say use you talent.

"So, guys, here's what I want you two to do starting today." Then she told them what she had in mind.

After they left, she signed on to her laptop and sent a message to the kill team. She knew one of them would be monitoring it 24/7. She waited a moment and read the reply. She sent her acknowledgment and signed off. Pam got dressed, checked her pistol, left the house, and headed for the team's safe house a two hour drive away. She didn't mind the drive; it gave her time to think. And with the convertible top down on her BMW, it was an enjoyable ride. She pulled onto the dirt road and drove up to the house.

She saw two of the men in the side yard practicing knife fighting with what looked like real blades. Another one was sitting on the porch cleaning some pistols, and a fourth man was standing watch at the other end of the porch. She entered the house and saw the fifth man sitting in front of a computer watching TV.

"Where's the woman?" she asked him.

"She'll be out in a moment. You ladies going to hang out for a while?" he said. Before she could answer the woman in the group appeared from down the hall.

"Never-the-fuck you mind. You just do your fucking job!" she barked. The man just smiled and flipped her the finger.

"You ready?" the woman said to Pam.

"Yeah, let's go," Pam replied, and the two of them headed out the door.

"Nice car, I hope we're going to a nice place. I'm sick of this country living with these pricks," she said as she got into the car.

"I don't know how nice it is. But it's not in the country and there are no pricks around," Pam said while putting the car in gear and gunning it. The wheels started spinning and kicking up a dirt cloud and the car fishtailed as it sped down the road towards the highway. Pam turned onto the highway and sped up taking the car up to 75 mph before letting up and cruising at that speed.

"Are we in a hurry?" the woman asked.

"No, not at all," she replied looking at her passenger. Judging from her reaction to the high rate of speed, her file was accurate about her fear. Pam slowed down. She could see her start to relax.

"What number are you? I mean how should I address you?" Pam said. "I'm Number Six on account I'm the last one to join the team. So you can call me Number Six," she said smiling at Pam.

"Okay, Number Six it is," Pam said then turned up the music. They listened to Beyoncé as they rode in silence. Pam didn't talk on purpose; she wanted this woman to think about what she may want from her. After all, she hadn't told them why they were here and what was expected of them. She needed the time to think. Now that she was alone with Number Six, she could start to figure her out. She needed to know what type of person she was dealing with. She knew contactors could be unreliable to say the least. Pam pulled up to the house and parked. They got out of the car, and Number Six stood in the yard looking at a tree. "I wonder how old this tree is?" she said.

"The people around here told me it's a hundred years old. And that every house built on this site was built around it. Come on, let's get out of the sun," Pam said as she walked up the walkway to the front door with Number Six following.

She unlocked the door, checked that the strand of hair she left in the upper left corner of the door was undisturbed, and then entered. She did her check so discreetly that Number Six missed the whole thing even though she was standing next to her.

"This is nice; it's cozy; I like it. You stay here alone," she said standing in the middle of the living room.

"Let's get to work. We have a lot to do, and time isn't our friend," Pam said as she walked past her to the kitchen. "Can I get you something to drink?" she asked as she opened the refrigerator door.

"Yeah, a beer and a smoke."

"No beer, just wine, and the other is on the table," she said taking out a bottle of wine.

She brought it with two glasses to the table, set them down, and then took her satchel off. Number Six sat at the opposite end of the table and prepared to roll a joint.

"If wine is what we have, then wine it is. This bud smells good. Is this the same stuff you gave us?"

"No, that is Thai Passion Fruit," Pam replied.

"You spies get all of the good stuff. I should've been a spy. Hell! I do a lot of the same shit you have to do without the steady pay check," she said as she rolled the joint. "So what's the deal?" she said as she lit the joint. She took a long deep pull and held it for a moment before letting out the smoke.

Pam opened the bottle of wine, poured two glasses, and took out the file on her along with a pistol from the satchel.

"Put your pistol on the table," Pam told her as she handed her a glass of wine. Number Six reached around to the small of her back and removed her compact 9 mm pistol. She placed it on the table and took a sip of the wine.

"That's not bad. I'm usually not a wine kinda of girl but this is pretty good. Now will you tell me what you want me to do?" Pam opened the file, took out a picture of Andikan, and slid it to her.

"This is your mark."

"Who's he?"

"He is your way into this man's compound." Then she slid a picture of Talaus to her. "So I can capture this man." Number

Six held up a picture of Royce. "And you have a particular skill that I can use to get this done."

Number Six got up and moved closer to Pam leaving her pistol behind but bringing her wine.

"This sounds like fun. Do tell," she said with a big smile as she sat down taking another pull of the joint.

"The first man is Andikan Rekening, a rich playboy but his sexual preference is BDSM and so is yours. I want you to get close to him and become his favorite sex toy. Think you can do that?"

"Yeah, sure that's easy. I'll need some things. But I think I can pull it off pretty quick."

"Good, tell me what you need, and I'll get it for you."

Pam spent the next five hours going over Number Six's assignment. She was very thorough going over it time and time again until she was sure that Number Six knew what to do. Number Six was very helpful; she provided a lot of information about the BDSM world as well as her knowledge about the special group which he belongs to.

"I know at least ten people who would give anything to be invited to one of their parties not just because of the toys and sex either because of the contacts. There are all kinds of important people invited ranging from government officials to rich pricks like him. I knew this was going to be fun. I never guessed it would be this much fun."

It was late when they finished. Pam made dinner. They drank another bottle of wine and smoked a joint. Then Pam showed her to her room.

"I hope you don't sleep walk; it's not a healthy thing to do around here." Number Six flipped her the finger as she went into the room and closed the door. Pam smirked, made a final check of the house, and went to her room. Pam sent her report and then went over her list again before sending it in. When she was done, she went to bed with her pistol tucked under her pillow.

Number Six awoke and came out of her room naked. She walked into the living room where Pam was having a meeting with Steve and Cal.

"Oh, I'm sorry. I didn't know we had company," she said standing there looking at the men who were looking at her.

"How about you go and clean up and put some clothes on. Then sit down to breakfast. You need to meet the guys," Pam said. Number Six turned around and headed back to the room down the hall as Steve and Cal watched every wiggle of her ass.

"Who-the-fuck is that?" Steve asked.

"That was Number Six in all her glory," Pam replied.

"She's definitely not shy. Is she?" Cal retorted.

"No, I'm afraid not. But she is the subject of this morning's meeting," Pam said. Number Six reemerged this time wearing a bath robe and drying her long auburn hair that looked red in the morning light.

"Well, you are certainly full of surprises," Number Six said as she looked at the two men. She walked over to the table and sat down. "Is anyone going to offer a girl a cup of coffee? You did get to look at my goodies. That alone is worth at least a cup of coffee. Don't yeah think?" she continued while smiling.

"You sure do, Miss. With a pussy like that, you deserve a lot more than coffee. I don't know when I last saw a sculpted pussy. Usually they're shaved bald."

"That's enough, Steve. Just get the woman a cup of coffee," Pam said. Steve got up and Number Six winked at him to say thanks. "That is Steve; this is Cal. Fellas, this is Number Six; she's going to be our inside person. So I'm going to need you two to wire a whole new house and set her up with devices that she can place in the targets home. The house you will wire is located here," she said as she folded the laptop flat so that they could see it better.

The house was located a mile from Andikan's place in Durban. It measured approximately three thousand square meters and had three huge bedrooms, three and half baths, a living room, dining room, patio, and an in-ground heated pool. The property was gated and surrounded by a six-foot-high wrought iron privacy fence and guarded by two male Boerboels weighing sixty three kilos each for added security. Immediately, Steve and Cal started to study the house plans as they looked up the exact measurements.

"When can we get in the place?" Cal asked.

"Right after breakfast," she said getting up from the table.

She liked cooking; it relaxed her. As they ate, she listened to her surveillance men tell her how they wanted to wire the place.

"Six, after the stop at the house we are going shopping," Pam said.

"For clothes?"

"Yes, and for some of those toys and equipment you said was needed. Then we are going to lunch to be seen. This is a special restaurant; it's where the people who enjoy your kind of sex hang out. They bring their latest sex kittens to be seen so you should fit right in," Pam said.

"Great! You just put me in my element and watch me shine. I'm going to love this assignment—fancy digs, expensive clothes, and all the toys I can play with. Where were you last Christmas?" Number Six said sarcastically.

Pam just looked at her and smirked; Cal and Steve laughed. After they finished eating, the guys left and the ladies prepared for their outing. Pam and Six, as she had taken to calling her, got into the car and headed for their first stop. Pam put in a rap CD and off they went. They didn't talk much; Pam was in deep thought for most of the ride into the center of Durban. She pulled up in front of a boutique shop and parked.

"This is our first stop; the shop specializes in cocktail dresses and evening wear."

"Who was that rap group you had on?"

"Fuck that group! Get your head in the game. We're going in here for clothes. Don't act like an ass, and none of your smart ass remarks either. Now get-the-fuck out the car," Pam said as she looked her in her eyes.

For the first time, Six looked at her. Pam's eyes said she had killed and she wasn't a pencil pusher. Six took note, got out of the car and waited for Pam to lead the way. They entered the store and were greeted by a rather tall woman who was dressed very smartly just short of corporate attire.

"May I help, you ladies?" she said with a broad smile looking at Pam who was dressed in a designer skirt suit and heels.

"Yes, you can. My friend here needs some clothes. Perhaps you can assist her," Pam said. The woman turned to face Six. As she looked down at Six, she smiled and said, "Of course, madam, I will do my best." Six looked down at herself. She wasn't dressed badly. And if she was, it was Pam's fault. She was wearing Pam's clothes after all. She thought the dress and heels she had on were nice, plain but nice. And she looked good in red. Six rolled her eyes at the woman.

"Lead on, my good woman," she said and winked at Pam as she walked away. Pam took a seat on a couch in the little sitting area used for viewing clothes. Another salesgirl asked her what she would like to drink. She told the salesgirl to bring her a coffee black as she waited. Six turned out to know fashion which wasn't a surprise to Pam but the head saleswoman was surprised. After her consultation, she ended up with seven cocktail dresses and six evening gowns. Pam paid for the purchase and instructed the shop to deliver the garments to the house address tomorrow.

Pam took her to two more boutiques for casual clothes and to three shoe stores where she bought eighteen pairs of shoes. Next, they were off to the lingerie shop where things slowed down, and Six seemed to thrive.

"I want you to start with colors that contrast with your skin really well. This guy likes colors. So let's keep that in mind as you make your selections," Pam said to her. Six nodded and told her not to worry. She went to the back of the store and worked her way forward. When Pam saw her, she had eight outfits in hand.

"Have a seat, and tell me what you think," she said and then headed into the dressing room. A few minutes later, she stepped out wearing a pair of black mules and red lace high cut panties with matching bra. "What about this one?" Pam looked at her; the color was perfect. Red really was her color. Pam noticed her frame: She was five-foot-eight, one hundred fifty-three pounds. Her measurements were thirty-six, twenty-four; thirty-four. Her caramel colored skin, hazel eyes, and auburn hair set the color off perfectly. More importantly, she realized just how beautiful she was. Her high cheek bones, full lips, and button nose gave her an innocent look which Pam knew men liked. And she was, after all, a world class thief. For the first time since she put this plan together, she felt confident. She believed Six could pull it off.

"That's a great color and I love the outfit. Let's see what else you picked out." Smiling, Pam sent her back into the dressing room. Most of the lingerie that she picked out was fine; only a few pieces were rejected. Pam paid for the items and gave the same delivery instructions. Afterwards, they left. As they sat in the car, Six said,

"I'm hungry. When do we eat?"

"I'm hungry also but we have one more stop. I think you'll like it the best. Then it's off to lunch," Pam replied. She started the car and headed to the upscale adult toy shop on the other side of town.

Pam and Six walked into the store. Six took one look around and a huge grin came across her face. A woman approached them. She was six feet, four inches tall, had pale white skin, and was skinny. She was dressed in a black leather miniskirt, red stockings, black and red trimmed corset, and four-inch heels. Her jet black hair was pinned up in a bun. The only jewelry that she wore was a black leather choker around her neck.

"Hi, welcome to Durban's best and finest fetish and adult toy store," she said with pride that Pam noticed. "How can I help you?" she continued. That's when Six spoke up.

"I'm new in town and I need a few things," she said softly and casually.

"Mistress or submissive?" she asked.

"Submissive," Six replied.

"Would you follow me, please? I think we have what you need. And if we don't, we will get it for you," she said as she led the two of them to that part of the store.

Pam stood back while she watched and listened to the interaction between the two women. It turned out the saleswoman was also a "sub" which was no surprise to Pam. She could clearly see that Six was in her element as she picked out leather straps for binding, paddles and clamps, and yards of silk rope. After they had finished with the restraining portion, they moved on to the dildo and vibrator section. At least in this area, Pam could keep up with their conversation and the saleswoman included her in the discussion for the first time. By the time Six was finished shopping, the woman had provided her with three contacts and an invitation to a party two nights from now. This time, they left the store taking the items with them.

"Did you hear her when I told her I was American?" Six said.

"Yes, I did. It's nice to know that a black woman from America will be in demand for her ass to be whipped, novel idea."

"Exactly! If these rich assholes want to beat this ass and get off, I bet this Andikan guy will be right up front." Pam looked over at her.

"I bet you're right, Six. So be on your game, no fucking up." Pam thought, "She's right and that is the break I was hoping for." Then Pam told her to tell everyone she meets in the BDSM world just that. It's something about fucking an American woman of African descent that these people find irresistible, and she was going to exploit that fact.

Pam drove to the house where Six would be staying. She hoped everything would be in place by the time they arrived. She stopped at the gate and put in the code.

"Is this my place? I mean for the time being and all," Six asked.

"Yes, this is it. I'll give you the tour once we're inside and the paperwork is completed," Pam told her as she pulled up to the front door. When they walked into the house, they observed a workman walking around and a short red-headed guy barking orders at them.

"Hi Greg!" Pam said. The man turned around. When he saw, her he smiled.

"I'll have this place finished in a half-hour, Pam" he said. "Who's your friend," he continued as he walked towards them.

"This is Six; she's the one all this is for."

"Well, she's pretty enough; that's for sure," he said as he looked her up and down with hungry eyes. "I have some paperwork for you to sign."

"For me or her?" Pam said.

"For both of you, so pull out your pens and get ready," Greg said and then laughed. He approached the women and looked at Pam. "First you," he said and showed her where to sign and initial. "Now you," he said to Six. "First, I need you to sign and initial these pages where you see an X," he explained. "Sign here for all of the clothes that were purchased today. It says simply that the items purchased belong to the CIA and that you are responsible for them. And that you will replace or pay for all damaged items. This page covers all equipment that is in the house now or anytime during this operation. This page states that you can keep all personal sex items like dildos, vibrators, and the like, basically anything that went inside you. Now do you have any questions?" He paused and waited for her reply.

"Do I get to keep the underwear at least?" she asked him. Greg turned a few pages then looked back at her.

"Yes," he replied. Then he handed her the clipboard and watched her as she signed making sure she didn't miss any page or item. "Well that's it for the paperwork. Here are the keys to the house and the car and here are the codes to the security system. My men and I will be out of here within the hour. With that being said, let me give you the tour."

Greg walked Pam through the house and showed her the playroom that had been equipped with all of the apparatuses that Six had ordered. Then they went to the backyard where he introduced them to the two Boerboel guard dogs that walked the perimeter. Pam took note of the security that had been put in place and so did Six. As they were finishing up, the workmen started to leave and Cal and Steve arrived.

"So what do you think? Meet your specks or what?" Greg said.

"It's perfect, Greg. You got everything I requested. Thanks buddy," Pam said to him with a big smile. She was really happy and surprised that Wilhelm let her have all of this stuff in the first place.

"Yeah Greg, and the modern furniture is beautiful. Thanks for the king-sized bed," Six chimed in. Greg said his goodbyes, did one more sweep of the place, and then got in the van with the rest of the men, and drove off.

"I have to talk to my men for a moment. Why don't you get cleaned up and ready for dinner," Pam told Six. While Six was in her room doing just that, Steve and Cal showed Pam where they placed cameras and microphones—The ones that Six wouldn't know about—. Then they showed her how the tracking device worked on the pearl-colored corvette. They assured her that she could not only track the car but also listen to the conversations taking place in and around the car up to fifty feet away. Pam was happy that this part of her plan had worked out so well. And if Six could get next to Rekening in a short amount of time, that would be even better.

℗

It has been two weeks since she set up this mission and placed Six in the trap house. She couldn't believe the amount of Intel she had gathered. Six had gone sex crazy in her opinion but with all of the right people. And finally, the invite came two nights ago during one of her crazy "beat me fuck me" session with Andikan. When she heard it on the tape, she did all she could not to jump up and down and act like a school girl who was just asked to the prom. Instead, she began her final preparations for the assault on Talaus' compound.

Pam made the two hour drive out to the farm house where the rest of the team was staying. She hoped that they hadn't gotten lazy. After all, it had been three weeks since she pulled Six. She hadn't made any face to face contact with them since that time. When she arrived, she found them sitting on the porch drinking beer and talking. She got out, walked into the house, and found the one they called their leader monitoring the communications center.

"Well, what can I do for you, stranger?" he said with a smile.

"Your men still ready for work? Or has the time off made you lazy?" she said.

"They're ready? Are you ready for us to do what we are getting paid for? I, for one, need to get laid. So the quicker we get it done, the faster I can get fucked."

"Call the men inside. You sound like a man who needs some ass real bad, and I don't want to keep you from it any longer than necessary." He got up, walked passed her, and called the men. Pam walked to the living room and sat down in a chair. She watched as the men filed in and sat down; none of them talked. They just looked at her. Pam reached in her satchel and pulled out a map that showed the location and terrain of Talaus' compound.

"This is the target area and map of the terrain. I also have a 3D image of this map." She handed the leader a flash drive. I need one guy from your assault team to work with my surveillance team. Study this and relay your action plan via this manner." She handed him a slip of paper. "Take all the time you need as long as I have your plan in twenty-four hours. Time is limited and we only have one shot at this," she said seriously.

"Who's the target?" the leader asked.

"That information will be given to you later. If you have any questions or something changes, contact me. I'll do the same." Pam answered some more questions then left with a sinking feeling in her gut. It was all becoming surreal, and the realization of what was about to happen hit her.

She drove back to the safe house and sent a report to Wilhelm. Then she showered and went to work fine-tuning her plan. She was several hours into it, when she received a message from her boss. She read it and then reread it. "He has to be out of his mind," she thought. Now he wanted her to conduct a full raid. What-the-fuck is this shit? Why would he change the objective at the last moment? This and a few other questions raced through her mind as she asked for confirmation. The reply came back to keep civilian casualties to a minimum but to eliminate all designated targets on the revised list.

Pam looked at the list. "This is doable," she thought as a sly smile crossed her face. She got off the bed and headed to the kitchen. She needed a good bottle of wine and a real big sandwich to help her work through the night. Somehow, she knew her team of killers would appreciate the change in plans. But she would wait until she reconfigured her plan of attack to accommodate the new targets before letting the kill team leader know about the change.

Pam watched as her team prepared their equipment and checked and rechecked their weapons and gear. As they worked, they listened to rap music, smoked spliffs, and laughed and joked with each other. Earlier she had seen Six. She went over her part of the plan and left Cal with her. Steve and the one they called Number Two were already on site monitoring the enhanced surveillance that they had setup the night before. Everything was in place. All she could do now was wait. So she rolled up some Congo Dank, sat back, and enjoyed the moment.


*Operation Royce*

Pam sat in the surveillance van that was parked a mile away from Talaus' compound. She monitored the team as they began their infiltration. She watched as the four-man team made their approach to the west side of the house. By using their head cameras, she saw what they saw and heard what the team was saying. Pam liked the plan that their team leader had devised. She hoped it would work. It was a good night for a party: The sky was clear. The temperature was perfect for running around naked in the outdoors.

She watched the guests as they swam and lounged around the pool. Some were having sex; others were watching and getting high. The real action was taking place in the house where she found Six. In the main room, she could see men and women dressed in the latest BDSM wear. The servers were dressed in thongs and nothing else as they walked around serving finger foods and drinks. Pam watched as the team reached their jump off point and lined up to prepare for the assault.

"Number 3 are you ready?" the team leader asked.

"That's a Roger, One," he replied.

"Then head out. We'll cover you," the team leader said. Pam observed as he made his way to the parking area. When he reached it, he crouched behind one of the cars and waited. When a guard came by on his patrol, he stood up quickly and stuck his knife in the man's throat killing and silencing him.

He then proceeded to place small metal magnetic discs full of explosives on the cars and motorcycles. He called for the others to join him and provided cover as they moved up very cautiously.

Pam checked the time; it was 0113 hours. In two minutes, all hell would breakout. She waited. When the appointed time came nothing happened. Pam checked her cameras and asked Steve if he saw anything. Three more minutes passed. Then she heard gunfire. The team had gained access to the main room through the sliding patio doors. When they opened fire, it was directed towards Talaus and Royce.

They happened to be sitting at a low table talking as the team opened fired. Talaus reacted first by hitting the floor hard and then scrambling away. Royce was a half-step behind him. Both men headed for the pool outside. The team split up looking for their targets: Two of them followed Talaus and Royce. The other two looked for the two women who worked for him. Six joined them. They gave her a pistol. She went to work killing three of Talaus guards as she moved through the room. The house team found Taylor first; she was headed in their direction firing a submachine at the three of them. The team cut her down with automatic fire and continued looking for the next female killer. They found Stacy on the lower level and dispatched her but not before she had killed one of them.

Pam switched to the drone cameras. The small drone was hovered over the area where a fierce firefight was going on. She watched as two assault team members took on eight of Talaus men. She caught a glimpse of two men leaving the pool area in a hurry so she followed them. She zoomed in to identify them. It was Royce and Talaus who looked wounded. Royce was helping Talaus who was hit twice, once in the side and shoulder. Royce looked to be hit once in the shoulder. She followed them and watched as the pair made their way down a set of stairs at the end of the pool area and into an underground room and closed a heavy door behind them.

"Pull out!" Pam said into the mic. "Repeat! Pull out!" She watched as the team started to disengage. Her surveillance team remotely blew up the cameras that were placed around the area and packed up. The man known as Number Two got behind his sniper rifle and provided cover fire for the team. Pam shut down the equipment in the van, got into the driver's seat, and left the area. She headed for the rally point and hoped the rest of the team would make it out okay.

*T and R wounded. Presumed to be alive. Whereabouts unknown at this time. Four team members KIA. Two secondary targets eliminated. Cleaning site. Awaiting orders. P1895V1220*

Pam sent the short report as soon as she had debriefed the lone survivor of the raid and released the money that the team leader and the communications man were owed. All she could do now was to wait for further orders. So she took a shower and went to bed.

239

# Ibizan Vacation

## *Chapter Fifteen*

Wilhelm read the message and smiled. It seems that Pam did better than he expected. Now he can turn his full attention to the upcoming mission. He picked up his phone and sent her a reply that read:

Good job. Take a few days then report to the station.

"As for Sanaa, she has proven she can work under pressure although I don't trust her for a minute. Anybody whom Rodney puts in his path is untrustworthy and should be viewed as an infiltrator," he thought.

### *Council Headquarters*

Number 1 sat on a modern style zebra print lounge chair and listened to Talaus. Talaus and Royce had recovered enough to tell him what had happened. He asked them pointed questions that caused him to come to their same conclusions that Libertaire was behind this. Number 1 read the report and saw the photos of the attack on Talaus' compound. The four dead mercenaries had been known to work for governments. In fact, it was their specialty. He was positive that there were more than four and his intelligence report suggested up to eight. These mercenaries killed both of Talaus' assistances and also killed or wounded three quarters of his security forces. This smelled and felt like Libertaire. Deep down, he knew Libertaire was making a move.

"Well, you two gentlemen will be out of commission for quite a while, the doctor tells me. So make yourselves comfortable. Of course, anything you need or want just ask. Also it would be a wise decision to hide out here during your recovery. I have my people working on this. We will find out who pulled off this raid," Number 1 said as he stood up and prepared to leave the room. Royce and Talaus expressed their gratitude and watched him leave before talking.

He went back to his office, poured himself a drink, and looked out the window where he saw the puma. The cat was sitting there looking back at him.

"Why do you come around when there is trouble? I'm starting to have thoughts about you," he said out loud and then drank his drink in one gulp. He sat behind his desk and got to work. If Libertaire was making a move, he had to be ready to strike back. He checked in on his Africa project. Then he contacted Number 2. He needed her network to get to work on this right away.

"What can I do for you, boss?" Number 2 said over the speaker phone.

"You can tell me where Wilhelm is right about now," he replied.

"He's at his farm where he's been for the last month and now getting ready for a mission."

"Are you sure his mission wasn't in South Africa killing a bunch of people?" he said sarcastically. Number 2 stared at the phone. She had missed that one or hadn't read the report yet. But at any rate, she didn't know.

"I'm sure my report says it was guns for hire, but I'm checking further. I will have something soon," she said lying and hoping he hadn't set a trap.

"Good! Let me know soon as you have something," he said. She exhaled. She had dodged that one she thought. "Now I want to talk to you about Linda and the operation your running. Royce reported that none of the agencies have made any major changes in their operations. It seems the removal of those agents has had very little effect," he said.

"I know it appears that way but trust me these agencies are feeling it. They just haven't figured out that it's Linda. But they will especially Wilhelm. He has already met with Scott from MI6 twice. I'm betting those meetings were off the books," she said.

"I want a full report tomorrow on your progress and Number 2 do not fail me," he said in a voice that made her skin crawl.

"I won't fail, sir. You'll have a full report as ordered," she replied. Then the line went dead. She leaned back in her chair and thought about how she could have missed a full assault on

Talaus. "There must be a report. Shit! I can't afford to slip like this again. Keep it together, girl. You're one step closer to running this organization. Don't fuck up now." Then she started to search for that report.

Number 1 was puzzled at this turn of events. It was true that both of these men had enemies ranging from governments to local thugs. But to hit a party with important people in attendance and whose families and friends had connections to strike back made little sense. Talaus hadn't retaliated for the death of his beloved Theresa although he knew he was waiting for the right time. And Royce's dealings with Libertaire was more personal than business. He picked up the phone and called Number 5. He gave him some instructions then hung up. He sat there thinking for a moment. He couldn't shake the thought that this was Libertaire. He had his sick way of sending a message, but what message.

*Ibiza*

Pam stepped off the plane onto the party island of Ibiza. Even though, it was late in the party season, the island still had that buzz. She loved this place not just for the gorgeous men but for the feel of it. There was no other place like it, and she had five days to enjoy it before she had to report to the witch. She checked into her hotel, bought an eighth of bud, and went to her room. She opened the patio doors and looked at the ocean. Her room gave her a perfect view not only of the ocean but also of the people. She rolled a joint, sat on the patio smoking it, let herself go, and enjoyed the scents that the breeze brought by.

That night, she went out dancing and trolled for only the finest male specimen. Around two o'clock in the morning, she found herself in a club with a dark-haired, beautifully tanned, muscled body, gorgeous man meat. When she paid attention to the music and the mix that the DJ was putting down, she grabbed his hand and half dragged him to the dance floor where she stayed for the next two hours. When she had danced enough, drank enough, and smoked enough, she kissed her date and whispered in his ear.

"Take me to my place and fuck me real good."

He did just that and managed to surprise her in that department. As they got started, she found out he was one of those special men not just in the size department either. He could come more than once and his recovery time was fast. After he announced he was spent and told her he just couldn't get it up anymore, she kicked him out and went to sleep.

Early afternoon, Pam awoke. She was sticky from the sweat of her activities the night before. She showered, had something to eat, and then dressed for an outing on the other side of the island. She got into her Mini Cooper Convertible, put in a dance mix tape, and took off. On a little stretch of rocky beach, she found herself sitting on a big rock, smoking a joint, and forgetting about life. As she relaxed, time had escaped her. Then she noticed the big bald burly black man staring at her.

"Oh shit!" she said when she noticed him standing there.

"Oh, sorry to startle you, miss," he said.

"How long have you been standing there?"

"A minute or two, you seem to be lost in thought or just really high. I couldn't tell which." She looked down at her hand and saw the half burned joint and smiled.

"Listen, if you're not doing anything at the moment, I thought you might join us."

"Join you were?"

"My house just up there," he said pointing to the house. Pam turned and looked. It was the house that she saw coming to this beach.

"You always invite strange women to your house?" she said with a smile.

"No, only the really pretty and really stoned ones; they tend to be more fun."

"Okay, why not. You seem like a nice guy. Let's party!" She climbed off the rock and headed for the car.

The burly man walked the short distance to his house as Pam drove and parked her car near the other dozen or so cars already parked. She got out and waited for him.

"Right this way, miss."

"Pam, call me Pam," she interrupted.

"All right, Pam. I'll introduce you around and the rest is up to you." He took her around and showed her the house as he introduced her to the twenty or so guests. She found a curious group of people representing a range in age and professions. She ate great barbecue, drank some really good wine, listened to a guy practice his comedy routine, laughed until she cried, smoked some killer bud, and watched the sun set.

It was late in the evening when she left. Upon leaving, she learned her host's name was Carl. He had recommended a club that she would definitely visit tonight. She went back to her hotel, showered, put on her party clothes, and prepared to repeat the night before. She continued this routine the rest of the week and went to every venue where Carl DJ'd. She loved the way he mixed; she could dance all night to his beats.

Her short vacation was over. On her way back to Spain, she checked her messages. She came across a message from Carl inviting her to a gig in Paris.

"Come, if you can make it," signed Carl Cox. She sat there shocked. He was the legendary Carl Cox, the greatest DJ in Europe, and she didn't know it until now. She smiled and laughed to herself. She would certainly be at that Paris show.

# Initiation

## *Chapter Sixteen*

*The Farm*

Wilhelm awoke early. He dressed and went downstairs to the kitchen for coffee. As he walked in, George and the chef were sitting at the table drinking coffee and watching the news. "How-the-fuck does he know when I'm getting up; it's creepy," he thought before speaking.

"Good morning, you two. Do you guys ever sleep?" he said.

"Yes, we do, boss. We have to be up to make sure you sleep," George said.

"This is true, sir. How else can you have a cup of coffee when you want?" the chef added. Wilhelm looked at the pair and smirked.

"Well, don't get up. I'll fix my own coffee, thank you. I wouldn't want to breakup your morning routine." He poured himself a cup and headed to the library.

Today was a busy day, more so than usual. First Wilhelm had his children's test, afterwards the final rehearsal of the mission, and later dinner with the Elder. The latter was always a big to do when he visited even though this was a business call. His wife and children adored the old man and so did he. But this still was business. He sat down behind his desk, opened a file, and began to read. He worked on his paperwork until he saw the first hints of day light. He turned in his chair and looked out the big floor to ceiling windows at the sunrise. He got up from his chair, went to the kitchen, and discovered that George was gone and the chef and staff were getting breakfast ready. So he left the kitchen and headed for the security quarters. On his way there, he was joined by George.

"Master Fuk and his two students have arrived. They are down at the training platform warming up. The team is suiting up and getting everything ready for the final run through. Is there anything I forgot?"

"No, George, that's fine. Would you double check the arrangements for tonight's guest and tighten security for it?"

Wilhelm kept going back to the security quarters and George peeled off to yell at a couple security guys. Wilhelm walked into the dining hall and looked around until he found the person he was looking for. He maneuvered his way to the table where one man and two women were sitting. The three started to get up when they saw him standing at the table.

"No, don't get up," he said. "Are you Pete?" he said looking at the young man.

"Yes, sir."

"Grab your medic bag and follow me," Wilhelm said, turned around, and started to leave. Pete got up from the table and fumbled for his bag at the same time. He was nervous; he had never been this close to his boss. Oh sure, he had seen him a thousand times always from a distance but not up close. Now he had to talk to him. Fuck! He hoped he doesn't fuck this up. This was a good job even if a guy could get killed doing it.

Pete followed Wilhelm as he walked around the house and down towards the gardens. He had been to that area once and only on patrols. So when he saw the platform, he knew the rumors were true. This was where the family trained. Only a select few of the security people were allowed to be back here. Wilhelm stopped and faced him.

"Listen Pete, your job is to patch up the fighters, nothing else. You don't talk unless it's to conduct your duties. Other than that, enjoy the show. Understand?"

"Yes, sir, I understand."

The pair walked into the platform area.

"Master Fuk, thank you for coming. I trust you and your students have been looked after properly," Wilhelm said in Cantonese.

"Master Libertaire, it is my pleasure to present my students for this skill test. We look forward to the contest. For my students to be tested against yours is indeed a great honor. All of Wu Long Gao holds its breath. It has been a century since this tradition was practiced."

"Master Fuk, this honor is shared by both of us. With your help, I shall bring back the traditions of our clan, and we will once again have a martial society we can be proud of." Then both men saluted each other. Wilhelm led him to a table which had a pot of tea and two Chinese tea cups on saucers. They sat down, and Wilhelm poured their tea.

Wilhelm looked at the two young people warming up on the platform. The young lady looked to be his daughter's age. The young man appeared to be a year or so older. She was practicing Whirling Wind style or Beijing Bagua. He was practicing the Muslim style Hsing Yi Ten animal style. He wondered how his styles would do against theirs. They were well-trained. He could see the skill in their movements. He noticed his children approaching. He watched them as they walked up to the platform and watched the pair. Wilhelm excused himself and went over to them.

"Good morning father! Who are they?" Connie asked.

"Good morning to you. They are your opponents. They are the students of *that* gentleman, Master Fuk from Malaysia. And this morning you have a skill test."

"What kind of skill test is it, Dad?" Junior asked.

"You will be fighting him and you, my dear, have her to contend with. The rules are very simple; they will be explained later. Don't worry; you are more than up to the task. I know you are going to do well, and you will thank me for being so hard on you when it comes to training. So warm up and stretch real well. Then we will begin," Wilhelm said smiling at his children. He knew they were good enough to beat these two. Their skill level

252

was higher. He didn't worry about the style difference. That would come down to who lost their concentration first and made a fatal mistake. It was the pole test that concerned him. Their opponents knew the same form.

He went back to his seat. Master Fuk's students came down from the platform as his children effortlessly jump up onto it and began stretching. While drinking tea, the two masters sat quietly watching them warm up. Now it was time for the test to begin. Wilhelm told his children to get down and get ready. Master Fuk rose. In a very dignified manner, he ascended the platform and addressed the fighters.

"Fighters, may I have your attention," he started. "This morning on this platform, you will be the first fighters to go through the rites of passage of combat as dictated by the rules of Wu Long Gao and carried out by you in personal combat. Listen well; hear these rules. There are no maiming, no crippling, no killing techniques allowed. If any fighter breaks any of these rules, the same thing shall happen to that fighter including death. The women shall fight first. The contestant who is downed three times or gives up or is knocked out loses. This is a full contact contest. We expect each fighter to do and give his and her best. Now will the first two fighters step onto the platform." Connie and the other girl walked up the stairs and faced Master Fuk. "Do you understand the rules?" They nodded. "Then go to separate ends and make ready," he instructed.

Wilhelm looked at their faces; they were downright scared. He smiled. They should be scared. They were about to see who was better at their art, and not knowing was the worst part. If they did well and gave it their all—win or lose, they both would become better fighters. The two contestants went to the opposite ends of the platform.

"Begin!" Master Fuk said. They both came out fast and crossed hands in the center of the platform. Then they walked the circle. On the third turn, they started. Connie initiated the first attack with a palm strike to the head as she simultaneously swept at her legs. Her opponent easily countered and attacked her with a fist to the ribs before spinning out of range.

Connie recovered and came back at her using a swimming dragon technique from her Emei Bagua style. Her rising toe kick caught the young lady under her chin causing her to stumble and nearly fall. But she regained her balance and started to move again. She circled Connie as she regained her composer. Connie had made a bad mistake and Wilhelm knew it. He wanted to call out to her and alert her to the problem but that was strictly against the rules. No interference or coaching was allowed. Wilhelm looked over at Junior who was riveted. His sight never left the stage on which his sister was fighting. His opponent was doing the same. Then he looked at Pete who stood there wide-eyed not believing what he was witnessing.

Connie's opponent attacked again this time with meaning. She was slower, more deliberate, more focused. Her attacks were relentless and backed Connie up to the edge of the platform. When Connie moved to her left to avoid falling off the stage, she was hit with a palm strike to her chest which stopped her movement. Then her opponent dropped down to get underneath her and pulled her legs out from under her. Connie hit the mat with a thud. She slammed the right side of her face on the platform and busted her bottom lip.

"Stop!" Master Fuk yelled. "Both fighters, back to your starting points. The match is one fall!" Both fighters went back to their starting points and made ready. Wilhelm looked at Pete and shook his head, no. Pete stood still.

"Begin!" This time both fighters came out much slower and more cautious. Wilhelm could see anger on Connie's face. Connie circled not changing palms. As she did so, her opponent did the opposite and changed palms several times. Connie attacked but kept her distance. She was just in reach and this made her opponent feel comfortable. The two young women exchange techniques for a full minute before Connie executed *fighting set #3*.

Her opponent attacked her with a right punch to the face. Connie intercepted it with her right hand which turned the girl's arm clockwise to lock it. Next she crossed stepped by crossing her right leg over her left and stepped to the right side of her opponent. Connie struck her with a yang palm alongside her head unbalancing her. Then she quickly walked behind her punching her kidneys before sweeping her legs and returning the face first favor. The girl hit the mat face first and busted her bottom lip by driving a tooth through it. Blood dripped as she got up and walked across the platform.

"Do you need medical attention?" Master Fuk asked her. She shook her head no and made herself ready. "The fight is tied one all. Fighters begin."

The fight had settled into a rhythm. Both women had one fall at this point. They had been fighting for eleven minutes. Both showed signs of fatigue. They came out, circled, and got right to it. They closed the distance and started punching and kicking. Two twirling masses of determination came down to this last bout and they were giving it their all. When her opponent made the mistake that Connie was waiting for, she executed the movement *plant the flower under the leaves*. Connie crossed her opponent's arms, attacked her knee, and threw her.

"Match! Fighters may leave the platform!" Master Fuk announced as he ascended the steps to the top.

"Miss Libertaire has won the match and so it will be recorded in the book. Now it's time for the men. Will the two fighters ascend the steps to their destiny?" Meanwhile, Pete looked after the girls. They looked worse than they actually were. Connie looked over at her father and tried to smile but it hurt too much. So she gave a painful wave.

Junior and his opponent walked up the stairs and took their positions.

"Are the fighters ready?" Master Fuk asked looking at each man as he answered. He turned and left the platform without saying another word. He returned to his seat but before he sat down, he said, "Fighters make ready! Begin!" Then he took his seat. The two men circled each other getting closer as they did so. The young man from Malaysia attacked first by using the Muslim martial art of Springy Legs. The attack caught Junior by surprise. He was expecting a Hsing Yi attack and had prepared mentally for just that. So this was genuinely a surprise. The first kick hit him in his mid-section; the second was to the chest. He managed to evade the third kick to his head and moved out of range.

Junior kept his distance easily blocking and dodging his opponent's next attacks. Wilhelm watched as his son gathered himself. He could see that he was thinking now. So he sat back and watched. He wondered what his son's response would be. Junior suddenly attacked using the *chicken step* but not the corresponding hand technique. Once he made contact, he switched to the techniques of An Shan Pi which forced his opponent to switch to Hsing Yi to cope. They exchanged blows while moving back and forth. As they stamped their feet, they sent energy to their punches. The young warrior from Malaysia broke contact and went back to kicking.

Junior stayed the course and settled into a rhythm. He countered the man's kicking attacks by attacking his upper body. Then he found an opening. With lightning speed, he moved in fast and caught his opponent with a *bong fist* to the solar plexus. This caused his opponent to gasp for air and lose his balance. Then he swept his legs and downed him.

"One fall!" Master Fuk yelled. "Fighters, to their corners! Begin!" he continued. Junior's opponent came out fast and cut the platform off which kept Junior on his side and boxed him in. He setup a close range fight perfectly and caught Junior right where he wanted him. The Malaysian fighter attacked with fists, elbows, and knees moving around Junior at will. In a short time, Junior was down and looked more than a little bewildered at what just happened.

The fight went on this way. Each fighter pulled out his bag of tricks and put on a very good show and showing. Wilhelm and Master Fuk could not have been any prouder of these young fighters than they were now. This was the last round and both fighters had two falls. The next one down loses. Junior still hadn't changed his style. He stuck with Hsing Yi thus far contrary to his opponent who had showcased at least three different styles and quite effectively. Yet here they were. Junior came out quickly and met his opponent in the center of the platform. To his and the observers' surprise, he switched to the *eighteen kicks* of Wu Dong and caught his opponent with a series of kicks. Next he attacked with a fist combination from the family style his father taught him. There was no answer to his attack. Before the fighter from Malaysia could mount a counterattack, he was down.

"Stop!" Master Fuk yelled as he stood up. Junior backed off and his opponent stood up. Both fighters turned and faced each other. Master Fuk walked onto the platform between both fighters and spoke. "Can the two ladies and Master Libertaire please join me on the platform." He waited as they did so. The fighters lined up and he and Wilhelm faced them. "This has been the best display of skill in boxing by any young fighters I have witnessed in quite some time. I am sure Master Libertaire will agree with me on this account. This contest has no winner or loser. It is designed to gauge the skill level of our fighters. This test is absolutely required if any fighter wishes to be admitted into Wu Long Gao. "Do the fighters before me wish to be known now and forever more as warriors in the society of Wu Long Gao?"

All four of them answered, "Yes."

"Then as a senior master and having witnessed by another senior master, I welcome you as our newest young masters of Wu Long Gao." Then he and Wilhelm saluted them and they returned the salute. At that moment, Wilhelm could see the pride in their eyes as it was just sinking in. They had fought their hearts out. They were sore and injured. Tomorrow they would feel even worse. But right now they were on top of the world. They had accomplished something few people can do. Now they were martial artists in the truest sense of the word.

"Pete, patch them up and send them on their way! Afterwards you can take the rest of the day off. I'll inform George. And Pete, good job!" Wilhelm shouted from the platform.

Wilhelm and Master Fuk walked down the platform and headed for the house. The master and the two fighters would stay a few days longer before heading home. He sure liked to know whose students they were because they had a high degree of skill. They would be even more formable in a couple of years. As he and Master Fuk walked to the house, he thought Colleen was going to have a few choice words for him later. But for now, he and Master Fuk would celebrate. Indeed, this was one of the best matches he had witnessed in a long while.

# Special Guest

## *Chapter Seventeen*

### *Final Briefing*

Wilhelm stood before the men and looked at them for a moment. He was wondering if they could pull it off.

"Alright! Listen up! Your target is this building!" he said. He pointed the remote at the clear Plexiglas screen in front of them. A building appeared that was situated in what looked like the middle of the jungle. The team looked intensely at the image but no one spoke. "The building you are looking at sits on the Bei Plateau 1,830 meters high surrounded by jungle. It's located in Angola. One side of the plateau slopes towards the Congo, the other side towards the Zambezi basin." He paused giving the team time to study the picture in front of them and to take notes. "The building is guarded by a special unit whose sole job is to keep what is inside this building out of *your* hands. This unit is commanded by this man, Major Yuen." He put up his picture. The picture of a solider appeared. He looked like a solider. Nothing was sloppy about this officer; he looked competent and dangerous.

"Major Yuen is head of special security. He comes out of the Chinese Special Forces and received additional training from their VIP Protective Services. He also was head of the Chinese Embassy security here in Washington. So this guy is experienced and deadlier than most. He's known for his interesting approach to securing buildings like this one." He looked at the men; they all had zeroed in on the major. They studied his face and searched for the signs of a professional; they weren't disappointed. They saw a professional looking back at them.

Wilhelm changed the slide. Now the screen showed an aerial view of the area. In heat signature mode, the satellite image showed the outside guards.

"Here, you are looking at the outside building guards. As you can see, there are four guards each with a canine. These three images out here are the three roving guards," he said pointing to the three heat signatures on the screen. "Each outside building guard has one side to watch and only one side. The dogs are an extra annoyance. The three rovers take care of the outer perimeter; they patrol out two klicks then back. Now here is an example of Major Yuen's approach to security. The rovers work in a spiral pattern. They leave the building complex always by a different route, go out two klicks, and then patrol the area spiraling back to the building. You can expect the usual defense—trip flairs, ground sensors. But our Intel tells me there are no mines.

"We never know how they will work the spiral nor predict the usual early warning system and booby traps. This is a very interesting perimeter security program. Inside are eight guards in all—two on each floor and two in the security room.

Strategically, your training has made you familiar with your equipment and the type of building you are going to assault. Now that you see what and who you are up against, you can make the necessary adjustments to accomplish this mission. Also once you start your assault, you will have fifteen minutes give or take a minute before the Angolan reactionary force arrives."

Wilhelm hit the button. A picture of a silver rectangle which was 8 inches long, 3 inches high, and 4 inches wide appeared. It had no markings, dials, or switches but had female plug-in connections on the back.

"Here is an image of what we theorize this object looks like since nobody outside of the Chinese has ever seen it. It is very important that you bring this silver box out intact and undamaged. You will find it here on the second floor in this room." Next he showed them the floor plans of the building. "After the Captain takes this box, you are to destroy any and all equipment in the room." Pausing for a moment, he waited for the men to finish teasing Tommy before he spoke again. "Now on to how you will extract once you have the item and have destroyed the equipment." The briefing lasted for two hours before he dismissed them to study the 3D map on the table and to talk among themselves.

Wilhelm left the training house, got into the awaiting jeep, and headed for the house. He had one more briefing to give before dinner, and he wouldn't be late for this meal. His friend and mentor was coming. This would be a rare occasion and he and the family was looking forward to it. The jeep pulled up to the front of the house. Wilhelm got out. Before he went in, he told the guard to get Sanaa and bring her to the library. He headed straight to the library. As he was pouring himself a shot of Bowman's scotch, Colleen walked in.

"Are you busy?" she asked.

"I have a minute," he said as he turned around and saw the look on her face.

"Good, I'll make this short and to the point. I just left my two oldest children who are black and blue with cracked ribs and who knows what else. They tell me that you had them fight in some kind of martial test of your society. I told you not to include them in your secret martial shit or any other shit you belong to. We had an agreement, Wilhelm, and you just fucked up royally with me on this. After dinner, we will continue this conversation. You aren't getting away with this one, mister. I promise you," Colleen said in her usual pleasant voice. She was always in control and never raised her voice.

"Okay," was all he said. Then he took a sip of his whiskey, walked to his desk, and sat down. Just then the guard and Sanaa appeared. "Perfect timing," he said as she walked in and Colleen walked out. "Have a seat," he said to her. As he got up, he nodded to the guard who stepped out of the room and closed the pocket doors. He walked over to the bar and poured himself another drink. "Would you like one?" he asked her.

"Yes, sir, a drink would be nice. I'll have what you are having, sir," she said as she sat on the edge of the couch.

"Relax, Sanaa. This is just a briefing." He noticed her posture as he approached her and handed her the drink. She took a sip.

"Mmmm, that's really good, sir. What is it?"

"Bowman's single malt special reserve, you like it?" he asked and then smiled to put her at ease. She nodded as she took another sip. "You better go over to the bar and bring the bottle back. I think we may have a few of these before this briefing is over." Sanaa walked over to bar and read the labels on the bottles until she found it. She brought it back, set it down on the coffee table, and sat down. This time she sat all the way back on the couch. Wilhelm took note, poured them another round, and then began.

"This man is Adilson Quarta De Carvalho; he is your target. He is the Deputy Minister of the Interior and a double agent who works for the Chinese and the Cubans. You will find all the information about him on this flash drive. Pay particular attention to his taste in women and his sexual habits. You are the honey pot on this op." Sanaa looked at the man's picture on the laptop screen in front of her and thought. "So this is why the dragon lady had beaten all of those sex techniques into my head complete with pictures and video."

"Your assignment is to get the information about the Chinese spy ring being run in his country and neighboring countries mainly Namibia and the Congo. Find out who his contacts are basically and who is running this guy. If you cannot retrieve the information by other means, you are to eliminate him. Are we clear?" he said giving her a hard look. "You'll work with this woman," he continued as he pulled up her picture. "This is Adalgisa Mantorras; she is a member of the FNLA. They are the people who will provide the location and movements of your target. Since she is the daughter of one of the ministers, she can move around freely. And you have just become her best friend," he said with a smile. "Your cover is this: You two met at college in this case Princeton. Both of you young ladies majored in international relations. So bone up on your Princeton trivia. You are also my trade assistant on this mission. We will be imbedded with the U.S. trade delegation. That's our way in. We have three days to get the information and get out. If you miss the ride or this goes south, Adalgisa will take you to an agent that we have there. That person will provide an exit for you. Do you have any questions or concerns?"

"Yes, sir, I have one. Will I be spending most of my time on this or will I be splitting my time with you?"

"You will be spending most of your time with her and your target. Once again we only have seventy-two hours to pull this off. So work quickly. If I need you, I'll let you know. Take this drive and study it. Pack the equipment you'll need and check back with me tomorrow." Then he looked at his watch. He had two hours before dinner. He dismissed Sanaa and headed upstairs.

Wilhelm walked into the master suite, undressed, and stepped into the twenty-head shower. After turning on the water, he stood in the center where the water would hit every part of his body. As he started to relax in the steam, the shower door opened and in stepped Afef.

"You're trapped and defenseless. So you can just guess what I have in store for such a man as you in this situation," she said. Then she snuggled up behind him and reached around cupping his cock and balls in her hands. "Oh, I feel you are liking this. Let me show you what else I have instore for my captive man." She stood in front of him kissing him passionately and sucking his tongue into her mouth with a hunger that beckons to be satisfied. He turned her around. She leaned forward, braced herself against the shower wall, and presented her round brown beautiful ass. As he entered her, she let the hot steamy water run down her back and over her head.

She grunted, moaned, and gasped all at the same time as her lover thrusted ever deeper inside her. When her body had the second earth shattering orgasm and her legs felt weak, Wilhelm pulled out and turned her around backing her up against the tile wall. Afef wrapped her legs around his waist and let out a deep sexy moan as he entered her again. This went on for the next forty minutes before she heard that satisfying moan in her ear which let her know she had emptied him.

"Thanks for the ride, baby. I needed that. Now hurry up. We don't have much time," she said. Then she gave him a kiss and left. He leaned against the wall for a moment and then started his shower.

Wilhelm dried off, shaved, and got dressed. Colleen had laid out his fall dinner jacket, French cuff shirt, and pants. He selected the platinum cufflinks with a sapphire center stone, a Moldavi watch, and his family crest stick pin. After completing the jewelry selection, he selected a pair Stacy Adams and silk socks. Happy with his choices, he laid back in the chaise lounge next to the fireplace in the center of the room and turned on the stereo. The sounds of European club music filled the room. Next, he took out a joint from the crystal box that sat on the Thai redwood pedestal table and lit it. He let himself get lost in the music, and the indica bud helped him forget the problems of the day.

## *Dinner Guest*

When Wilhelm walked towards the living room, he found his family had gathered—all of the children, his three wives, and of course, George. Bubble Bee, his youngest, saw him first and ran over to him with her arms stretched out indicating she wanted to be held. He picked her up and continued into the room.

"My, don't we look nice this evening even George dressed for the occasion," he joked. Bubble Bee laughed and pointed at Junior. Then she whispered in his ear, "Somebody hit Junior in the eye."

"Yes, I see that Sam. But he'll be alright. Okay," he whispered back and then put her down.

He went over and sat down with his wives on the couch. This was a rare time for him; he didn't get the chance often to see them all at once. He sat there and enjoyed it. He listened to his children and answered their questions about tonight's guest. Only Colleen knew the Elder. Afef and Afra hadn't had the pleasure to meet him as of yet. Meanwhile, George took drink orders from behind the bar when Afra told him to turn on some music. Wilhelm knew this was going to be truly an occasion to remember. He took his drink, relaxed, and enjoyed his family.

A guard appeared at the door and talked to George. When he left, George gave his boss the signal and Wilhelm stood up. He straightened his dinner jacket and told Colleen that their guest had arrived. Then he left the room. He walked outside, stood at the top of the stairs, and waited for the car to pull up. He saw the headlights coming up the long driveway first illuminating it and then casting fleeting shadows of darkness. The dark colored continental pulled up in front of the sweeping front steps and stopped. The driver got out. As he went to open the back door, he noticed the guards closing in with weapons at the ready. So he stopped. George waved his hand and the guards stopped. Then the driver opened the back door and helped an elderly black man out of the car.

Wilhelm walked down the steps and stopped one step above the rose that was carved in the step below. He waited. The elderly man walked up the steps and stopped in front of the rose and looked down at it.

"All who enter here is safe and welcome," he said looking at Wilhelm.

"*All who come to rest and leave the world behind are welcome and protected*," he responded. Then the Elder walked around the rose careful not to step on it. When he was face to face with Wilhelm, he embraced him. George and the guards stood and watched. Clearly, this man was special. But what they just witnessed was something different. These two men were part of some secret society. The words they said were powerful, very special, and held great meaning.

Wilhelm and the Elder walked up the steps and into the foyer where he stopped and allowed the attendant to take his hat and coat. Then he walked over to the mahogany table in the foyer and placed his colt 32 ACP pistol on it. Afterwards, George took charge of it. The three men made their way to the living room with Wilhelm and the Elder talking the whole way. When they entered the room, his family stood up and faced them.

"Mr. DuBois, may I introduce you to my family," Wilhelm said. He began the introductions starting with Colleen. DuBois looked at Wilhelm's family; his wives were dressed in fall colors. Colleen was wearing beige. Afef was dressed in a muted copper, and Afra was wearing a soft gold dress with matching heels. His wives wore matching jewelry, platinum necklaces with rose and yellow gold pinecone pendants, matching bracelets, and earrings. They stood with the younger children around them, and Afra held the baby. After the introductions, they sat and had cocktails. Mr. DuBois talked with the wives and children who asked him many questions. He tactfully answered some of them and he managed to avoid the majority. They laughed and drank for the next hour until dinner was announced. Then they moved to the formal dining room.

The family walked the short distance down the hall and into the dining room where the head server greeted them. The children went to their places at the table and stood behind their chairs that matched the long hand carved hardwood Spanish style table that was set for twelve. Afra placed Bubble Bee in her high chair. When Colleen reached her chair and waited to be seated,

Wilhelm sat down. Then the family followed. The attendants and George helped the women, children, and their guest be seated. DuBois looked at the plate. He knew it was fine china and expected no less. The autumn scene painted on it looked familiar.

"What scene is this?" he said to no one in particular.

"It's the northeast pasture; you like it?" Afra said. "I picked out that scene," she continued.

"Yes, I do. It's very peaceful," he said. Then the chef interrupted by announcing what was on the menu for tonight's meal.

"Tonight, we have Mediterranean seafood paella with a nice 1995 Rojas wine. And for the children, we have cheeseburgers and French fries with milk shakes and juice. Dinner is now served," he announced. The servers started to bring out the food and fill the glasses with water, wine, juice, and milk shakes. They ate and engaged in lighthearted conversation for the next two and a half hours.

"That was a fantastic meal, Chef," Wilhelm said to the chef who was standing by. He smiled and nodded in acknowledgment. "Shall we adjourn for after dinner drinks," Wilhelm continued. This time, he was looking around the table. "And you children go to the game room until it's time for bed." They got up from the table, said "nice to meet you" to Mr. DuBois, and left the dining room. One of the daughters stopped and collected Bubble Bee from her high chair. They went down the hall laughing and talking about dinner.

The adults went to the living room but settled in a different section of the great room where the large fireplace was located and the furniture was arranged to facilitate conversation. They sat down, and George went to the bar and made the drinks. When he returned, he handed the women sherry and gave his boss and their guest scotch.

"Shall I hand out the cigars now, sir?" George asked.

"Yes, please do. And don't forget yourself," he replied. George went over to the cedar wood humidor and took out six cigars that were made entirely from cannabis, in this case Neville Haze. He placed the cigars on a small silver tray along with six silver butane lighters. He served everyone starting with the wives. After everyone received a cigar and lighter, George sat down and lit his.

As they slowly inhaled and exhaled, the six of them sat back and enjoyed the smooth smoke that the Neville Haze produced. A peaceful silence lasted for about five minutes before Wilhelm spoke.

"Look at you. All of you are a bunch of potheads." His comment caused them to laugh. The conversation soon flowed as they puffed on their cannabis cigars and drank. Wilhelm got up and put on some music. Suddenly, the room was filled with beautiful sounds. He held out his hand towards Afra. She put down her cigar and got up to dance with her husband. They danced to an instrumental track sometimes doing a two-step, sometimes free dancing.

"I think your husband is fucked up," Afef said to Colleen, and they both laughed.

"I heard that," Wilhelm said. "Now you have to dance with me." Afef got up. But she didn't put down her cigar as she danced her way over to him. The song changed and she started to move her hips in rhythm with the beat. The Luther Vandross song brought out her sexy. She and Wilhelm danced a semi-slow dance. Then the song changed and so did the beat. They danced through that one as well before he called Colleen to the dance floor. They two stepped through three tracks. This went on for the next hour. Wilhelm loved dancing with his wives and did so every chance he got. When he finally sat down, he had danced his high off so he started again by relighting his cigar.

"Mr. DuBois," Afra started to say.

"Please call me Chauncey," he said.

"Okay, Chauncey. How did you come to work for the company?"

"Afra, you shouldn't ask him that!" Colleen interjected.

"It's quite alright, Colleen. She's curious. I haven't told this story for some time now. I suspect even you are a little curious so I'll tell her. I don't mind. And with this cigar, it might come out better than ever." They all laughed. George refilled everyone's glass, and he began.

"I was recruited in 1965 four months after graduating from college. It seems the agency didn't have people to go into Africa—the right color of people that is. So I joined. It seemed like a good idea and I needed a job. So there I was down on the farm learning my craft to be a spy. At the time, there wasn't a lot of black spies in the agency especially field agents. So there I was with about thirty or so other Americans of African descent training to become field agents." He paused to pour himself a double shot of Bowman's special reserve and dip the tip of his cigar in it before placing it back into his mouth.

"Well my first assignment was in the Congo. I worked Africa most my career. I did a few jobs in Europe and South America, but Africa was my beat so to say. And that, young lady, is about it. You have now heard the exciting story of Chauncey M. DuBois. Now I have a question for you."

"You may ask," she replied.

"What is the name of the little one you call Bubble Bee? I heard Wilhelm call her Sam."

"Her name is Samantha. Her father is the only one she responses to when she is called Sam," she said. Then the conversation turned to another subject. The night went on like this.

# Operation Algorithm

*Chapter Eighteen*

*CIA Headquarters*

Wilhelm sat at the long conference table and listened as his contemporaries discussed his final plan. They were having a bit a trouble with the time table he had laid out, and they didn't understand why he had such a short one.

"I, for one, think it can't be accomplished in three days," the CIA deputy director said.

"If he says he can pull it off in that time frame, then he can. So let's get back to the main purpose of this thing. Shall we?" Rodney stated. Then the director of the Africa desk for that area spoke up.

"This man is a double agent working for the Chinese and Cubans. We have reason to believe that he entered into an agreement with the Russians to sell them the device. A message intercept has informed us that his contact is this woman."

Wilhelm and the others looked through the file in front of them until they found the photo. "So this is why Rodney wants Sanaa on this mission," he thought after seeing the woman in the picture.

"Adilson hasn't met his contact before, but she will be identified to him by a mark under her left armpit. We've already removed the contact. I'm told the agent who will replace her is ready to go and up to speed," the director of the Africa desk stated.

"Yes, she is. Wilhelm has personally trained her and she's up to speed," Rodney said before the director could answer. Wilhelm sat there going through the plan in his head and nowhere was this training. So when did she get her training? Better yet, how much does she really know about this operation? He suddenly felt set up by Rodney and this didn't sit well. Wilhelm looked around the table. He was looking for something; his gut told him Rodney wasn't alone in this. He focused on pig face. That's what he called the NSA deputy director. Wilhelm noticed he wasn't looking at the picture. In fact, he hadn't studied any of the photos like the other members at the table.

This was making sense now. He thought about the reasons behind Rodney wanting Sanaa on this mission, arranging the late night visit by the president, and sending him personally on this mission. In fact, Rodney insisted he run this mission, argued that the stakes were too high for him to send a less experienced man, and needed his specific talents "on this one." Now Wilhelm would have to add an element from his backup plan—the one he withheld. If he was right, Sanaa was the spy to spy on him more specifically on his security forces and he had housed her right where Rodney wanted her.

Wilhelm answered their questions and went over the plan one more time with them before he left the meeting. He went straight to his office and then upstairs to where the planning guys hung out. He walked into their office and found it empty. So he went to the back room where he found them. The four of them were sitting around a table playing cards and drinking beer.

"What's up boss?" one of men said as they all looked up.

"I need some info on an agent name Sanaa; here's her photo. Run it and check everything and I mean everything!" he said. Wilhelm went downstairs to his office and called MARs. He gave her some instructions and left the office. He was headed home to a questioning session with Sanaa.

## Peru: Council Headquarters

Number 1 sat behind his desk listening to the report that Number 4 and Number 5 were giving him about the attack on the convoy. Number 2 sat in a chair facing the large glass screen watching Number 4 and drinking a martini.

"I have the information on that warlord, Number 4. I will send it to you and Number 5 as well," she told him.

Number 4 told them that a shipment of food and ammo had been hijacked and all the guards had been killed and beheaded. This particular warlord hadn't bothered them before this incident. Actually, he had made a point to avoid their convoys. Number 4 wondered why now and why this convoy when last week's convoy carried weapons and explosives, a much better target.

"It isn't important why he hit this one or the next one. I can't have anyone thinking they can do this and live. Number 5, I want you to send a unit to deal with this. I want no survivors," Number 1 ordered.

"I expected such an order. I have a unit on standby. I'll let you know as soon as it's done," replied Number 5.

"Good! Now is there anything else, gentlemen?" Number 1 asked. Number 4 and Number 5 said,

"No," and signed off.

"Now for your report," he said to Number 2 turning his attention to her. He looked at her sitting in the chair. Her legs were crossed. Her emerald colored dress highlighted her milky white skin and had slid back to reveal her thigh. She sat there gently swinging her crossed leg back and forth playing with her shoe that clung to her painted toes for dear life.

He got up and walked over to the bar.

"Refill?"

"Yes."

He walked over and took her glass. He filled it from the martini tumbler and made himself one also. Then he took out two joints. When he handed her the drink, he gave her the joint.

"Hash Berry," he said as he lit it for her.

"One of my favorites, you never cease to amaze me."

"It's my job to amaze you and the others. Otherwise, one of you might get to be the boss," he replied looking at her. She uncrossed her legs and pulled down her dress casually yet very ladylike. Then she took a sip of her drink and took a pull of her joint before replying.

"That problem comes with the position but I doubt that is a problem for us," she said then took another sip.

"Now tell me the news," he said matter-of-factly.

"Wilhelm is headed to Angola mid-week. He's going as a member of a trade delegation of all things. It's suspected he is after a double agent. This could be a good opportunity to get rid of him. Don't you think?"

"I think you're right, Number 2. This may be a good time to get rid of Mr. 'pain in the ass' Libertaire. Put a plan together and I'll look it over. If I like it, it's a go."

"I hoped you might say that so I took the liberty." She took the file that was sitting in her lap and handed it to him. "Thanks for the drinks and the joint; I'll leave you to your reading," she said as she left the office. Then, he called for his office girl.

"Yes, sir," she said as she stood just inside the doorway.

"I have a terrible headache; come and relieve it for me."

"Yes, sir," she replied softly. She picked up a pillow on her way to his desk. She walked around it, placed the pillow on the floor in front of him, got on her knees, unzipped his pants, and proceeded to give him head. Meanwhile, he reclined back in his chair and looked out the large picture window at the puma looking back at him.

*Tajikistan*

Shadow One arrived in Tajikistan in the middle of the night. Although there was a slight breeze, the air was stale. This was his last assignment on this job. He was glad. He wanted to go home, see his dogs, and relax. This had been a difficult mission not because the targets were hard to handle but because the mission kept changing. First Wilhelm wanted them interrogated; then he wanted them tagged and released. At least, this target was a firm kill—no doubt about this one and no changes. Kill him and go home. He checked into his hotel room and went to sleep. He got up early. After his morning workout, he went down to the lobby for breakfast. As he ate, he reviewed his target's information.

*Name: Chiao Yun Fen:*
*Description: 5' 10" tall, 220 lbs., black eyes,*
*black hair, white tiger tattoo on his back*
*Position: Assassin for the Chinese government*

As he read on, it was obvious that this guy was well-trained which was no secret. What he needed was an edge and so far he hadn't found it. Well, he could go looking around town for him. Or, he could enjoy himself with a little sightseeing and let his target find him for a change. Besides, flying into this hole was tiring, and he could use a nap. So he went back to his room and did just that.

Shadow One wandered around town. He was doing much of nothing but made sure he was seen in public. This went on for three days with no contact at all. But that changed on the fourth day when a man who fit Chiao's description was sitting at a café table drinking tea and eating a small plum cake. Shadow One kept walking and passed by the man. He went to another café halfway down the street and sat down. He ordered tea and a sweet cake and watched his target who was watching him.

The two killers sat casually at their perspective perches and carried on as if they didn't have a care in the world. Shadow One even picked up a pretty tourist and took her back to his hotel for an afternoon romp. When he came down several hours later to see the young lady off, a message was waiting for him at the front desk.

*"Meet me at the bar for drink, Chiao,"*

it read. So he headed for the bar. Jonathan sat down and ordered a drink. He scanned the room but Chiao wasn't there. Shortly after, the bartender brought him his drink and told him a gentleman at the end of the bar would like a word with him. Jonathan looked down the bar and saw Chiao standing with a drink in hand. Jonathan got up and walked to one of the tables in the center of the room and sat down. Chiao walked over and did the same.

Chiao signaled to the bartender who he came over with an unopened bottle of whiskey. He placed in the center of the table and left.

"I thought we could have a drink or two before we try to kill each other later," Chiao said as he unwrapped the seal and opened the bottle.

"Why not?" Jonathan said. Chiao poured them a stiff drink, sat back, and proposed a toast.

"May the best warrior win." Jonathan raised his glass and both men drank the entire content. Then Jonathan poured the next round of stiff drinks.

"Now that we have done whatever it is we just did when do you want to do this?" Jonathan said sarcastically.

"Not so fast, there is no rush to kill here. We should talk and enjoy the whiskey. Come tomorrow, one of us will be dead."

Jonathan looked at the man sitting across the table. He looked like a business man. Like millions of Chinses businessmen, he was in his early thirties, fit not overly muscled, clean-cut and well-mannered. In fact, he was a Chinese business man, and he thought of himself in that way. This made Jonathan take notice; he had just found his angle. He had met other killers like him, and they all had a quirk of some kind. This one's was etiquette.

"Why not? The whiskey is good and the company is acceptable. Let's drink. We'll fight another time," Jonathan said while pouring another drink.

"I'm glad you agree. Here are the GPS coordinates to a nice spot for our contest. No one will disturb us there and the scenery is fantastic. I believe you know the place. It's the meadow you visited yesterday," Chiao said. Jonathan didn't respond. He just looked at him and drank and waited for him to continue which he did. "Your file indicates you're an expert swordsman, so here's my proposal and the reason for this talk. I am also a swordsman and some consider me an expert as well. It's not often I have the pleasure to cross swords with such a high caliber opponent. If you did not bring a sword, there are several bladesmiths in the area." He paused and drank while looking over his glass at Jonathan and waiting for his response.

"That was unexpected, I must admit. I knew you had something up your sleeve but not this. You're telling me you are willing to fight with swords instead of guns. I really don't know how to answer."

"I fully understand. It sounds a little crazy to me also. I mean you could show up and start shooting and I could do the same. That being said, I am serious about my proposal. And if you accept, there wouldn't be any tricks on my part, I promise you." Jonathan looked into his eyes and spoke.

"I accept your offer. I will fight you at the proposed site. It's a beautiful place to die. I will meet you there just after sunrise tomorrow. Agreed?"

Chiao agreed. They drank on it. Jonathan got up from the table and left. He had to get use to the sword that he bought two days ago. He wondered if Chiao knew this and if this was the reason for his challenge. Anyway, it didn't matter. He had to get a feel for this blade and fast. Otherwise, this could end badly for him.

Shadow One entered the time and date in his log. It was 3:00 a.m. on the morning of October 5, 2015. He was about to leave for his match. He picked up his black cloth backpack and sword and left the hotel. It was easy sneaking out. They had nothing in the way of security, and at that time in the morning, the clerk was asleep anyway. He rode his motorbike until he was two miles away from the meadow. There, he hide it and walked the rest of the way. The night was pitch black. By being dressed in all black, he was virtually invisible as he eased his way into the meadow. He chose a spot and sat down. He closed his eyes, slowed his breathing, and waited.

About an hour before sunrise, he felt a presence. He opened his eyes and listened. Hearing nothing, he put out his feelers. He felt it again; he knew it was Chiao. He was close by but he didn't feel threatening. So he closed his eyes and continued to meditate.

Chiao had approached and enter the meadow much in the same manner as Shadow One; he too was dressed in all black. After he entered the meadow and was making his way to its center, he felt Shadow One. He felt a calm but powerful presence somewhere in the field. As he kept walking, it got stronger. So he stopped and sat down to wait for the dawn and his fate. Both men sat patiently. When the sun began to rise, they stood up. To their surprise, they were only fifty yards apart but neither man showed any expression on his face.

They stood looking at each other. Neither man moved a muscle while standing like statues under the early morning sun. Then Chiao began to walk towards Shadow One slowly. He stopped when he was ten yards away and spoke.

"I am glad we can face each other this way, Shadow One. I know of your reputation as a skilled killer and Libertaire's number one agent and student." He paused and studied Jonathan's face. Finding no reaction, he continued. "My main reason for this request is so that when I kill you, I want full credit. And killing you with a gun just wouldn't be as much fun as using my sword," he said then flashed a truly sadistic smile.

Jonathan stood watching him. He looked at the sword that he held in his right hand. He also scanned for a firearm. He was surprised that his target knew whom he worked for as well as the student part. The Chinese had more information about him than he had expected.

"Are we going to fight or talk the morning away?" Jonathan finally said. "That is the only way you are going to find out if killing me is all that you dreamed of. As for me, you are the last asshole standing in my way of going home and relaxing. So the sooner we start, the sooner I can go home. Let's get started, dick head, and enough of the running of the chops," he said then smiled at him.

Chiao stared at him for a moment and then he took off his backpack and laid it on the ground beside him. As he was doing this, Jonathan was also preparing for the fight taking his backpack off as well. He kept his pistol on and in place at the small of his back and another one in an ankle holster. He was sure Chiao had done the same.

When Chiao was finished, he turned his attention back to Jonathan. This time, his sword was in his left hand. He gave the martial salute and held it as he spoke.

"I am Chiao Yun Fen ranked fighter of the White Tiger Clan. I challenge you to a match to the death." Now Shadow One understood this was more than an assignment, thus the reason for the special request.

"I am Shadow One ranked fighter of Wu Long Gao. I accept your challenge," he said as he held the salute.

Both men unsheathed their swords. As Jonathan suspected, Chiao's sword was in the spring autumn style. Jonathan's sword was single-edged with a bone handle that he wrapped in silk cloth for a better grip. His sword also had an edge on the top quarter where it curved upward. The two men worked their way into range. Chiao attacked. It was fast and powerful causing Shadow One to back up as he defended against it. Then he returned the favor except his attack was precise attacking Chiao's legs and wrists. Chiao caught on. His next attack was more deliberate using techniques that cleared his sword path with the attack.

This went on for five minutes until Shadow One changed styles and went into the Eight Immortals style. He managed to cut Chiao twice, once on the upper left arm, the second on his left side. Neither cut was deep enough to do much damage or stop him. Chiao countered with a cut to his upper chest. Chiao attacked low at his legs and then came up with his cut stopping halfway up his body before he turned his blade horizontal and thrusted. He stabbed Jonathan in the right side just missing a rib. Jonathan's quick movement backwards kept the blade from entering too deep.

"Fuck!!" he said as he circled Chiao. Jonathan watched him closely. Chiao was bleeding pretty good but then again so was he. If they kept this up much longer both of them would be too weak from blood loss alone. So he decided to try something that he didn't think Chiao would fall for. But if he did, it would give him an opportunity to get in one good strike and end this fight. So he attacked to the chest. When Chiao blocked it, he withdrew his sword. Then stepping to his right, he cut at Chiao's midsection. Chiao blocked it. By attaching to Jonathan's blade, he stabbed forward. Shadow One changed directions going back to his left letting Chiao's blade pass by. As Chiao withdrew his blade, Shadow One executed *silver dragon descends from the heavens* striking Chiao on the right side of his head and cutting it in half. The blow killed Chiao instantly. The blade cut through him so fast, he just stood looking at Jonathan with his left eye. The other half of his head lay on the ground. Then his body collapsed in a dead heap in the middle of the meadow. Jonathan stood there for a moment looking at him. He wasn't thinking of anything special; he just looked at him. He walked over to his backpack, sat down, and opened it. Next, he took out his medical kit and began working on himself.

When he had patched himself up, he went over and looked through Chiao's bag. He took out what he thought was important and left the rest. He went over and picked up his sword, cleaned the blood off with a handful of grass, and re-sheathed it. He headed up the road where he had left his motorbike. "Now I can go home," he thought as he walked.

### South Sudan

Number 5 and his twenty five commandos lay in wait in the darkness three hundred meters away from the warlord's camp. It was 5:20 a.m. and the sun would be up in twenty minutes. He called his radio man over and got on the horn. A minute later, he was reassured that all the men were in place and they had not been detected. All he had to do now was to wait. So he laid back, looked at the stars, and watched the sky slowly light up.

Then the radio came to life:

"25! This is strike force, over."

"This is 25. Go ahead, over."

"We are ten minutes out. You should hear our rotors soon, over." Number 5 checked his watch—seven minutes to jump off.

"That's affirmative, strike force. Commence run, over."

"Strike force commencing run, over and out." Number 5 readied his men. Then they heard the helicopters. The gunships began their attack with rockets. They targeted the warlord's camp buildings. As the two gunships flew over the camp, they machine gunned it with three mini Gatling guns killing soldiers as they passed. The two gunships made several attacks before heading off.

As they left, he ordered his seventy-five-man attack force to sweep through the camp. No survivors or prisoners were his orders. They encountered a few soldiers willing to fight and engaged in a brief firefight. Their three-sided assault was successful and the battle was soon over. Number 5's men found the warlord hiding in his personal bunker. They brought the warlord to him. When he arrived, Number 5 personally cut his head off and ordered the others killed. They destroyed the small base, boarded their trucks, and headed home. All of this was done by 9:00 a.m. Number 5 lit a joint of Malawi Gold and settled in for the ride home.

# Mission Begins

*Chapter Nineteen*

## Dulles International Airport

It was 8:00 a.m. on the morning of October 13, 2015. It was cool and clear—a typical autumn day in the capital. Wilhelm sat in the government VIP lounge at Dulles International Airport and read while he and Sanaa waited to board. As usual, there was a delay of some kind so he kept watch on the various diplomats whom he didn't know. He did have a file on the three CIA officers who were imbedded as a matter of policy. But he paid attention to the fifteen men and women that made up the actual trade delegation. Rodney had really shuffled the deck this time. He was pitting the Angolans against the Cubans, and don't forget the Chinese. He had a lot of players to be mindful of, not to mention watch and follow. No one in the delegation seemed to know him, and the agents definitely didn't have a clue.

So he sat there reading and watching until it was time to board the plane. He and Sanaa choose seats in the middle of the plane on opposite sides. The agency had upgraded them. This plane could seat twenty passengers comfortably and the seats folded down into twin beds. He overheard two of the diplomats comment on how this must be more important than they had figured since they had been given such a nice plane. The flight attendant came along and made sure they were buckled in and then the plane started to taxi.

*Council Headquarters*

Number 2 put down the report on Jonathan. It seems his skill had saved him this time. She shouldn't have trusted the Chinese to get rid of him in the first place. Now that he was back home, he was too hard to hit. She would have to wait for another opportunity. So she turned her attention to the Angola operation where she had a team of five in the capital—three to do the hit and two as backup. She wanted to send more but Number 5 rejected it. She placed them in the country for a full week before Wilhelm would arrive. They were all set. This plan should work; it's a simple kill mission. Even more, she didn't expect them to escape or survive thus leaving no trace back to her or the Council.

*Cape Town, South Africa*

Captain America sat outback behind the hanger at an out of the way airstrip operated by the CIA. He was drinking a beer and sharing a joint with Paul. He had received word that the mission was a go and they would take off as scheduled. The other guys were checking equipment or firing their weapons for practice. He and Paul sat there getting higher and higher while discussing the code names that they had been given.

"Where does he come up with these code names? I can hardly pronounce the damn thing," Paul said.

"They're African from the mythology of the continent. I bet if you looked it up, it probably means god of war or some shit," Captain America said; then he took a hit of the joint and passed it.

"Have you heard them? I'm called Faro; Daniel is Gamab; Jhon is Eshu; Lee is Dongo. You are, get this, Tsui, and Sanaa is Haiuri. But there is no wild or fucked up code name for Libertaire," Paul said and then took a long hit of the joint and sip of his beer.

"Stop your bitchin'. What would a code name do for him? Fuck! Man, everybody that's somebody in this game knows who he is. And if you don't and you're in this game and run afoul with him, you're a dead son-of-a-bitch. So I say go with the flow and keep this Zulu/Swaziland sativa coming. This shit is outer this world, man."

*Luanda, Angola*

When the plane landed at Luanda International Airport everyone on board looked fresh and rested. This was due to the showers and grooming stations on the plane and all onboard took advantage of them. When they exited the airport, a line of SUVs from the embassy waited for them. Wilhelm and Sanaa got in their assigned vehicle. As they rode, the pair received the weapons that he had requested, an updated Intel on their target, and the team readiness report. He read the report as they rode. The convoy turned towards the embassy and his car continued to the hotel. When they arrived, the hotel lobby was alive with people moving about in a hurry. He went straight to the desk to check in.

"Ah, Mr. Libertaire! Welcome to Angola. We have you and Ms. Haiuri in rooms 516 and 515 respectively. Please sign here," the head clerk said. He turned the guest book for his signature, and Wilhelm signed in. The clerk handed the keys to the awaiting bell hop, and they followed him to the elevators.

They rode in silence and walked to their rooms. First Sanaa went in room 515 across the hall from Wilhelm. Once the bellman left his room, Wilhelm swept the room for bugs. He knew Sanaa was doing the same. As he went through each room, he found three listing devices. One was planted in the living room in the ceiling light. The second was in the bathroom, and the last bug was in the bar area of the suite. All were concealed very cleverly. He examined them and discovered that two were Chinese and one was Soviet.

Just then, Wilhelm heard a soft knock at the door. He took out his pistol and went to answer it. It was Sanaa. He let her in and placed his finger to his lips. She nodded in understanding.

"My room is bugged. I found two—one in the bathroom, the other in the headboard," she whispered in his ear. Wilhelm held up three fingers and then walked her through the room pointing out the three bugs. He put on some music: *Button Legs by Cindy Bradley* and her trumpet filled the room.

"Go back to your room and destroy the bugs. Once you have done that, meet me downstairs later."

"Do you want me to do anything else?"

"No."

Sanaa returned to her room. She looked at the two guards, one at each end of the hall. They stood there looking back at her as she went in her room.

She removed and destroyed the listening devices as ordered and ran another sweep for peace of mind. Then she sat down and reacquainted herself with the target for the next three hours. Sanaa checked the time; she had a few hours to get ready for the welcome dinner. So she put her outfit together: She laid out a lavender color satin cocktail dress, shoes, and under garments. Then she turned her attention to the hard part—hair and makeup.

After preparing, she stood in front of the full length mirror and went over her outfit and checked to see if she hid her pistol well. The cocktail dress was doing a good job drawing attention to all the right places. The dress was formfitting and fit her like a glove. Her shimmer stockings and heels made her legs look sexy as hell. Her makeup made her look five years younger. The dragon lady's makeup techniques worked. She raised her left arm and looked at the birthmark on her armpit. Ever sense

Wilhelm questioned her about it at the farm, she felt sub-conscious about it. Lastly, she set her security measures at the patio sliding door and prepared to go downstairs to the festivities.

She placed her room card in her clutch bag and left the room. As she waited for the elevator, she wiggled her ass just a little for the guard since he was staring. Judging by the guard's response, her outfit was a hit. The elevator arrived, and she got in. When she turned to face him, she noticed the growing bulge in his pants. She smiled and winked at him as the elevator doors closed.

Sanaa attached herself to a small group of people who were entering the banquet room. She showed the guard her badge and waited as he scanned it and read the readout before allowing her to pass. After entering the room, she conducted a quick scan looking for her target. She didn't see him or Wilhelm, so she took a glass of champagne and started to mingle.

She made the rounds by meeting people, making small talk, and all the time keeping an eye on the door. Her target still hadn't arrived, and she was beginning to think he would skip the event. As she chatted with one of the many diplomatic aides, a young lady walked up to her and introduced herself.

"Hi, I'm Adalgisa. You must be Ms. Haiuri," she said as she extended her hand.

"I'm pleased to meet you, Ms. Mantorras," she replied as she shook her hand to let the young woman know she had made contact.

"Can we talk over there?" Adalgisa said as she pointed to an empty table.

"Yes, that would be great actually." They waited until they were seated before speaking; Sanaa spoke first. "Is Adilson coming to this dinner?"

"He should be here soon; he's entertaining a young lady at the moment."

"How do you know this? Are you sure about your information?" Sanaa questioned; she was starting to push her.

"Quite sure, Ms. Haiuri. We keep constant surveillance on Quarts. So relax," Adalgisa said and then took two champagne glasses from a passing waiter.

"Why did you call him Quarts just now?"

"Oh that's a nickname for him. The women say he comes a quart and he's not hung to bad either," Adalgisa said with a sly smile as she took a sip of her drink. Sanaa looked at the young lady; she couldn't be more than twenty maybe twenty two years old. Yet to look at her, she could past for a sixteen year old without the makeup and the very sexy cocktail dress.

"Great, now I have to deal with a double agent who thinks he is a sexual legend. Now if he just shows up I can make a better assessment of him and definitely take this child's Intel with a grain of salt," she thought as she smiled at Adalgisa from across the table. Adalgisa looked back at Sanaa and thought, "She thinks I'm a child, the big bad CIA agent. I've been a member of the FNLA for years. She's in for a big surprise. Wait until she has to deal with asshole and his cronies then she'll find out how childish I am."

They continued to talk. Sanaa asked about certain people, and Adalgisa told her about the area and what she could expect. Later, dinner was announced, and they headed for their assigned table. After being seated and just before the speeches began, Adilson walked in. Sanaa watched as he strolled in dressed in Armani; he was better looking in person. Now she understood what Adalgisa was saying. Adilson Quarta De Carvalho went straight to his seat. Meanwhile, Sanaa caught Adalgisa's eyes that were looking at Adilson with hate. Wilhelm still hadn't showed up. She knew she was on her own so she settled back and enjoyed the evening.

Wilhelm left the hotel on foot. He strolled casually down the few blocks to a taxi stand where he looked for and found the taxi he wanted. He walked up to the cab; the driver was standing with the other drivers smoking.

"Hey! Take another cab. I'm done for the night," he said to Wilhelm.

"I want this one and you to drive it," he replied. The cabbie threw down his cigarette and started towards him.

"What! Are you so some kind of idiot? I said I was done for tonight!" he said angrily as he approached. When he was standing in front of Wilhelm, Wilhelm spoke.

"I hear you have the best collection of Jimmy Hendrix tracks of any cabbie." The cabbie halted from what he was about to say and do.

"Yes, sir. That's right. I guess I can take one last fare before calling it a night," he said with a big smile on his face this time.

He opened the door for Wilhelm who got in. The cabbie jumped into the front seat, started the car, and drove off.

"I am sorry for that, sir. I thought you were one of those pushy businessmen," he said as he looked in the rearview mirror.

"I look like one of those people. Do I?" Wilhelm retorted.

"Pardon me for saying so but in that gray pinstripe designer suit, yes. Who are you wearing if you don't mind me asking?"

"It's from my tailor. So I guess you can say it's my design."

"Very classy, sir! Very classy! By the way, my name is Conrad. We will be at the meeting place in a few minutes," he continued.

"Thank you, Conrad."

"You're welcome. Mr. Libertaire, it is my pleasure, sir," he answered then he concentrated on driving. Wilhelm sat back and looked out the window as the city lights started to fade and they headed out to the country. He listened to Drake and some other tracks as they rode. The cabbie's stereo system was better than he expected. Then again, *this is* Africa. After a forty minute ride, the driver pulled up in front of a house and stopped.

"They're expecting you, sir. Go right on in. I'll be here to take you back."

Wilhelm got out of the car, walked up the walkway, and stopped at the bottom of three steps that led to the porch. A young woman opened the front screen door and stepped out onto the porch. She stood there for a moment before speaking.

"Are you Libertaire?"

"Yes."

"The Elder said you were a man of few words. Come in. There are some people you should meet," she continued. Then she turned around and went back into the house. Wilhelm walked up the old steps that gave a little as he stepped on them and went into the house.

## Lay of the Land
*Chapter Twenty*

On his way back to the hotel, he listened to Conrad's choice of music, an interesting mix of American and African rap. Then Hendrix blared through the speakers just as they hit the city limits. They were just starting to enjoy the music when unexpectedly Conrad turned down the music and said to him.

"We are being followed. Do you wish for me to get rid of them?"

"Are you sure?"

"Yes, it is the same car that followed us to the city limits before stopping. Then they picked us up again when we returned. They are the same two men."

"Then we should do something about that, Conrad. Any suggestions?"

"Yes, sir. I do. Just sit back and watch me work." He picked up his cell phone and made a call. He spoke in Bantu to someone briefly and then hung up. "It's all taken care of, Mr. Libertaire." Then he made a left, drove into a neighborhood, and made a couple of easy turns so as not to lose the car following them. They came upon what seemed to be a street party with young people dancing and drinking to the music. He slowed down as they made his way through the crowd. When they emerged on the other side, he stopped.

"You may like to see this," he said to Libertaire. So they got out of the cab, stood there, and watched. As the car which was trailing them entered the crowd and slowed down, two people—a woman and a man—approached it from both sides. They didn't raise their AK's until they were close; then they open fired. The two men in the car were killed instantly. The shooter on the driver's side opened the door and pulled the dead man out. He took his place, stopped the car, popped the trunk, and then got out. He looked up the street at them and waved. Then he and the woman began to put the bodies in the trunk. Wilhelm got back into the taxi, and Conrad drove off.

"My orders are to keep you safe while you are with me and to assist you if I can. So how do you like the protective service?"

"Very efficient, Conrad," was all Wilhelm said. He arrived at the hotel with no more excitement and walked through the quiet lobby. He noticed two women sitting and talking so he took a quick note and kept moving. When he got to his room, he called Sanaa and told her to come over. Then he made a sweep for listening devices. When Sanaa arrived, he put on a podcast of Mongo Land and the music filled the room.

"How was the party? I hope the food was good at least," Wilhelm said as he started to roll a joint.

"It wasn't bad, and the food was really good," she replied.

"Did you make any new friends?"

"One, a young lady. I believe she is the daughter of one of the ministers." Wilhelm paused from lighting the joint to listen to the opening of a song. Then he lit the joint and walked behind the bar.

He handed the joint to Sanaa as he poured two scotches. She took a toke and coughed.

"What is this?" she asked him as she took another pull this time not so deeply.

"It's some local bud not bad, huh?" he said while handing her the drink. "Now tell me all about your new friend." Sanaa gave him her report as they smoked the joint and drank scotch. After she returned to her room, she planned her strategies on how to handle Quarta and Adalgisa.

Sanaa and Adalgisa had breakfast as planned. Now Adalgisa was showing her around town and especially pointed out the places that Adilson liked. As they rode from place to place in her tricked out jeep wrangler, Sanaa noticed that having an American car gave a special status. Not everyone in her circle had one; they mostly drove BMWs, Mercedes, and the like. She did find out that Adilson drove a gold corvette and would be at his favorite hunting grounds later in the day.

One of the women that Libertaire saw sitting in the lobby last night was waiting for Sanaa to leave the hotel. She and her partner had been told about the incident last night and the demise of their colleagues. Tonight, they would be successful in killing

Libertaire as soon as his assistant left for her date. At the bar, two men sat drinking and talking to two women; the couples were laughing and ordering drinks. The two men were seated where they could see the lobby and the first set of elevators. They were part of the three-man team that Number 1 sent to kill Wilhelm and anyone else who may try to prevent that from happening. That put Sanaa square in their sights as well. Although they didn't see her as a threat, she was to be removed only if necessary.

Wilhelm and Sanaa stepped out of the elevator and started across the lobby when Wilhelm steered her towards the bar.

"Adalgisa hasn't arrived yet. Let's have a drink. She'll be late like all women are," he said jokingly as they headed for the bar. The two men took notice. They had watched him since he stepped off the elevator. The woman in the lobby also perked up, sent her partner the signal, and kept a watchful eye on him until she arrived. Wilhelm chose a table that gave them not only a good vantage point to view the room but also allowed for a quick exit if need be. They sat down. The waiter came over and Wilhelm ordered champagne and scotch.

As they sat drinking and talking, Sanaa saw Adalgisa walk by. So she yelled to her. Adalgisa stopped and looked. She recognized her and walked over. Adalgisa was dressed to party with a sexy short dress that had a very low back in soft yellow which really highlighted her complexion. She strutted in open-toed black ankle strap heels and wore minimal makeup that let her natural beauty shine while showing off her high cheek bones. She wore a choker with an ivory craving of a cat in its center. Her hair hung straight and black and shiny down her back. Dangling sparkling earrings and a clutch bag completed her look. Wilhelm watched her walk towards them. "She is beautiful," he thought as he watched the sway of her hips and the gentle bounce of her breasts.

As Adalgisa approached, she noticed the older man sitting with Haiuri. "He is handsome," she thought. He had an important look about him. By the looks of his suit and shoes, he was a wealthy man. She didn't date older men as a rule, but she was known to break that rule from time to time. For this man, she would break it in a heartbeat. She sashayed up to the table and spoke.

"Are you ready to party, Haiuri?" she said addressing her directly but looking at Wilhelm. "I see you found some company. Sorry I'm late. Who's your friend?" she continued not giving Sanaa a chance to say anything. Wilhelm sat there taking in this lovely picture of a woman with a sly smile on his face. Sanaa looked at Adalgisa. "She's in heat; the girl is hot to trot. How does he do this? He hasn't even spoken to her yet," she thought.

"You look nice. But won't your jeep mess up our hair and makeup?" she said snapping Adalgisa out of her stare.

"No, don't worry. I brought the mustang. You ready to go? I mean I don't want to rush you," she said as she wiggled her hips a little.

"Yes, I'm ready. And by the way, this is my boss, Mr. Libertaire." She watched the expression change so slightly on Adalgisa face. She didn't stop smiling but she did stop wiggling. The name rang instantly. Her commander had told her who he was and how important he was in the CIA, not to mention he was a very dangerous man and she should be careful around him. His reputation was well earned.

"Nice to meet you, Mr. Libertaire," she said regaining her composure and extending her hand. Wilhelm stood up to shake it, and as he did he spoke.

"It is nice to meet you, Ms. Adalgisa. I see you are dressed for dancing. Those young men are in for a treat when you show up tonight," he said in his baritone voice as he looked into her large brown eyes.

"I'm ready if you are," Sanaa said as she stood up. She couldn't take it anymore. If this continued, the girl will be coming in her panties. Sanaa said goodnight and pulled Adalgisa along as she headed out of the bar. Once in the car and all the way to the club, Adalgisa talked about Wilhelm.

"You know he is older than you," Sanaa said as they sat in the parking lot of the club smoking a joint.

"So what's that have to do with anything? You American women are too uptight."

"He has three wives."

"Are they as old as him?"

"No, he has two that are younger than him and one about your age," Sanaa said.

"That's encouraging. That means he is still in the game, girl. And I'm telling you if I get the chance, I'm going to fuck his brains out," said Adalgisa, and they both laughed.

"Let's get out of this car and get this party started. Are you sure Adilson will be here tonight?"

"Yes, he'll be here. Why? You're curious to find out if he really shoots a quart? After your first meeting, I'd say that will be the easy part. Getting him to stop is the trick," Adalgisa said pulling on the joint.

"I'm not worried about that, and you sound like you have given it a ride."

"Girl, with a rumor like that what red blooded woman wouldn't want to find out. Come on! If you play your cards right tonight, you can find out too."

They got out of the car and headed into the club. The music was loud, and the club was crowded with the beautiful people. This wasn't a place for the weak of pocket. This was Angola's version of big ballin.

Wilhelm sat at the table and ordered another scotch. He glanced at the two couples seated at the bar. The men seemed to be totally into the women and vice versa so he only kept a casual eye on them. Unexpectedly, a tall lean woman, dressed in a black business suit, walked into the bar, and sat down at a table. He thought she was with one of the delegates here for trade negotiations. But something about her didn't fit that profile. He shrugged it off, stayed a little longer, and then got up to leave. As he was signing for his tab, the two men paid their bill and the four of them headed to the elevator.

Wilhelm waited for the elevator with them. When it arrived the five of them got in. Wilhelm maneuvered himself to the rear right corner and waited for one of them to press the elevator button.

"Number 5, baby," one of the women said and pushed the button. The doors closed and as the elevator went up, the couples continued their playfulness. Wilhelm unbuttoned his suit coat and waited. When the elevator stopped and the doors opened, the two couples got off. As they did so, Wilhelm took two steps to his left and changed positions.

He put his hand on his pistol that he was carrying in a cross draw setup and watched them as they got off. Suddenly, the men turned, pulled their guns, and opened fire where they last saw him. They fired their first volley into the right corner. Having already drawn his weapon, Wilhelm returned fire. He hit one man killing him instantly. As he stepped into the center of the elevator, he hit the door's open button and fired at the second man missing him. The killer fired back and then took off running down the hall firing as he did so. Wilhelm gave chase following the man into the stairwell. He fired at his assailant. As he ran down the stairs by taking three and four steps at a time, he dodged the assailant's bullets. They shot at each other for five flights of stairs; the chase ended in the underground garage. When Wilhelm arrived, he was just in time to see the man jump into an awaiting dark sedan with no license plates and speed off.

Wilhelm holstered his gun, buttoned his jacket, and walked out of the garage and back into the hotel. He was going to his room. When he got off the elevator, the guard told him that it would be best if he stayed in his room because there had been a shooting on the fifth floor. Wilhelm told him he would and went to his room. Once there, he made a phone call. He called the FNLA commander, informed him of the incident, and told him what he needed by noon the next day. Then he poured himself a drink, lit a joint, and sat down in a chair to begin his decompression process.

Sanaa had been at the club for a couple hours now. She was beginning to think Adilson wasn't partying tonight at least not here anyway. But that didn't mean she wasn't enjoying herself. On the contrary, she was having the time of her life. An attractive black woman from America was a rare occasion in

Angola and every man in the place wanted a piece of her. She and Adalgisa enjoyed the attention. It seems her status had gone up having Sanaa around. They drank and danced and played with the men who came by to try their luck. Then Adilson arrived but Sanaa missed his entrance. She didn't know he was there until Adalgisa told her.

She picked a guy and took him to the dance floor where she put on a special show for him. Afterwards she went back to her booth and waited. It took him all of five minutes to make his way over to her.

"I saw your dance; you are a very good dancer, Haiuri," he said.

"Sit down, Adilson. Join me," Sanaa said patting the seat next to her. He sat down, and she poured him a glass of champagne.

"Are you having fun? Is Adalgisa showing you a good time?" he asked leaning close to her ear.

"Yes and yes. Let's dance," she said in his ear and then licked his ear lobe. Sanaa slid out of the booth and headed to the dance floor with Adilson right behind her. Sanaa sexually teased him until the club closed. Afterwards she talked to him by the car as she waited for Adalgisa. Finally she showed up. Sanaa kissed Adilson, said goodnight, and got into the car.

"Where have you been?"

"Getting some dick, how about you? Get any tonight?" Adalgisa said giggling.

"No."

"Too bad, I just had some good dick after dancing, drinking, and thinking about your boss all night. I had to get that itch scratched and scratched good. You should have given Adilson some."

"Not tonight, tomorrow night, remember we have a job to do," Sanaa said seriously. Adalgisa started the car and took her back to the hotel.

## House of the Flying Snakes

*Clever, ruthless, charm*
*Fight elusive spy master*
*Teach, protect, pass on*
By Claire L. Hand

# Three Attacks

## Chapter Twenty-One

Sanaa waited until their morning meeting to ask about last night's incident. Wilhelm half explained and left out a lot of information. Sanaa told him about her plan of how she would extract the information from Adilson. Wilhelm told her that he wanted the Chinese to kill him not her. She will plant this device in his home, then call this number, and leave this message exactly as written. He gave her the items and one last piece of advice.

"Sanaa, today is going to be very busy and dangerous. Trust your gut, rely on your training. We are being hunted, and I'm not sure by whom yet. So until I get more information, rely on Adalgisa. She's not the amateur you think she is."

### South Africa: CIA Airfield

Lee brought the communication that he just received to Paul. Paul read it, got up, and headed out to the lounge.

"Listen up! We are a go. The hybrids are in place, briefing in 10 minutes," he said and then went back in the space that they used as an office. The men gathered and waited for him to begin. "We take off at 1700 hours; we jump at 2300 hours. We should be at the target by 0100 hours no later. The guard numbers haven't changed but stand by. You know how this shit can change on a dime. Now pay attention! Let's go over the plan one more time. Smoke'em if you got'em," he said. Then he began. After Paul had finished the briefing, he told the men to lay out their equipment for inspection. He went through each man's kit slowly and methodically not missing a single thing not even a loose thread. "Okay! The kits are in order, now for the weapons check." The men laid out their weapons. Each man was issued a PPX 9 mm (Navy SD) with a threaded barrel tip for a suppressor, the M416 CQB carbine in 7.62x39, and the DP 12 gauge pump shotgun that held 16 rounds. Satisfied all was in order, he told the men to hang loose until jump off. Then he went back to his office.

### Council Headquarters

Number 1 sat and listened to the report his spy was giving him. He didn't like the news so far. Two of his men had already been killed in an ambush and one of Number 2's men had also been dispatched by Libertaire personally. He was told that the remaining hitters will try again tonight. He signed off and went to find Number 2. They couldn't blow this opportunity to kill Libertaire. He wanted to know if her team of assassins could pull this off as well as the backup team he sent. They had tonight and tonight only to kill him. Tomorrow, he'd be gone and out of reach. On second thought, he would let it ride and see if she can pull this off. If not, it wouldn't change the equation or the final outcome of his plan for Libertaire. Then he turned around and went back to his office.

*Lunda, Angola*

Conrad was waiting outside in his cab. When Wilhelm came out, he called to him,

"Cab, sir?" Wilhelm headed for the cab and got in. Conrad drove off.

"Where are we going this morning, Conrad?"

"I have the information you requested. There is no identification on the man you killed as yet. He only had a tattoo on the back of his left shoulder."

"Let me guess, a globe with the number five in the center."

"Yes, how did you know? Here's a picture." Conrad handed him the picture. "Who are this council? I have never heard of them," he continued.

"Oh, just someone who is starting to piss me off, is all. Say, you know a good place for breakfast?"

"Sure do! If you like good food, good company, and safety," Conrad said.

"Yes, to all of those things." Conrad took him to a house in a quiet suburb, pulled into the backyard, and got out.

"Come on! Man, this place has the best food in the city and the woman who cooks is very pretty also," he said as he led him up the back stairs and into the house. Wilhelm was introduced to

Alice, a full figured woman with plenty of curves and a pretty face.

"So you hungry? You don't look like you missed any meals," she said as she looked him up and down. "Sit on down, take off your coat, stay awhile, and tell Alice what you want to eat." Wilhelm did just that and sat at the table with Conrad. "Have you decided yet, Mr. Libertaire?"

"Yes, whatever is the house special, Alice. And please, call me Wilhelm."

ℙ

Sanaa was spending the morning in her room. She ordered room service. While she waited for breakfast, she was revising part of her plan. With the changes the boss gave her last night, she would need Adalgisa to play a much bigger role. She only had a few hours to work up a plan. Adilson would be picking her up at 1:00 p.m. in the lobby for the first part of their date. Before he arrived, she would need to tell Adalgisa. She called her, but the phone went straight to voicemail. So she left a message. Sanaa ate, took a shower, and got dressed. It was close to the time for Adilson to arrive and Adalgisa still hadn't called.

ℙ

Wilhelm sat there listening to Alice tell him how she became a home restaurateur. The story was funny and full of crazy antics; he loved it.

"That was great, Alice. I loved the story and the food wasn't bad either," he said making her laugh. He loved her laugh; it was hardy and shook her all over when she did so. "What I owe you?"

"Seven dollars ought to cover it." Wilhelm stood up, put on his suit coat, reached in his pocket, and pulled out some money. He counted out fifty dollars and handed it to her.

"Now that's *too* much, Wilhelm."

"Consider the rest a tip. I could not have had a better breakfast in better company." Then he kissed her on the check, and he and Conrad walked out the door.

"Where to?" Conrad asked.

"How about you show me around since you have to hang around anyway?" Wilhelm said as he got in the cab.

Conrad did just that. He took Wilhelm to one end of the city and back again. They went everywhere from markets to cockfights to bars. Wilhelm even bought a few gifts for his wives. All along, he was looking for a tail. He knew the Chinese and Russians would be keeping an eye on him. The listening devices confirmed that. But it was the hit team that was foremost on his mind. They would try again, and it had to be tonight. At every place they went, Conrad pointed out the security. His people were in the most likely places. Shop workers, street workers, people riding on motorbikes, and men and women blended perfectly into their environment. Wilhelm was impressed. He would take this lesson with him and put it to good use.

It was 4:00 p.m. when he told Conrad to drop him off at the hotel and to pick him up at 11:00 p.m. sharp. His plan was to draw his assailants out and on the ground of his choosing. They had their shot; now it was his turn. When he got back, he found out Sanaa hadn't returned yet. So he went to his room and cleaned up.

Adalgisa was waiting in the bar when she saw Wilhelm walk through the lobby. She didn't say anything; she let him pass by. She had missed Haiuri's call, and she didn't want him of all people to scold her. So she stayed hidden at the bar and waited. Sanaa came in an hour later but Adilson was with her. He didn't leave until she was on the elevator.

"Fuck! Fuck! Fuck! How am I supposed to get to her now?" Adalgisa thought. She tried the number. The phone did what it had been doing all afternoon—two rings and then it went dead. She hung up and sat there. She was up shit's creek, and it didn't matter if she had a paddle. Just then Sanaa appeared. Adalgisa was startled.

"Where did you come from?"

"That's not the question. Why didn't you answer your phone!" Sanaa said sternly.

"I was…" Adalgisa started to say but Sanaa stopped her.

"We can't talk here. Come with me."

Sanaa took her up to her room. The guard who had patted Adalgisa down really enjoyed himself since she was wearing a mini skirt.

"That guard grabbed my pussy like he wanted to take it home," she said after they entered the room.

"Good, he got a cheap thrill. If you were doing what was expected of you, that wouldn't have happened," Sanaa snapped.

"Sorry, Haiuri. It won't happen again," Adalgisa said sincerely.

"Alright let's move on. This is what I need you to do tonight. Somethings have changed." As Sanaa put together her outfit for tonight's date and mission, she told Adalgisa the plan. After two joints and several rehearsals Sanaa thought she was ready and sent her home to prepare.

## South Africa: CIA Airstrip

At 1640 hours, the men were loading onto the C17 that sat with its engines idling. Paul was watching and counting men. Even though only five of them were on this mission, he still counted—old habits.

"Where-the-fuck is the Blasian?" he said above the engine noise to Daniel.

"Here he comes!" he said pointing to him waddle running towards the plane.

"Hurry your ass up, Jhon! Now is not the time to let your Korean side out, you slow motherfucker!" he yelled to him.

"I had to get a new copter," he replied pointing to the miniature. Paul and Jhon walked up the ramp together and sat down. The ramp started to close, and the crew chief began his check as the plane started to taxi.

Paul looked at his watch; it was 1700 hours and right on schedule. The plane lifted off and climbed. When they reached altitude, the crew chief told them it was okay to relax. Then they began to spread out. It would be a few hours before they had to jump. So they just relaxed and were shooting the shit with each other and the crew chief.

*Luanda, Angola*

Conrad was waiting for Wilhelm who walked straight to the taxi and got in. Conrad drove off without Wilhelm telling him to. Wilhelm had told him the route to take earlier after the tour of the city. Now he was putting his plan into action. The first stop would be a club which they were on their way to now. As they pulled up and parked, Conrad noticed a rent-a-car parked on the side of the building. It had three people in it but they couldn't make out if any were women.

"You want me to send someone over to check it out?" Conrad asked.

"No, if they are the hitters, it will fuck up the plan. If they are not, we might tip our hand. Just chill; let it play out." They got out and went into the club.

℗

Sanaa sat across from Adilson and his friend sat across from Adalgisa who sat to Sanaa's right. The double date was going as planned. She kept her cover as a proper government employee. The restaurant was really nice. The atmosphere said relax and enjoy, and the food was delicious. Adilson put some thought into this, and he expected a hot wet pay off at night's end. He had no doubt about that. So far, Adalgisa was playing her part perfectly. Sanaa smiled and acted as if she was paying attention to what Adilson was saying. She couldn't let him bed her before 2:00 a.m., and she had to have this rapped up by 5:00 a.m. She had to be on time; she couldn't make any mistakes.

*Bei Plateau Assault*

Paul walked up to each man and checked him. Then he stood in front and spoke through his helmet headset.

"Everyone knows his job. Let's get it done and get paid," he said and then he turned around and faced the open ramp. The crew chief watched the red light. When it turned green, he yelled, "Go! Go! Go!" He waved his arm in a circle for emphases. The mercenaries took their time and walked off the plane.

"Faro here! Sound off!"

"Gamab here!"

"Eshu here!"

"Dongo Longo here!"

"Tsui here!"

They floated in formation until it was time to open their chutes. Then they broke apart and landed.

The men gathered and buried their parachutes and headed up the plateau. The field that they landed in put them 3800 meters away from the target. Paul led them at a steady pace for the next hour before calling a halt to look over the map. He had Lee contact the C.A.A. and notify them of their position. He stayed just long enough to accomplish this. Then he pushed on. The team zigzagged its way up the plateau avoiding the small villages along the way. When they arrived at the target, he had ten minutes to catch his breath and set up. Paul didn't waste any time. He started giving orders by using hand signals only. His team went into action. Jhon unpacked his mini-copter and set it up. Daniel fell back to set up booby-traps that would cover their escape. Then he worked his way to the southwest corner of the building. The Captain took up a position to cover them from the roving guards. When they were set, Paul told Jhon to send the copter. It was 0100 hours.

## Three Attacks

Eshu launched the spy copter. He watched his handheld monitor as the copter cleared the roof. Then he started his inspection.

"Roof clear!" Eshu said into his mic.

"Roger," Faro replied. "Faro to team, take up second positions, over," he whispered into the mic.

The men started to move. Tsui came in to cover his corner of the building. Dongo and Gamab did the same. Eshu directed the spy copter finding each guard and alerting the corresponding team member. After the men reported, they were in position. Faro began the count down. When he reached zero, they fired. Each guard went down simultaneously on the first shot. The second round was for the dogs.

"Move out!" Faro said and the men made a beeline to the front entrance, all except Gamab who headed for the generator and electrical boxes. They waited until he returned.

"All set?" Faro asked.

"Yes. After I set this to the door, we'll be in business," Gamab said as he set the explosive. He gave the ready signal and they pulled back. "Three, two, one," he said and then pushed the button.

"Boom!" was heard. As the lights in the building went out, the heavy front double doors blew in. The team rushed in. Faro and Tsui turned left and headed for the stairs. Gamab and Dongo turned right and headed for the communications room. Eshu stayed put. Roving patrols were still in the area, and they would be heading back at a run after hearing the explosion.

On the second floor, Faro was engaged in a firefight with two guards but his shotgun kept them at bay. Tsui kept going. He had to get to the computer room on the third floor, and the other staircase was at the other end of the hall. He had less than ten meters to go when two more guards rounded the corner and opened fire with their submachine guns. He ducked into an office door space and returned fire. The shotgun's first six rounds were mixed. The left barrel was firing double-aught (00) buckshot. The right barrel fired slugs. The mixture was doing a great amount of damage to the walls and large glass windows by blowing some out completely and causing the Chinese guards to retreat back around the corner.

Tsui pulled a grenade and rolled it down the hall. It bounced off the wall at the end of the hall, exploded, and killed the two guards. He ran down the hall towards the stairs. When he turned the corner, he slipped and fell in the blood and guts of the dead soldiers. Tsui jumped up and continued taking the stairs quickly but carefully. Four guards were still in the building.

"Tsui, wait! I'm right behind you," Faro said in his earpiece. So he stopped at the top of the stairs and waited for him.

Gamab and Dongo had reached the communications room. Gamab started to set charges on the door hinges. They took cover. He blew the doors open. Then Dongo charged in and shot the radio operator as he tried to get up off the floor.

"Hurry up! I hear Eshu. He sounds awful busy," Dongo said.

"Go and help him. I got this," Gamab told him. Dongo took off. When he arrived, he found Eshu in a full-fledged fight. From what he could tell, Eshu was fighting at least six soldiers. So he joined in, firing his M416 on three round bursts towards the muzzle flashes that he saw coming from the woods.

"I hope the others are having as much fun as us," Eshu said to Dongo.

"I think they are." Then they heard the explosion. "Gamab's fun is just starting. He should be along any minute," Dongo said.

"And not a moment too soon, I'm running low on ammo," Eshu said.

Faro and Tsui reached the main computer room and ran inside. A hail of submachinegun bullets just missed them.

"Find that thing fast. I'll take care of the help," Faro told him. Tsui nodded and started looking for the algorithm machine. He went past the computers and up and down four aisles before he spotted it.

"Got it!" he yelled. Tsui disconnected it and put it in his pack in a waterproof bag. "Let's get-the-fuck out of here. I've got the damn thing. Let's go!" Tsui said as he knelt at the door and fired his rifle on full auto. They both threw grenades down the hall and ran for the stairs not stopping until they reached the others.

When they arrived, the other three were positioned at the front door and window and were firing on the few guards left in the fight.

"Change to nightlight," Faro said. The guys took out the mags that were in their rifles and replaced them with two thirty-round magazines attached together. Just as he was about to give the assault order, Eshu heard the C.A.A. in his earpiece and alerted Faro.

"This is home base calling, over!"

"Go ahead, home base. Eshu here, over."

"You have FANA and river patrol headed your way, ETA twenty mikes, over."

"Message received. Over and out," Eshu said. Eshu relayed the message.

"Listen up! We have company on the way. So let's get rid of these guys and catch our ride. On one, alright! Here we go. Three, two, one, go!" Faro said. The men began firing as they exited the building. Once outside, they lined up and assaulted the guards' holding position just inside the tree line. The green tracer rounds kept them on target and lit up the area.

"I love this shit; I truly do," Dongo said into his mic as he fired his rifle on full auto and sprayed from side to side making the green tracers dance. When they reached the spot where the soldiers had dug in, they found three bodies. Faro didn't waste time. He picked up one of the soldier's radio, and they moved out at a trot.

"I hope those ATV/Skidoo's are there," Gamab said.

"Shut up!" was all Faro said, and they ran in silence. When he was close to the equipment, Faro called a halt and gave the hand signal to circle him. "Gamab, I want you to go about fifty meters in that direction and come back. Do not get caught. Do not engage. Got it!" Gamab nodded and walked into the jungle. While they waited, the team formed a circle. All muzzles were pointed outward; everyone was down on one knee. Dongo heard a noise to his front and raised his weapon.

"Don't shot me, cocksucker," Gamab said. He walked in and took a knee. "The ATVs are thirty meters ahead; the area is clear," he reported.

"Take the point, Gamab," Faro said. As the men stood up, there was a loud explosion. Faro looked at his watch and then gave the signal to move. He knew that was one of their claymores which meant the enemy patrol was ten minutes behind them. They moved quickly and quietly. When they reached the ATVs, the men removed the camouflage and checked the vehicles. The ATVs had a resupply of ammo, explosives, and batteries. They reloaded and jumped on. One by one, they started the super-muffled engines that made the ATVs very quiet.

Faro turned on the GPS. Its dim lit screen seemed bright in the darkness of the jungle. He punched in the coordinates and waited. A second later, the route came up. He looked around at each one of his men. They gave him the thumbs up. He pointed to Dongo and then straight ahead, and they took off. Dongo slowed down as he approached a dirt road. He turned off his headlights and cruised up to the road and stopped. Looking both ways and spotting nothing, he gave the okay and the team crossed.

"Ganja Jim to Eshu, over."

"Eshu here, go ahead Ganja Jim. Over."

"I'm seven minutes out. Will you be late to dinner? Over."

"Negative, dinner party will be on time. Over."

"That's a roger. Eshu, see you at the table. Ganja Jim out!"

Eshu informed Faro of the radio call. In turn, he ordered Dongo to speed up. The team followed. Dongo came across a second dirt road. This one wasn't on the map so he stopped and waited. He told Faro what he found as he waited for the rest of the team to catch up.

"What do you think?" Dongo asked.

"Give me a minute," Faro answered as he searched his GPS to see if this road intersected anywhere close to the river. "This must be a new road. It's not on the map and doesn't intersect with the river. Keep to the route," he told Dongo. So he took off back on point.

"Faro, how far are we from the river?" Tsui asked.

"About five minutes, why?"

"Because I see headlights on our left."

Faro looked over to his left. He had to look behind him so he slowed down. Then he spotted two sets of headlights. He called a halt and took a look through his night vision binoculars.

"You're right, Tsui. Except, we have two vehicles coming fast. Lights out; goggles on," he told them. They pulled down their night vision goggles and resumed. The draw back was they couldn't go as fast. The goggles restricted their view, and they were forced to slow down. This caused them time. So far, they had not been spotted, and it wasn't far to the river. They kept going slowly and steadily with everyone at the ready.

"They're coming this way!" Tsui said into his mic to no one in particular. Faro looked over and confirmed it. The two jeeps had changed course and now were headed straight towards them at an intercept angle.

"Eshu, you and Tsui keep on to the river and wait for us there. If we aren't there in ten minutes, head to the pickup point. Also count to five and turn on your headlights. You too, Tsui! Then count to three and turn them off. You got all that!" Faro said.

"Yeah, got it and good hunting," Tsui replied.

"Gamab, Dongo, on me. Now take off, Eshu." Eshu and Tsui started off. Faro watched. When their lights came on, he turned his attention to the jeeps. Then the lights went out, and he waited to see if the men in the jeeps bought it. After a moment, he saw them turn; they fell for it.

"AP rounds," Faro said. The men reached into the saddle bags attached to their ATVs, pulled out the magazines with armor piercing bullets, and reloaded. "On my signal, we're going to hit them from the side. Don't turn on your lights until I start firing. Make sure they're your high beams." As he watched the jeeps accelerate towards the other two ATVs, he was busy calculating his angle of attack. Then he said, "Go!" They tore off fishtailing as they did so. "Concentrate on the jeep closest to us, first," Faro said into his throat mic. He waited until he was just about to run into the jeep before opening fire. The three of them concentrated their fire where Faro's tracers were hitting. The red tracers slammed into the jeep enveloping it in a red blanket of bullets. The jeep swerved and then flipped over several times before coming to a stop. The team kept going past the second jeep and turned off their lights. Now the machine gunner was firing blindly into the darkness. The team turned around, put in a fresh mag, and started their second run. "Split up and hit it from three sides," Faro instructed. The men in the second jeep couldn't see them in the dark field so the driver turned on his lights, turned the jeep around, and headed back into the field. The machine gunner and soldiers started shooting into the field in front of the jeep and from its sides.

Red and green tracer rounds flew through the air in all directions as the jeep barreled along in the field. Dongo was headed straight for the jeep. Faro was on its left side and Gamab on its right. Then Dongo opened fire and the machine gunner answered. Tracers passed by Dongo's head and pommeled the ground in front of him. Faro and Gamab heard him laughing in their headsets and say,

"So you want to play chicken. Then come and get some, motherfucker!" They opened up on three sides, decimated the jeep and its passengers, and set it on fire as it rolled to a stop. The trio met up and in the fire's glow took their helmets off.

"You're some kind of crazy," Gamab said to Dongo.

"You stupid son-of-a-whore, if you want to fulfill some kind of death wish or fucking thrill do it on your own time. I have to agree with Gamab; you're some kind of crazy," said Faro.

"I couldn't help it–the trill of it. Something came over me. It won't happen again," Dongo said.

They put their helmets on and with headlights on headed to the river. Eshu and Tsui saw them coming and started their vehicles.

"Hell-of-a show from back here," Tsui said.

"Yeah, looked like a touch-and-go sort a thing," Eshu chimed in.

"Enough with the small talk! If we ride this river like a twenty dollar Bangkok ho, we'll just make our pickup," Faro said. Each man entered the river. As they did so, their ATVs turned into skidoos and their GPS panels switched over to radar. The team quickly brought their vehicles to 40 mph. They started to cruise. The Cuanza River was calm and smooth. But it wouldn't be in a few weeks when the rains came. For now, it was a peaceful ride. The team was speeding along. Faro crossed his fingers and thought, "A few more miles and we are home free."

"Ganja Jim to Eshu! Over!"

"Eshu, over."

"You have a patrol boat half-a-klick behind you. Over."

"Hold Jim. Over." Eshu switched to a channel that allowed him to talk to Faro privately. He then told Faro what he just learned. Faro told him what he wanted to do, and Eshu switched back.

"Eshu to Jim, over."

"Jim here, over!"

"We're on time for pickup. Can you cover? Over."

"That's a positive, Eshu! Making preparations, see you on the river. Over and out!" Eshu informed Faro, and they continued down the river at full speed.

As the men came out of a slow long bend in the river, their radar picked up the seaplane. They were a few hundred yards away. There was no sign of the patrol boat. As the men pulled up to the plane's side door, they were met by Hashish Henna.

"Welcome aboard, warriors!" she said with a big smile that showed off her perfect teeth.

"Well, who are you?" Eshu said as she helped him into the plane.

"Me, baby? I'm the co-pilot," she replied as she helped the men aboard. Meanwhile, Gamab set charges to the skidoos and pushed them into the middle of the river.

"I got that patrol boat on radar. It's time to go!" Ganja Jim yelled from the cockpit.

Henna secured the door, and the men groaned with delight as they watched this slim dark-skinned woman make her way to the cockpit. She was wearing short-shorts that showed more cheek than it covered and a halter top that was struggling to hold in her large breasts. Ganja Jim brought the idling engines up to full speed and started down the river for takeoff. The patrol boat was just straightening out from the long bend in the river when they spotted the plane. The machine gunner opened up, and the patrol boat sped up.

"Hit the deck!" Henna yelled to the men. The plane took a couple of hits as it became airborne. No one was hit. Ganja Jim banked the plane to starboard and started to climb.

"Watch this!" Gamab said to the guys. They all looked out the starboard window.

*"Boom! Boom! Boom!"* Then a big fire ball rose up.

"What was that?" Tsui ask.

"The water bikes! The charges went off, and that patrol boat must have been close by. Look at it burn!" he said laughing.

The seaplane leveled out and continued to climb as Ganja Jim came over the PA system.

"For your traveling pleasure, Hashish Henna has prepared a little snack. In the blue cold case, you'll find sandwiches. In the red case, you'll find some fine craft beer. But on the side of the red case, there is some fine smoke. It's one of mine and Henna's favorite, *Arjan Haze #1.*"

"Enjoy, warriors! If you work for Libertaire, you certainly earned it," Henna added.

The men all went for the red cold case and side pouch. With wide smiles on their faces, they sat back, lit up, and enjoyed the ride. While chilling, the loudspeakers belted out *Black Betty* in honor of the lady painted on the side of the plane.

*Luanda*

Wilhelm had led the people who were following him all around town from one night club to another. Now that it was 2:00 a.m., it was time to spring his trap. He hoped Sanaa was on time. He could do nothing but trust that everything on her end was going according to plan. At the last club, he had picked up a pretty young woman who reminded him of Adalgisa and had her hang around. He had Conrad do the same but Conrad didn't understand Wilhelm's plan. In fact, he didn't know his plan. He was just as much in the dark as the woman whom he was kissing on at the moment.

"Let's go!" Wilhelm said to Conrad.

"Where to?"

"To that tree-lined section near the eatery. It's a nice place to make out," Wilhelm explained. Conrad leaned over to the woman who he was with and told her they were leaving. Wilhelm whispered something in the young woman's ear that made her smile and nod her head in agreement. The four of them left the club. Once outside, Wilhelm and Conrad scanned the parking lot and found the car that had been on their tail. Conrad drove to the spot that Wilhelm wanted and parked. He was nervous because he didn't like being bait or a sitting duck. He looked in the rearview mirror and saw Wilhelm kissing the woman. It looked as if he had forgotten all about the danger.

"Come on, baby. Don't you like me?" the woman in the front seat said to Conrad.

"Yeah, baby! I like you." Then he kissed her. In no time, Conrad and the woman had the windows steamed up and the smell of sex filled the car. Conrad suddenly looked up trying hard to see out of the passenger side window.

"What is it, baby?" the woman asked.

"I thought I heard something."

"That was me, baby. You lovin' me good," she moaned. Conrad looked in the backseat at Wilhelm who was looking back at him with his gun in his hand. Conrad sat up and pulled up his pants.

"Are you done, baby?"

"Quiet, woman," he said in a hushed voice and continued to get dressed. "Put your panties back on and pull your dress down," Conrad told her then he looked back at Wilhelm who was sitting in the back seat cool and calm. He was lightly rubbing the young woman's clitoris as she lay there with her legs over his lap, her skirt up around her waist, and no panties on.

Wilhelm was completely dressed. By the woman lying down, he had a clear shot through the passenger window. He saw a shadow then another. He knew it was the hit team. They had approached just where he wanted them to. He waited until the shadow got closer and he could determine if the person was armed. He fired shattering the window which caused the women to scream. Conrad pulled his gun but Wilhelm yelled for him to hold his fire. Wilhelm's security detail emerged from hiding. They yelled at the assailants to drop their weapons and put their hands up. Conrad yelled at the women to shut up and stay in the cab as he and Wilhelm got out. They walked to where the team was holding three assailants, two women and one man. The man was shot in the left arm and was covering his wound as he stood there. Wilhelm watched as the men searched them, bound their hands behind their backs, covered their mouths with duct tape, and placed a hood over their heads.

Then they led them off without talking. Conrad instructed a man to drive the women home. Before they left, Wilhelm walked over to the cab and leaned in the back window that he had shot out.

"I'm sorry about the commotion ladies. I really had a nice time especially with you," he said as he looked at the woman sitting in the back seat. He reached in his suit jacket's inner pocket and took out two envelops and handed them to the women. "I hope this makes up for it and assures that this stays between us."

The women took a quick peek inside the envelope and then said, "Yes." Wilhelm turned and walked into the darkness as the cab left.

Wilhelm entered the room where the three killers were hanging from a beam by their arms. It was just high enough that only the tips of their toes touched the concrete floor. They had been stripped of their clothing, hosed down, and blindfolded.

"You obviously know who I am. So the mystery question is who are you three. I see you have matching tattoos. I am most interested in that particular club. The first one to fill me in will win their freedom. Do I have any takers?" Wilhelm waited a minute then nodded to the man standing off to the side. He walked over and touched each of them briefly with an electric cattle prod. The man repeated this several times, and the three killers screamed and convulsed with each touch.

Wilhelm asked them again and again, and they all held fast. So the torture continued until one of them broke. One of the women decided to talk, so Wilhelm had her taken down and removed from the room. He personally interrogated her. She told him that they worked for an organization known as the Council of Five and exclusively for a woman they called Number 2 in that organization. That woman had once worked for one of the western intelligence services. Even though, she didn't know which intelligence agency, she was certain that the Council was located somewhere in the Andes Mountains. Then she told him that the leader of the Council had a personal hate for him. She didn't know the reason, but he was determined to kill Wilhelm at any cost. After she told him all that she knew and he was sure that she hadn't held anything back, he told Conrad to shoot her and the others and dispose of the bodies. Then Conrad took him back to the hotel. During the ride, he was hoping that Sanaa had completed her mission.

*Haiuri's Mission*

Sanaa looked at her phone; it was 2:00 a.m.

"Adalgisa, accompany me to the ladies room," she said. They got up from the table and walked towards the bathroom. When they were sitting in front of the vanity, she spoke.

"It's time to go to his place and get some lovin'."

"I'm more than ready. His friend is really cute, and he's primed and ready to blow." The words meant nothing to the other women in the bathroom who were listening; they were thinking the obvious. But Adalgisa knew it was time to go to work as she looked in the mirror and applied fresh makeup.

"I want to go, Adilson," Sanaa said as soon as she sat down.

"Where to? Another club?" he asked.

"No, your place, I'm horny and wet, and my coochy needs some attention," she said making Adilson smile.

"Let's go, man!" he said to his friend and stood up. Sanaa followed suit and then Adalgisa, and the four of them left the club.

"What club are we going to?" his friend asked as they got into Adilson's car.

"We're going to Adilson's house. Aren't you horny, baby?" Adalgisa said to him as she rubbed his crotch. On the drive there, Sanaa listened to Adalgisa make out in the backseat. It was making her horny. She looked down at Adilson's lap and his growing bulge told his story.

He pulled into the underground garage of his apartment building. It was located in an upscale neighborhood. As they rode the elevator up to his 15th floor apartment, he and Sanaa watched Adalgisa and his friend kiss and feel each other up.

"Can you believe your eyes, Haiuri? They are as bad as when they were in the car. Come on, guys. Get a room!" he said making them all laugh. When she walked into his apartment, she was surprised it was decorated with contemporary furniture. It looked like a bachelor's pad yet was professionally done. "Make yourself at home, Haiuri. You two, stop and sit. Anyone for a smoke? I sure could use one," he said as he walked to the bar. He came back with a small box and sat next to Sanaa on the couch. When he opened it, the aroma instantly filled the air.

"Oh! You've pulled out the stank," Adalgisa said.

"What's the stank?" Sanaa asked looking over at Adilson. Before he could answer, Adalgisa chimed in.

"It's the sex plant! Smoke that and off with your panties," she said and laughed so hard she started to cough. Adilson rolled a joint, lit it, and then passed it to Sanaa. She took a short light hit. She tasted a peppery, earthy, spicy flavored smoke that was smooth and didn't burn her throat on the way down. Then she exhaled, and a strong skunky smelling cloud rose up.

"What strain is this?" she asked between pulls.

"Pass it and I'll tell you," Adilson said.

"Yeah, Haiuri. Share," Adalgisa retorted.

Sanaa passed the joint. When the circle returned it to her, she asked again.

"Oh shit! I must be high. I forgot that quickly. This is Congolese crossed with a local landrace strain. It's grown on the plateau by a few farmers."

"The Bei Plateau?" Sanaa asked.

"Yes, do you like it? Is it having any affect?" he said jokingly.

"Yes, it is. I'd like to get some before I leave. I have some friends who would really like this strain. And yes, it is kinda working. How about you, Adalgisa?"

"Hell girl! I was activated on the ride over. This shit is making it worst. Besides, I'm way pass horny. I need sex and right now." She got up, grabbed the guy's hand, and said, "Which way to the bedroom, big fella? I hope that statement is true." They went down the hall. Adilson's friend was leading the way to the guest room.

Adilson stood up and extended his hand. Sanaa took it. He helped her up. She continued to smoke the joint as they went his room. His bedroom continued the modern theme with a king-sized bed in the center of the room. He took off his clothes and let them lie where he threw them. Then he flopped down on the bed on his back with his legs open and his half-hard cock hanging between them. Adilson lay there and looked at her with a drunken smile. Sanaa looked at him and smiled back. She was so high from the bud that that was all she could do. But now, it was time to end this mission and get out of there. So she began to undress. She put on a show for him as she slowly took off her clothes. Next she bent over at a right angle and laid her clothes on a chair to cover her pocketbook.

Naked, Sanaa walked around the bed. As she passed the night stand, she picked up a condom and slid onto the bed. While snuggling up next to him, she began kissing him and rubbing on his cock. When he was fully erect, she started to kiss her way down to it. On the way, she stopped to suck each of his nipples. Sanaa unwrapped the condom and put it in her mouth. As she started to give him head, she slipped it on.

"Hmmm, Haiuri!" he moaned as she sucked his cock. She kept up her technique until he started moving his hips wildly.

She stopped and only messaged his balls to calm him down and keep him from cumming. When she had accomplished this, she straddled him. At that very moment, she realized just how wet she was and how good that long hard pole felt. She rode him fast and slow while leaning over him, kissing him, and reaching behind him to squeeze his balls periodically. When she felt him about to blow his load, she would stop and delay him. This game went on for a half-hour before he just couldn't stand it any longer and rolled her unto her back. After putting her legs up on his shoulders and sinking fully into her, he pumped hard, fast, and deeply which caused Sanaa to orgasm several times. She heard him grunt and then stiffen followed by a full body shutter. It must have taken him a full minute to finish cumming.

Adilson looked down at her then kissed her forehead before rolling off. He said,

"Haiuri, if all black American pussy is as good as yours, our women are in deep shit." Sanaa laid there and listened to Adilson's breathing slow down and regulate. When she was sure he was asleep, she slipped out of bed, gathered her clothes, and left the room. As she entered the hallway and started towards the guest room, she heard someone call her name. She turned around. Adalgisa was already dressed and standing in the living room.

"Well, how was it?" she asked and smiled as Sanaa approached.

"Not bad," Sanaa replied as she got dressed. "Did you make the call?"

"Yes, Haiuri, and I said what was on the card exactly," Adalgisa replied.

"Good, one more thing to do." Sanaa picked up the table lamp, unscrewed the bottom, placed the flash drive in it, and reassembled it. "Is your guy asleep?"

"Like a baby...that man sure knew how to treat a horny girl but he's out for the night. How about Quart? He done for the tonight?"

"In more ways than he knows. Now let's get out of here. I have a plane to catch." They left and got in Adalgisa's car that had been placed there earlier. Sanaa looked at her phone; it was 4:00 a.m. She got out of the car and walked into the hotel straight towards the elevators. When she got out of the elevator, she asked the guard if Libertaire was back.

He said, "No." So she went to her room and jumped in the shower.

After Wilhelm stepped out of the elevator, the guard told him that Haiuri asked about him and she was in her room. Wilhelm elected not to talk to her at the moment and went to his room, showered, sat at the bar, and smoked a joint. It was 5:30 a.m.

Later that morning as Wilhelm and Sanaa walked through the lobby, they were met by Adalgisa.

"Good morning!" she said cheerfully as she fell into step with them. "In case you hadn't heard, Adilson was found dead in his apartment this morning. He was shot in the head twice with a small caliber bullet; his friend was not hurt," she told them. They stopped just before going out to their awaiting cars. "It was a pleasure meeting you, Mr. Libertaire."

"It was a delight meeting you, Adalgisa," he replied in a soothing baritone voice that makes women's knees weak.

"Is there any way I can come work for you? I really like this spy business," she continued.

"I'll see what I can do, Adalgisa. Goodbye," Wilhelm said and then walked off.

"It was nice working with you, Haiuri," she said sincerely.

"It was nice working with you also, Adalgisa," Sanaa said with equal sincerity. The two women walked to the awaiting car. Before Sanaa got in, Adalgisa said,

"You think your boss can get me in?"

"If he says so, it will happen."

"Good, I just have to taste that man just once," Adalgisa whispered and then walked away.

At the airport, Wilhelm kept a watchful eye while they waited to board the plane. He didn't spot anyone who was a threat. After the three days that he just spent, he wasn't leaving anything to chance. The delegation boarded the plane, and they took off. As the passengers started to relax, Wilhelm sat there and went over the information that the assassin had told him. He wondered who was the Council of Five, and why had they targeted him specifically. He had enemies—good ones. But they all understood the game. No one who he could think of hated him as much as she said they did. As soon as he got home, he would dedicate his time to finding the answer to those questions. Then he sat back and pictured Adalgisa naked.

# Home Invasion

*Chapter Twenty-Two*

It had been seven months since the Angola operation. Wilhelm hadn't been out of the country since then. Rodney had kept his word for a change and allowed him to work on bullshit assignments that kept him around the office and home. He enjoyed the time off from planning and worrying about missions. His efforts and discoveries about the Council were starting to pay off. Shadow One had fully recovered from his wounds, and his training in Wu Long Gao's special techniques was going well. Shadow Two had been busy. The work was mostly stateside which made her happy, plus he got to spend more time with her as he promised.

Captain America and Derek had finally cracked the late Stanleys' encryption. The information from those papers was both frightening and informative. Wilhelm was learning a lot from reading the first five thousand pages. The Captain told him thousands more were to come, and the section he was reading only covered five years of operations. Wilhelm was also considering releasing Derek. The man had done his job and couldn't cause him any problems. Besides Derek had some old scores to settle which would take years to finish if he survived at all.

But for the time being, Wilhelm was going to sit back and enjoy this car ride with his wife. He looked over at Afra singing along with the radio and then back at the road. As he shifted into third gear, his corvette sped up effortlessly.

### Andes Mountains

Number 1 was looking at a mother puma and her cubs as they played and she sunned herself. He stood thinking as he watched them on this warm spring day in the mountains. He felt like the puma and he had survived once again. This was a good time to be alive. They both had endured the long harsh mountain winter. Number 1 stayed for the winter at his headquarters never leaving it. He had been busy planning a very special operation. And now, he was ready to put his plan into motion. He would inform the other members later this evening after it begins. He checked the time and looked at the clock that showed U.S. Eastern Standard Time. It read 10:00 a.m. It was Saturday morning there. "Good, a little morning excitement is good for the digestion," he thought.

### Libertaire Manor, Virginia

Wilhelm turned onto the side road headed for home. He saw the old barn and knew he was twenty miles from home even though all the land he passed by belonged to him including that old barn. Technically he was already home. Afra was still singing this time to Tupac. He glanced over at her. She was happy as she looked out the window and sang. Then he looked in his side mirror and saw a motorcycle. Next he looked in his rearview mirror and saw two motorcycles. Wilhelm shifted gears and sped up. His gut was telling him they were in danger.

He was glad this road was empty this time of morning. Its long flat runs and gentle rises made it a favorite thoroughfare of drivers. He could see them steadily gaining on him, and he was going 90 mph. He also knew he couldn't out run those bikes. Then it happened—his worst nightmare. They were firing on him. He saw a muzzle flash then heard rounds impacting his car. Wilhelm turned down the music and spoke to his wife.

"Sweetheart, your husband has to go to work. I want you to open the glove box and take out the pistol. Then I want you to hunch down in your seat and keep your head below the back of the seat. Okay, baby?" he said to her in a calm, matter-of-fact tone.

Afra slid down in the seat while holding the pistol at the ready. Wilhelm turned his attention back to the bikes. He pressed a button on the consul. The corvette's rear lights folded away and short barreled machineguns appeared. Using the aiming sights on his windshield, he lined the bikers up and waited. He was approaching a low rise in the road and wanted to use it to his advantage. He held his speed as his car dipped in the road and came over the rise. Then he watched as the bikers hit the rise and their speed caused them to lose contact with the road. As they landed, he fired a short burst from his 30 caliber machine guns. He kept his eyes on his targets as the bullets slammed into one of the attackers and knocked him off his bike. But he missed the other one who immediately went into evasive maneuvers firing as he did so.

One of the rounds hit the rear passenger side tire causing the vet to fishtail. The automatic stabilizing system kicked in and helped him keep control while the tire re-inflated. When it did, he stepped on the gas. The motorcycle had gained ground and was moving fast. But the rider wasn't ready when Wilhelm released the spikes. He ran right into them which blew out his tires and sent him and his bike flying. Wilhelm watched as the rider's body bounced along the road before coming to a stop. Then his communications panel lit up. He hit the intercom button and spoke.

"I'm a little busy at the moment. Afra and I are under attack."

"Sir, so are we! There are mercenaries dropping from the fucking sky and hitting us from the ground as well! I have all personnel engaged, and the family has been sheltered. I suggest you enter through the west entrance, sir."

"I got that, George. See you in seven, out."

Just before he was about to turn onto the western road, two jeeps appeared in front of him and both were firing at him.

Wilhelm kept going and headed straight at the oncoming jeeps. He switched to his front machineguns as his headlights retracted. Then he began firing. Both jeeps' machine gunners had misjudged the height of his car. So their rounds struck high on the windshield or missed them all together. Wilhelm aimed for the jeeps' engines and let loose a long burst. The rounds hit the radiators and engines causing the vehicles to smoke. He raised his sights and fired again this time into the windshields. The bullets ripped through the men. Next he merged with them. As he passed them, he saw their bullet riddled bodies and blood splattered throughout the cab. He down shifted, executed a J-turn, and headed back to the western road. When they arrived, he saw a full-fledged battle in front of him.

"Stay close to me. When you get out, shoot anyone who's not us. We are going to the house. Okay."

"Okay." Then they were out of the car and headed towards the house at a run. Wilhelm was firing at targets as they appeared. Afra was doing the same. She shot three people within the first five yards. There were so many mercenaries; it was a target rich environment. It seemed like hundreds. When they reached the west entrance to the house, he paused.

"How's your ammo?" Afra took the magazine out and looked.

"About three rounds left."

"I'm out. So when we enter, find yourself a fresh gun and get to the bunker."

Afra nodded, and they went in. A short distance down the hall, he ran across a dead guard and two dead attackers. As he listened for any approaching attackers, he gave Afra the guard's rifle, pistol, and ammo. He took the rifle and ammo along with two grenades from one of the dead attackers. They continued moving down the hall. This wing housed the pool, spa, and other rooms with tile and marble surfaces. The blood on the floor made walking a nightmare. As they passed the pool area, they received fire. Wilhelm immediately returned fire; Afra joined in. By him yelling directions over the noise, they managed to kill the seven men in the pool area.

They continued down the hall towards the living room. They approached the T-section at the end of the hall which linked it to the east wing where the living room was located. He told Afra to go to the other side of the hall and move only when he moved. They did this without further incident. When he reached the T-section, he gave her the signal to stop. Wilhelm slowly looked around the corner. He saw one of his guards fighting with an attacker. Wilhelm suddenly took off running at them. Afra was close behind. The attacker looked over and saw him which gave his guard an opening. The guard didn't waste the opportunity. He kneed him in the groin, yanked his left hand free, grabbed the man's hair, pulled his head back, and then sunk his knife into his neck. The attacker gurgled as the blood squirted from his neck. He fell dead.

"Sir, I'm glad to see you; you too ma'am," the guard said.

"Report!" Wilhelm snapped.

"Well, sir, they just fell on us literally, sir. We looked up and there they were."

"My family?"

"They are all in the bunker, sir, except your wives. They're fighting somewhere on the grounds," the guard explained.

"I want you and Afra to find the other two and get them in that bunker.

You understand!"

The guard said, "Yes."

He and Afra took off. Wilhelm headed to the front door and ran into a couple of invaders at the T-section. He killed them in short order. Crouching down, he opened the door and looked out. He saw dead and wounded guards and attackers. As he started to go out, a burst of gun fire hit the thick wood door causing him to fall backwards. As he did so, he closed the door.

He got up and cracked opened the door again. This time, he was looking for the shooter. He found him behind the fountain in the driveway. Wilhelm took one of the grenades, pulled the pin, but held the spoon. He flung the door wide open. The man jumped up and began firing, and then ducked down. That was when he threw the grenade. It landed beside the fountain and exploded throwing the man out into the open where Wilhelm shot him. Then he dashed outside and followed the sound of gunfire. He was hoping to find George or Anthony. There was smoke and fire and explosions going off everywhere. As he made his way across the lawn, he could see pockets of fighting going on. His men were attacking in some instances or defending in others, but everybody was fighting. He was proud of them. At that moment, they were holding the line.

Then he saw a group of his men pinned down around a stand of pecan trees so he headed that way. He found some cover and looked over the situation. He spotted George in the group of men. To get George's attention, he fired at him. The two rounds impacted just above his head on the tree that he was laying behind. George ducked his head down and looked over to where the firing originated. He saw his boss waving his hand at him. George pointed to the four assailants and to the five guards who were pinned down. Wilhelm took the last grenade and threw it at the invaders. The explosion drew their attention, and they started firing at him. That was when George and his men jumped up, and in true legionnaire fashion lined up and assaulted the position.

They walked through the attackers and tore their bodies apart with the volume of bullets they fired into them. Wilhelm joined them. They knelt as the men reloaded. Wilhelm got a situation report from George.

"Sir, I have enemy on three sides of the area. Their main force seems to be coming from the southwest. I figured the bulk of them landed in that field. They had a small force land right here at the house. That force caught us off guard. Sorry about that, sir. The family is in the bunker. That is all of the children. Afef and Colleen are off fighting somewhere, sir. I tried to get them in the bunker but Ms. Afef pulled a gun on me and said she was defending her home and children and not hiding like a helpless bitch in a bunker."

"She said that, George?"

"Yes, sir, and she meant it. That's all I have, sir."

"Alright, George, you and the men follow me. We're going to sweep towards the stables and clear that area," he said and they headed off.

After a few engagements, they reached the stables and found it on fire. Wilhelm hoped the horse's got out.

"Sir, the horse were turned out this morning; the stables are empty," George said as he stood beside him. Wilhelm kept moving. He couldn't stand here. There were people to kill and chase off his land. So they headed for the back of the house. That was when Wilhelm saw a woman in a turquoise colored sundress. She was running across the lawn with twelve female guards. They were assaulting a group of attackers who looked like they were retreating.

"Is that Afef?" Wilhelm asked.

"Yes, sir. It is," George answered.

"Well, let's give them some help. Looks like they have them on the run." They joined in and started firing at the retreating attackers. Wilhelm caught up with Afef and she hugged him real tight.

"Where's Colleen?"

"She was headed to the back of the house the last time I saw her."

"You and your army stay with George. Don't you leave his side until this is over. Understand!"

"Yes, my husband," she answered. Then she gave him a quick kiss. Wilhelm and two guards took off towards the maze gardens. As they got closer to the gardens, he slowed down. There, they ran into the bodies of dead attackers. He could see the concern on his men's faces. He was concern as well. He didn't want to be shot by his wife and neither did they. They passed nine bodies already and were approaching her special garden. This was the one she designed, the kill box as the men called it. He approached the entrance very carefully. When he reached it, he got down on one knee and peered in. He saw five more bodies lying in and around the refection pool.

"Colleen!" he yelled. "Don't you shoot me. Where are you? You in here, Colleen? Answer me."

"Stop your yelling, Wilhelm. I'm okay," she said as she walked out to where he was standing with her rifle in hand. He hugged and kissed her.

"What are you doing out here? Why aren't you in that damn bunker?"

"Me and Afef wanted to fight! It's our home after all, and who-the-fuck did you piss off? Because it's somebody who really hates you if they broke this rule."

"We'll talk about that later. Right now, I have a fight on my hands."

"You mean, we have a fight," she retorted.

"Don't give me any shit right now, Colleen. Your fight is over. You will go with these men and link up with Afef and George," he said sternly. Colleen nodded in compliance.

"You kill every one of those motherfuckers, baby. They really don't know who they're fucking with. Do they?"

"No, baby, they don't. Now go. I'm going to finish this fight."

Wilhelm went back to the front of the house. His guards had finally secured the front section including the garage. They were pushing the attackers back to the southwest where George said it started. Then he heard singing machineguns; they were his men. He could hear the medium machineguns taking turns firing; it sounded like a song. So he headed in that direction. He was joined by Anthony who had seven men with him. Then George showed up with five more. When they arrived, he found two machine gunners, one man on each gun. Wilhelm split his small force in two and directed each section to support the machine gunners. They laid down a base of fire on the force in front of them.

Afra didn't go to the bunker instead she and the guard started to clear the upstairs by moving from room to room. As they came out of one of the children's room, they ran into three attackers in the hall. The guard was hit and killed immediately. But he also killed one of them. The remaining two attackers concentrated their fire at Afra which forced her back into the bedroom. Afra stuck her rifle out into the hall and fired blindly on automatic. Then she reached out and grabbed a hold of the dead guard's leg and pulled him into the room. She took his ammo and reloaded. Next she looked for and found his canister of tear gas. She remembered what her husband told her.

"If you don't have a mask, run through it and don't breathe until you have to." Afra readied herself, pulled the pin, and threw the tear gas canister down the hall as the two attackers approached. Seeing the canister and thinking it was a grenade, they turned and ran down the hall.

Afra came out of the room firing. She ran through the smoke attacking them and hit one attacker as he tried for the backstairs. She put a few more rounds into his head as she stepped over him. Then she ran after the last attacker. She knew he could only hide in two places since these stairs led to the kitchen and the ancient weapons collection room. She swept the kitchen and found nothing. So she moved on to the collections room. She pushed the door open but didn't enter. She looked across the wide empty floor to the far wall. Seeing nothing, she crossed the doorway to the other side and surveyed that side of the room. On that side, the room was laid out in an L-shape bend, and she couldn't see into that area without going in. Afra resisted rubbing her eyes. Now they stung from the tear gas, and she knew it would only make it worst. By staying low to the floor, she entered the room and moved to her right until she could she the corner.

*Pop! Pop! Pop!* The resound of a rapid firing pistol made Afra fall flat and return fire. But from that angle, she couldn't get a clear shot at her assailant. So she crawled out of sight and waited.

"Give it up! Throw out your gun and come out!" she ordered and then waited for a reply. Not hearing one, she tried again. "Come on. Give the fuck up. In a few minutes, my guards will be in here, and then you will die. Give up to me. At least, you'll live. What do you say to that?" Then she heard a voice that she recognized.

"I'll give up if you give me a fair fight and a chance to escape, Afra."

"Fuck! That's Linda Banally's voice," she thought."

"Is that you, Linda?"

"Yes, Afra, it's me. I'm coming out. Here's my weapon," she said as she slid the pistol across the floor. Meanwhile, Afra was on one knee with her rifle aimed in her direction.

"Alright, come out, Linda." Linda appeared with her hands up and a nervous smile. She walked to the center of the room and stopped. "Why, Linda?" Afra asked as she stood up.

"You mean the attack? Well partly because I didn't have much of a choice and partly because the money was *too* good to turn down."

"Why should I give you a chance? Not that I couldn't kick your ass. Why shouldn't I just shoot you? After all, you did attack my home, bitch; you put my children in danger and fucked up the décor. You deserve to be shot like the dog you are," she said and aimed the rifle at her chest.

"It's the spy game. You should know this. You're married into it and at a high level. Yes, your husband will kill me or the CIA will kill me. And they will do it in the most evil way they can think of. At least with you, I get two questions answered." Are you really that good? And is the Libertaire family sword style that good? Here's my chance to find out and what better place than here," she said smiling.

"Okay, Linda, take off that gear." Linda unbuttoned her web gear and dropped it to the floor. "Take off that outer shirt. You can keep on your undershirt," Afra instructed.

"Don't trust me, huh? All I want is a fair chance to get out of here, Afra. Besides I don't have to cheat to kill your ass." Afra told her to turn around. Satisfied that Linda didn't have a hidden knife or pistol, she ordered her to sit on the floor with her hands on her head. Afra kept her rifle pointed at her while she walked over to the sword wall and took down two sabers. She selected Russian Shasqua twin sabers with blades 32 inches in length, a deep fuller, and spear point. The special feature of these weapons was no hand guard. Afra walked back to within ten feet of Linda and placed one of the sabers on the floor. Then she backed away. She put her rifle down but not before she unloaded it.

"Pick up your sword, Linda, and let's get this over with," she said as she whirled her saber around her body.

The two women immediately started to circle each other. After a full turn, Afra attacked. She started with a basic four strike combo. Linda either blocked them or parried the strikes away. Then it was Linda's turn. She attacked with all the fury of a trapped animal and a woman fighting for her life. Her attack caused them to move around the room putting Afra on the defense. Linda was doing her best to kill her fast.

When Linda's attack slowed, Afra went on the offensive using the *five element saber technique*. She managed to cut Linda twice, once above her left breast, the other on her arm. Both cuts were short and deep. Linda resumed her attack by using an English saber movement that caught Afra on her right upper arm. The slash opened up a short but deep wound. Linda followed this up with a low lunging thrust to her pelvis. Afra jumped straight up and executed a mid-air split while chopping down on Linda's head. Linda brought her sword up above her head and supported it with her other hand to ensure that she would absorb the blow. Afra's strike caused Linda to go down on one knee. Then Linda rolled out of the way. She came up fast and swung her blade which caught Afra on her thigh.

"Oh, that had to hurt," Linda said smiling as she circled.

"Shut up, bitch, and keep fighting. Your time on earth is running out," Afra said and then attacked. Afra managed to return the cut to Linda's leg. Other than that, this fight was dead locked. She had to end this and end it now. Afra waited for Linda's next attack. She blocked and answered everything Linda threw at her. Then Afra realized Linda had used a series of lunge attacks so she set herself up for the perfect lunge. Linda took the bait. She not only took it, she swallowed it whole. Afra couldn't believe it; Linda had over-extended. Even more, her recovery would be slow which gave Afra her chance. Afra executed *black dragon pins his prey* and stabbed Linda in the chest. Linda's body instantly stiffened. As she dropped her sword, her dying eyes fixed on Afra. Afra removed her blade and before Linda's body could fall, she cut her head off.

Afra watched her head roll a few feet away and then come to a rest with Linda's surprised look staring at the ceiling. Afra sat down in a chair and looked at her wounds. Her arm was worse than her leg. "This is a good time to check on the children," she thought. She got up, reloaded her rifle, and started for the bunker.

During her fight, Wilhelm had gathered a few more men and women from his security force. They had maneuvered on the last pocket of attackers. He saw some of them heading for their helicopters which sat waiting with rotors spinning. But he had to get past this holding action that was keeping him and his men pinned down. Whoever these guys were, they were highly trained and dedicated. They were not only putting up a good fight, but also a smart one. Then Wilhelm heard sirens, and so did his attackers who broke contact and made a mad dash towards the awaiting helicopters. Wilhelm and his men gave chase and shot as many attackers as they could before they reached the helicopters and safety. Surprisingly, it turned out he wouldn't have that problem because the three awaiting copters took off and left a force of twenty men behind. Wilhelm and his men killed them all.

Wilhelm gave his men their orders. He told George to find his two crazy, brave wives and to check on the children. He told Anthony to take care of the dead and wounded and to coordinate with the arriving emergency personnel. He reminded everyone to just do their job and not to talk to anybody that wasn't family. His men understood and said so. Wilhelm headed to the house. There would be a lot of questions. He didn't have the answers; he had no idea who had attacked. Hell, he had enemies all around the world but only a hand full came to mind. Talaus was at the top of that very short list.

## Council Headquarters

Number 1 walked into the conference room. The other four were already there and drinking. He walked to the bar and made himself a stiff drink. Then he walked over to the long glass conference table and sat down. The others started to walk over and sit down while they listened to Number 3 tell them how glad he was to be back in the cool mountain air. Everyone was dressed casually. They were wearing sandals or went barefoot like Number 2.

"I have an announcement to make," Number 1 said. The others quieted down and looked at him. "At 10:00 a.m. Eastern Standard Time, I ordered an attack on Libertaire Manor," he said and then paused to let his words sink in for a moment.

"You're telling us that you attacked Libertaire at his home. Have you lost your fucking mind?" Number 5 said.

"You know you've broken the most sacred rule we have. In this business, he has a rose for Christ sake," Number 2 added.

"Why would you start a war with the CIA?" Number 3 asked.

"If this blows up in your face, you know the rules of this Council and its consequences," Number 4 said.

"Now that you have had your say, what is done is done. As for the CIA, I haven't declared war on them. I've simply made this a personal matter. And believe me, Libertaire will treat it as such. I have seen to that. This is between me and him. It's high time for Wilhelm Libertaire to retire permanently," he said and then drank his drink down in one gulp.

# About the Author

P. W. Hand is a scholar, an all-around adventurer, and outdoorsman. He is an avid golfer and sailing enthusiast. He earned three degrees from the University Nevada, Las Vegas, which are a master's degree in educational leadership, a B.A. in history, and a B.A. in Asian studies. As an expert in Asian history and culture, he is a skilled calligrapher and teacher of Chinese internal boxing arts and swordsmanship. He has studied and practiced Chinese martial arts for fifty-two years as well as French and Italian swordplay for fourteen years. He teaches the arts of Yang Style Tai Chi Quan, Hsing Yi Quan, Classical Northern Wu Style Tai Chi Quan, and European swordsmanship.

His travels have taken him to the four corners of the globe which has inspired his research on exotic peoples, cultures, and places. In Egypt, he conducted research for his espionage series, Wilhelm Libertaire.

He has chaired creative writing sessions at the Far West Popular Culture and American Culture Associations conventions held in Las Vegas, Nevada. He is a member of the Golden Key International Honor Society. Presently, he and his wife Claire live in the Henderson area of Nevada with their two French mastiffs. He can be contacted by email at pwhandbooks@gmail.com.

www.ingramcontent.com/pod-product-compliance
Lightning Source LLC
Chambersburg PA
CBHW051553250626
47157CB00001B/284